DIRTY
LITTLE
LIES

JULIE LETO

Pocket Books

New York   London   Toronto   Sydney

An *Original* Publication of POCKET BOOKS

 POCKET BOOKS, a division of Simon & Schuster, Inc.
1230 Avenue of the Americas, New York, NY 10020

This book is a work of fiction. Names, characters, places and incidents are products of the author's imagination or are used fictitiously. Any resemblance to actual events or locales or persons, living or dead, is entirely coincidental.

ISBN-13: 978-1-4165-0163-3
ISBN-10:   1-4165-0163-0

This Pocket Books paperback edition September 2006

10   9   8   7   6   5   4   3   2   1

POCKET and colophon are registered trademarks of Simon & Schuster, Inc.

Cover design by Min Choi
Cover art by Craig White

Manufactured in the United States of America

For information regarding special discounts for bulk purchases, please contact Simon & Schuster Special Sales at 1-800-456-6798 or business@simonandschuster.com.

"What do you think you're doing?" Marisela said, her voice a raspy whisper.

With a flick, Frankie unbuttoned the waist of her jeans. He leaned into her neck and inhaled. "I'm touching you. I've wanted to all day. You're torturing me, you know that, *¿sí?*"

"Your own damned fault," she replied, her eyes drifting closed as his fingers danced along the lower edge of her belly. "You can't beat your chest around me, Frankie. Get all jealous and macho. That doesn't turn me on."

He stroked a finger across the top of her panties. "Maybe not, but I know other ways to make you wet, *vidita*. I know you, Marisela. I know your body. I know how you think. No other man will ever give you what you need the way I can."

He wasn't talking about a vague, unnamed "other man." He was talking about Ian Blake.

She arched a brow, holding back a pleasured gasp as his fingertip twisted around her tight pubic hair. "You think so?"

"I can prove it."

"Julie Elizabeth Leto's *Dirty Little Secrets* is one of the sexiest books I've ever read, with fun, fast writing. Fizzy as a flute of Clos du Mesnil champagne. As a guilty Latina pleasure, *Dirty Little Secrets* ranks alongside silk Eberjey negligees, Blanxart Spanish chocolate bars, and Maria Evora black soap."

—Alisa Valdes-Rodriguez, author of *The Dirty Girls Social Club*

Dirty Little Lies is also available as an eBook

To Helen Breitweiser,
agent extraordinaire.

ACKNOWLEDGMENTS

Setting a book in a city I've visited only three times in my life (two of those times I was just playing tourist and not really paying attention to the details) was a challenge. Luckily, I absolutely love Boston and pouring through pictures and maps and notes to refresh my memory was not a chore. Special thanks go out to my consummate tour guide, Bill McDunough, founder of BostonPrivateTours.com and his amazing driver, Larry Constanzo, for my crash course in Boston history, lore, and layout. Forest Hills Cemetery wasn't even supposed to be in the book—but they made me fall in love. I also thank Boston residents Marley Gibson and Barbara Keilor for answering my many questions about everything from the life cycle of apple trees in the Northeast to the proper way to talk about JP. Their insight, knowledge, and humor was invaluable. Same goes for my incredibly smart, incredibly talented editor, Amy Pierpont, whose knowledge of Boston is only surpassed by her expertise in editing. This book would never have made it to print without her.

A special thank-you to the moms at Carrollwood

Elementary school—especially Melissa, Annett, Christy, and Jeanine—who listened endlessly to my tales of woe during the writing of this book and never once slapped me in the face and told me to "snap out of it." Friendship like this is hard to come by and I hope our kids are in the same class or have classrooms near each other for at least three more years because if not, I may never write another book without mental health assistance. Same goes for the ladies of the Tampa Area Romance Authors (TARA), particularly the stalwart writers in the Book Challenge, who cheered me on during every stage of this book's production. Writing is a solitary pursuit, so having the support of such amazing women is invaluable.

Which leads me to the Plotmonkeys—Janelle Denison, Leslie Kelly, and Carly Phillips—and my critique partner, Susan Kearney, without whom I could not function—as a writer or as a woman. You are my sisters, my friends, my colleagues. You all know what went into writing this book and I couldn't have done it without you.

Last but not least, I must acknowledge my amazing family—first, my husband, Tim, and daughter, Alyssa, who for the first time in twenty-something books, finally saw what a true ugly deadline is and not only lived through my madness, but also celebrated the completion of this project with a trip to Hawaii. *Mahalo*, from the bottom of my heart. Second, my parents, Sam and Nilla, and brothers, Chris, Tim, and Jason, for encouraging me all those years ago when I said I wanted to be a writer, for buying all my books, for giving books to clients and talking me up at every opportunity, caring about my progress at every step—best illustrated by Jason challenging me to go home and write when I was visiting him in the hospital. (No more of that hospital crap again, okay?) I also couldn't have made this book happen without my sisters-in-law, particularly Joy and Jeannette, who listen to me, read for me, tempted me away from the computer for the occasional lunch out and also understand when I say, "No, I can't, I have to work." And to my nieces and nephews who remind me how much fun life can be. And of course, my aunts, particularly Anita Durand, for checking all my Spanish and for generally reminding me that family is what life is all about.

DIRTY
LITTLE
LIES

Prologue

"DON'T STOP, MARISELA. God, don't stop."

Ian Blake forced his eyes open, pushing aside the languid fog coursing through his brain. No matter how heavy his muscles, no matter how dry and parched his throat, he fought to focus on this fantasy come true.

Marisela in his bed.

As she moved atop him, he swallowed deeply, the mingled tastes of bourbon and woman lingering on his palate. The rows of richly scented candles behind her created a halo against her luxurious black hair. Her skin, so naturally brown, glistened with the sheen of sweat, tempering the friction that sparked between their naked bodies. Her thighs tight on his waist, she pumped them closer and closer to orgasm, a forbidden end to a mating that never should have begun.

"*Eres tonto, tu no sabes quién soy yo.*"

Tonto? Fool? He couldn't disagree. He'd lost his mind. He'd drunk too much. He'd been in the wrong place at the wrong time with a woman so wrong, she should have come with a warning label.

She leaned forward and captured his mouth just as his groin tightened and pulsed. He groaned and surrendered. To the lust. To the insatiable need. To Marisela, the woman who'd made it her mission in life to drive him insane.

Once he was spent and fell instantly to sleep, Yizenia Santiago climbed off her lover and sighed appreciatively while working out the kink in her back. He was handsome, this *hombre*. Maybe even more dashing than his father, a man she'd known so long ago. And even high on too much *whisky americano*, he'd been sinfully proficient in bed, even if he'd called her by some other woman's name.

As she slipped into the living room and prepared to close the pocket doors behind her, Yizenia stopped and looked at Ian Blake's lithe but well-muscled body draped across the sheets in glorious male splendor. She hadn't happened upon him in that Back Bay bar by accident. But the state of his sobriety had come as a surprise—one that she'd immediately exploited for both of their pleasure.

In the burgeoning morning light, Yizenia dropped the window blinds, closing out the view of the impressive pond glistening outside her window. She hadn't expected such beauty in the middle of a big city like Boston, but then, the last time she'd come here, she hadn't stayed long enough to see the sights. She vowed to explore this Jamaica Plain area, where the vast influx of Hispanic residents would allow her to blend in and go unnoticed.

That is, until she wanted to be noticed.

She quickly brewed and poured her morning *café cortado,* then reached for the newspaper sent to her months ago; she wanted the article close at hand when she contacted her client. She stretched, working out another of the knots in her lower back, then punched the prearranged number into her phone.

Despite the early hour, the client answered on the first ring.

"Señora Santiago?"

Yizenia sneered. The voice on the other end was mechanically disguised. A sign this client didn't trust her. Did her reputation mean nothing?

"The altered voice device offends me, señor," she said.

"I apologize, Ms. Santiago, but I cannot be too careful. Until our arrangement is settled, such precautions protect us both."

Yizenia tapped her red-tipped nails on the table beside the phone, noticing yet again how wrinkled her skin was becoming. She reached for the bottle of French lotion she'd purchased on her last holiday, and worked the emollient into her hands as she spoke.

"You will reveal yourself to me before I commit to your cause," she insisted.

"Of course."

The answer came quickly. Without hesitation. She supposed that her potential client could be ruined if anyone found out they'd engaged the services of an assassin. Or, as Yizenia preferred to think of herself, a minister of justice.

"*Bien,*" she agreed. For the time being, she had the upper hand in this negotiation.

"Did you receive the information I sent?"

Yizenia eased into the chair beside the phone, the dossier nearby. "*Sí,* but I will need to know more before I decide whether or not these men deserve my attention."

As the client offered to send her any information she required, Yizenia glanced at a photograph she'd unpacked a few days ago, frowning at how the watercolor hues had faded, how the smiles of her mother and father and younger sister seemed so . . . forced. Far away. Dead, even though the image had been created nearly a year before they'd been slaughtered by Franco's secret police.

"According to what I have read, Rebecca Manning received no justice from your courts," she said finally.

"I thought we would agree on that point." Even with the mechanical camouflage, she could hear the smile in the client's voice. The relief. "I've lived with this injustice for too long. Now, to watch these men receive accolades and monetary rewards when a beauti-

ful young woman I dearly loved died at their hands . . .
it turns my stomach. I cannot live with this any longer.
I'll pay any price."

Yizenia listened keenly. The desperation she heard
seemed genuine. She should know. She had once attempted to live with the knowledge that the monsters
who murdered her family had gone unpunished. When
living had become unbearable, she'd decided to take
justice into her own hands and mete out the retribution
her country's regime had denied her. Her tragedy had
turned her life in a new, powerful direction. For nearly
forty years she'd traveled the world, killing on behalf of
the victimized, risking her life to ensure that God had
His chance to punish the unforgivable acts of the arrogant and the cruel.

But now, she was tired. Old, really, though she
could still push her slender body and keen mind when
she needed to do so. When the price was high enough.
When the retribution was swift and sweet.

And this particular case brought an added incen-
tive, one her potential client need know nothing about.
She glanced at the pocket doors leading to the bedroom
and was satisfied by the sound of snoring.

"My price will be *exorbitante*," she assured.

"Name it."

She did. With no hesitation, the client agreed t
her terms.

"We must meet," she demanded. "I insist on shaking the hand of the person courageous enough to engage me."

Yizenia smiled as the voice described several sites in Boston where they could rendezvous unnoticed. She had fond memories of this quaint American city. Contacts born here. Rivals she'd acquired. And now, the possibility of finding someone to pass the torch to, someone to carry on her mission to right the wrongs of the world.

She committed the meeting place and time to memory. "Then I say *hasta luego*," she concluded. "You will have your justice soon, I assure you."

And ultimately, so would she.

One

"SILK SUITS YOU."

Marisela Morales tried not to jump at the sound of Max's voice, but his sudden, unexpected presence was the final stomp on her last nerve. It was bad enough being dragged to some society soiree where she stood out like, well, like a Cuban American ex-gang chick amid a mansion full of blue-blooded Boston big shots. But she didn't appreciate Max, Ian Blake's right-hand man, reminding her that no matter how honed her instincts were, he could trump her. Every time.

"Would . . . you . . . stop . . . doing that," she insisted through clenched teeth.

"Doing what? Complimenting you?"

She leveled her gaze into Max's steely gray glare. She knew he was laughing at her. Gloating. She dropped the subject. Max was a mystery she had no interest in solving tonight.

"Where's the boss?" she asked.

"Mr. Blake will be along shortly."

"He can take his time," she said with a sneer.

Max frowned. "Time to let go of the past, Marisela."

Marisela's jaw dropped open.

Max's expression froze and not surprisingly, he didn't say a word. Max was nothing if not loyal. But on Marisela's last mission, Ian Blake had used the life of one of his agents as a bargaining chip against her. And not just any agent, either. Some nights, she still could feel the slick gloss of Frankie's blood on her hands. And Max expected her to just up and forgive Ian for calling her bluff? Not likely.

"He nearly let Frankie die."

"But he didn't die, did he?"

She glanced aside and blew out a frustrated breath. No, Frankie hadn't died. He'd recovered. Not that she knew how he was doing since he hadn't bothered to contact her in three months.

"Mr. Blake asked me to bring you this," Max explained, handing her a flute of pale gold champagne.

"Fancy hooch isn't going to erase what he did, Max."

"No, but it might erase that god-awful look on your face."

"What god-awful look?"

"The one that makes me wonder if you didn't step in a pile of dog shit on the way up the red carpet."

Marisela took a long sip of the sparkling wine, rolling her eyes at Max's earthy assessment. Okay, so she didn't want to be here, in blustery Boston, at some highfalutin shindig fund-raiser, acting as arm candy to Ian Blake, who, so far, hadn't even bothered to show his face. She wanted to be back in Mexico, where she and Brynn Blake, Titan International's majority stockholder and Ian's twin sister, had been finishing up a case involving the kidnapping and rescue of a corporate CEO who should have known better than to venture into some quaint Chihuahua village just to pay for a piece of ass. The retrieval operation had been dangerous and bloody. She was still riding on the high of their success. Marisela had wanted to stick around when the Titan contingent handed the perpetrators over to the authorities, but she'd been recalled to the home office instead.

"So where are these jewels we're supposed to be protecting, anyway?" Marisela asked. Several women attending tonight's masked ball were wearing borrowed jewels as if they were actresses at the Oscars rather than the trophy wives of bloated politicians who showed their generosity toward those less fortunate by planning parties. Thanks to the guest list, security for the event was under the jurisdiction of the state police and the Secret Service. But the guy throwing the party had wanted extra attention paid to the jewels, so he'd hired Titan.

"You have half an hour until your shift," Max informed her. "Finish your champagne. Mingle. Get a feel for the layout of the place. But stay out of trouble."

She turned to blast him for his parental tone, but not surprisingly, Max had disappeared. She found some measure of comfort in the fact that she caught sight of the back of his head as he eased through the crowd.

He wasn't a ghost, but he sure as hell acted like one sometimes.

Mingle, he'd said. Get a feel for the layout.

She'd rather get a feel for the dark-skinned, long-haired *hombre* on the other side of the dance floor, staring at her as if she were the only woman in the room.

He wore a sequined black mask, but with the slim line of a beard tracing the hard edge of his chin, he oozed machismo. His tuxedo emphasized his physique—not too muscled, but by no means slim. She arched a brow, intrigued. With a cool stride, he walked from the foyer and into the ballroom, stopping to raise his champagne toward her in invitation.

Moving in his direction, she downed the rest of her own champagne and deposited the empty flute on a passing waiter's tray. She did look hot tonight. And she still had a good thirty minutes before Max would miraculously find her and escort her to her post. Might as well find someone . . . er, something . . . interesting to do until then.

As she moved, she enjoyed the soft friction of her silk gown against her skin. One perk of working for Titan was the wardrobe. She'd been hustled from the private airstrip where the Titan plane had landed from Mexico, to an exclusive Newbury Street boutique, where she'd chosen the most expensive gown in the shop. Royal purple and spaghetti strapped, the dress curved deliciously over her body from the plunging neckline to the fitted bodice to the skirt that flared at the hips with just enough Latina swish to hide the LadySmith revolver she had strapped to her inner thigh.

But she doubted she'd need the piece tonight. Anyone who tried to rob this bunch would have to be certifiable. As she wove through the dance floor seeking out the sexy man in black, she noticed security guards posted near every exit. The Secret Service had blocked off access to large portions of the expansive grounds, and even Titan's operatives had to check in through a special clearance procedure.

But none of that mattered to her when she caught sight of her mystery man talking to the bandleader. A few seconds later, the music segued into a Latin beat. A salsa. Not a boppy, cheerful salsa, but a sensual, sultry one. The music instantly pulsed deep in her belly. A crowd surged around her. Even the *gringos* couldn't resist such an undeniable rhythm.

She closed her eyes. Listened. Son of a bitch. He'd requested *"Reina de Reinas."* Queen of queens. She moved the bangle bracelet she wore on her left wrist and glanced at her tattoo, the only physical evidence left of her gang days, except for the scar behind her ear, hidden by her thick, dark hair. The brand at the base of her hand was a small purple crown, tipped with red jewels—the color of rubies, the color of blood. The color *las Reinas* wore when they wanted their enemies to be very, very afraid.

Her eyes flashed to the man in black. He stood in front of the stage, his face hidden behind a mask she could now see was tied with a bloodred ribbon. He raised a hand toward her, beckoning, inviting, demanding.

With an intrigued smile, she stepped nearer, inviting the music into her blood. The bongos beat a sway into her hips and the horns blared the shimmy into her shoulders. The minute the flesh of her fingers finally slid into his warm palm, he tugged her forward against his chest, rock hard and flowing with pure male power. She'd just danced herself into danger of the most carnal kind.

And after one glance into his hazel eyes—flecked with slivers of deep jade green—followed by the tandem swivel of his hips pressed close to hers, she knew.

Danger with a capital *F*. She smiled cryptically. The *cabrón*. Did he really think she wouldn't recognize him?

He grinned, emphasizing the thin, sculpted line of facial hair that traced from his sideburns down his strong chin, then spiked up toward his full lips. The dark streak of a moustache dashed across his upper lip and the wicked triangle below his bottom lip made him look like *el diablo* himself. To anyone else, his disguise might have been convincing.

But not to the girl who'd given him her virginity.

"So, where have you been all my life?" she asked him in Spanish.

Or more specifically, for the last three months. On their last mission together, Frankie Vega had taken a bullet that had nearly cost him his life. Before she'd left for Mexico, she'd stayed by his side, making sure that he lived long enough to turn her life upside down at least one more time.

He didn't answer her question, but instead, spun her skillfully beneath his arm, then stepped into the dance with sure and certain fire. Marisela matched him twist for twist, turn for turn, and kicked-up heel to kicked-up heel. Gazes locked, they danced the full breadth of the song until just before the final verse, when he slid his hand to the small of her back, yanked her flush against him, and then spun them off the dance floor into a corner behind the bandstand.

He pressed his palm against the paneled wall and a door slid open. Marisela bet the cops out front didn't know about this hiding place, though she wasn't surprised Frankie had found it. He had a talent for finding places he wasn't supposed to know about. With a slight gesture, he invited her inside. Once they were through a narrow archway, a steep and winding stairwell emerged from the shadows. Marisela freed herself from his bone-melting embrace and placed her palm squarely on the center of his chest.

"Where do you think you're taking me?" she whispered, her nose skimming the rough texture of his chin.

"A cielo, encantadora."

She laughed. Frankie had called her many things over the years, but "witch" had always been one of his favorites.

"To heaven, huh?" She traced his slim beard, enjoying the textures beneath her fingertip—the smooth heat of his skin, the prickly pinch of his razor-thin beard that effectively covered the scar she knew lingered beneath his bottom lip. "You look more like *el diablo* than any angel I've ever known, señor. But then, that's the idea, isn't it?"

He tilted his cheek into her palm, then turned to kiss the sweet spot on the inside of her wrist, squarely on the tattoo he had watched her get over ten years ago.

"Venga con mi, mi amor. Tengamos una noche divertida."

Come with him and have a wild night? She could think of worse offers. Like listening to Ian Blake schmooze with plastic politicians. Or watching over a bunch of rich women who didn't have the sense not to flaunt jewelry that could finance a few small third-world nations. Still, if she'd learned one thing from Brynn, it was that the job had to come first.

"I'm supposed to be working," she said, glancing over her shoulder. Darkness enshrouded them, but she could hear the music just beyond the wall.

With an insistent touch, Frankie turned her chin toward him. His mouth curved into a half-frown, half-pout as he took her hand in his and led her up the stairs. *"¿En que trabajas?"*

Only half reluctantly, she followed, amused at Frankie's game, asking her what she did for a living when he'd been the one to get her this gig in the first place. But tonight, he was leading her astray and likely enjoying every minute. She figured he'd be damned happy if she got fired. Again. Without Brynn to run to her rescue this time.

"I usually spend my time looking for bad guys," she answered.

Her comment inspired a smile that cracked beneath the edges of his mask. *"Tu a encontrado."*

Yeah, she'd found a bad guy, all right. One of the baddest around—and damn if that didn't thrill her to the bone.

At the top of the staircase, Frankie led her into the darkness of a shadowed niche. To her left, Marisela could hear the sounds from the ballroom drifting upward. He'd led her into the dome above the dancers, where a balcony, hidden by velvet curtains, kept them from view. From here, they could watch the activity below unseen.

If they were interested.

Which Marisela was not.

Frankie tugged her in close so that her body, covered in silk so delicate she'd eschewed traditional undergarments in favor of a skimpy thong, instantly molded to his hard, unyielding muscles. She leaned close and inhaled the scent on his neck. The fragrance was musky and male. The aroma curled around them, drawing her so close, his breath brushed her neck only seconds before his lips followed the same erotic path.

He whispered in Spanish, but the words didn't matter. Her mind was a swirl of color and sensation and she could focus only on the press of his hands over her hips, the scratch of his moustache across her neck, the heat of his lips on her shoulder. Against her ribs, the familiar jab of his sidearm heightened the polarity of safety and danger she felt in his arms. She speared her fingers into his hair, breaking the string that secured his ponytail. Suddenly, she realized that the hair she'd always known to be thick and wavy flowed through her fingers like threads of silk, fine and polished.

Doubt slammed into her. She opened her mouth to question his identity when he captured her lips with his own. The kiss was classic Frankie—possessive, urgent, and oh-so-thorough.

She yanked off his mask. With a push against his hard chest, she forced him back so that his cocky smile emerged in the shadowy light.

"You didn't know it was me, did you?"

She wanted to slap that smirk right off him. "I knew it was you the whole time!"

"Sure you did, *vidita*. I'm thinking a couple of months without me in your bed made you so hot, you'd do any guy with dark skin and an accent to make up for what you've been missing."

Keeping her rage in check, Marisela stepped farther into the alcove above the ballroom. The salsa music had given way to a disco tune. "Turn the Beat Around." They'd escaped just in time.

"What the hell are you doing here?"

"Getting you excited," he answered, reaching forward and flicking her tight, aroused nipple.

She'd backed up against the velvet curtain, biting the inside of her mouth to keep from pushing this challenge too far.

"You're some piece of work," Marisela claimed, borrowing one of Brynn's favorite phrases. "You think just because I'm back you can take up where you left off, with your hands in my pants?"

"Worked last time."

"You don't know what I've been up to the last few months," she claimed haughtily. "Maybe I've moved on."

"Don't make a fool of yourself, Marisela. I know everything you've been doing the last few months, right down to the vibrator you bought at that little sex shop in Tijuana with the *horchata* lollipops shaped like dicks in the window. I could give you a play-by-play of what happened next. Want me to?" He eased closer, and unless she planned on performing a backward flip out of the curtained archway onto the dancing crowd below, she couldn't retreat any farther.

Not that she wanted to. It seemed silly to protest when the feel of his hand inching up her inner thigh ignited a fire that hadn't been stoked in entirely too long. His eyes narrowed when he found her thong, and with a hard snap, he invited a rush of blood and sensation to the intimate lips of her *concha*.

She let her head fall back, inviting Frankie's lips to taste the sensitive skin of her throat. He complied, and the mixture of the soft, moist heat of his mouth with the stiff, cool friction from his beard nearly drove her plummeting over the edge. Her eyes fluttered open just in time to realize that she was leaning so far back, she was halfway outside the curtain, exposed to the crowd below.

With a startled laugh, she glanced down, hoping no one—particularly Ian Blake—had witnessed her indiscretion. Confident they hadn't been spotted, Marisela turned back toward Frankie—just in time to see the flash of a gun barrel—a gun trained on the crowd below.

Two

WITH A SHOVE, Marisela sent Frankie flying out of her way, his Glock now gripped tight in her hands. She aimed and pulled the trigger—a split second before the rifle across from her fired. Or maybe a split second after. She wasn't sure. But the curtain flared and from the other side, she heard a startled curse.

A cacophony of screams erupted from below and the music stopped mid-note. Marisela looked down. A man lay on the ground, blood pooling behind his head on the polished dance floor, his eyes staring blankly upward.

She tossed Frankie his gun and retrieved her own from beneath the folds of her skirt. Pointing to the curtain she'd fired at, Marisela then jerked her thumb to the left while she started down the circular hallway to the right, gun leveled ahead of her.

Behind her, she heard authoritative shouts spiraling upward, likely inside the narrow, hidden stairs she and Frankie had taken earlier. Great. What if some rent-a-cop confused her with the assassin, shot first and asked for ID later?

She met up with Frankie, both of them having completed their half-circle of the balcony. The opening to the main staircase mawed in front of them, brightly lit and covered in plush carpet. The ultimate escape route.

"I found this," he said, flashing the spent cartridge in front of her.

"Security's coming up behind us," Marisela said.

Frankie grabbed her arm and tugged her toward the wall. "If security in this place was any good, the congressman wouldn't be dead."

"You know him?"

Frankie shook his head. "Heard him introduced earlier. His wife is wearing several hundred thousand dollars' worth of ice around her neck."

When the cops appeared, Marisela and Frankie held their weapons above their heads and identified themselves as Titan operatives. While two uniformed officers from the state police checked out their names by walkie-talkie, the rest of the contingent headed downstairs via the open stairway.

"They had the main entrance guarded," Marisela said to Frankie, her mind racing. How could an assassin get in to this party armed and then escape nearly unnoticed? Thanks to Frankie's sensual diversion, she hadn't had a good look at the mansion's layout, but she had noticed high ceilings, wide-open foyers, and few odd-angled curves. Seemed an ideal place to protect. Big, but with mostly unhampered views inside the main areas. Of course, the place was probably loaded with secret passageways and hidden halls. Look at the staircase concealed behind the bandstand. How many other hidden nooks and crannies did Houghton House possess?

"The dome was the perfect hiding place for a shooter. Security sucked," Frankie assessed, inducing the ire of the cop still holding a gun on him.

Thanks to Frankie's outspoken remark, checking out their story took twice as long, but when the police decided that finding the shooter was more important than harassing two private investigators, they took quick statements, recorded their contact information, and then told them to get lost. One officer immediately dashed down the stairs. The other remained behind, protecting the area Marisela pointed out as the shooter's perch.

Marisela pulled Frankie around the opposite side of the circular balcony, where the cop wouldn't hear them.

"Why didn't you give him the casing?"

Frankie grinned and shrugged. "Cooperating with badges ain't my deal no more."

Marisela smirked. For years while in prison, Frankie had survived twenty-three-hour days behind bars by working as an informant during the one hour he was in the yard. He'd never ratted out his home-boys, but specialized in putting a crimp in the foreign-run drug trade. And while his service had shaved a few years off his sentence, he tended to look back on his time as a mole with disdain, probably because his dirty deal with the DEA had led him straight to Titan and Ian Blake.

"Let's find the shooter ourselves," Frankie offered.

"Our gig is just to watch the jewels," Marisela pointed out.

Frankie tossed the casing into the air like a coin he intended to flip. "No harm in us taking a look around. Maybe if we catch the shooter, Blake'll give us a raise."

Marisela rolled her eyes. "Bored a little?"

Frankie's grin was pure sin. "Not now that you're back, *vidita*. Where do we start?"

Marisela took a quick look around. "Where does the main staircase lead?" she asked, pointing to where the officers had disappeared.

"Down to the main entry hall. Two doors lead into that hall. Both had two guards at each site. The cop at the foot of the stairs was just backup. No way the shooter got in through there."

Marisela nodded. "Then there's another secret entrance up here. Like the one we took. Could the shooter have used—"

"No," he interrupted. "The secret staircase wasn't

on any of the blueprints. I found it by accident earlier when I was checking things out. I'd been using it all night to get a bird's-eye view."

"Couldn't someone have seen you use it?"

He looked offended. "The cops were sweeping the balcony every fifteen minutes. I was timing myself around them. No way anyone got past me."

Marisela walked along the balcony, running her hands along the wall panels that encircled the inner part of the dome. On her second pass, she started to count. Belinda would be so proud of her. Her math-whiz little sister was forever preaching to Marisela about the virtues of using numbers to solve all her problems. Unfortunately, most of the time, Marisela needed a calculator to figure out a twenty-percent tip. But something about being surrounded by curves in the circular balcony sparked an idea. She counted the panels between the main stairwell and the secret stair-case she and Frankie used to ascend to their private rendezvous.

The numbers didn't add up. On the left side, where they stood, there were too many panels.

"Damn, where's Belinda when I need her?" she said in a whispered hiss.

"*¿Tu hermanita?*" Frankie asked, clearly surprised. Marisela didn't talk about Belinda much. Mostly never.

"There are twenty-three panels between the main staircase and the one we used. And forty-six . . . "

As she spoke, the problem's solution popped into

her brain. So simple. She counted twenty-three panels from the main stairwell in the opposite direction of the secret staircase and stopped. She stretched up and smoothed her fingers into the grooves around the wood. She pressed on the left side. Then on the right. A spring released the panel, revealing another private staircase.

"*Madre de Dios,*" Frankie said.

Marisela shushed him, but inside did a mental salsa step. "Come on."

She could feel Frankie venturing away from her, exploring the darkness beyond the panel, which she closed so the cops wouldn't follow. After a few seconds, their eyes and ears adjusted. Light glimmered from below. In the faint distance, they could hear footsteps moving downward.

Frankie grabbed her hand. "This way."

Marisela followed, wondering how the hell she was supposed to walk quietly down creaky wooden steps in stiletto heels, but did her best to balance on the balls of her feet. She gathered the bulk of her skirt over her arm, preferring not to rip the damned thing to shreds chasing an assassin she hadn't even been hired to find. But she couldn't deny the rush of adrenaline pumping through her veins. This was the stuff that had led her to Titan in the first place. The thrills. The excitement. The risk.

At the bottom of the stairs, a partly opened panel led into a short, narrow service hall. Not too far in the distance, pots and pans clattered, steam and grease sizzled, and raucous conversations in rapid-fire Spanish rent the air. Marisela moved quietly toward the door and listened.

What did she have in that bag? How much did she give you to stay quiet?

Whoever had just sneaked through the kitchen had the tongues of the staff wagging.

"Frankie," Marisela whispered. "She went through here."

"*She?*"

"According to the kitchen staff, yeah."

"Let's follow her," he said, his eyes twinkling.

Marisela barred her arm across the door. "I'll follow her through here. You double back and get outside. Cut her off."

Frankie narrowed his eyes and she blew out a frustrated breath. He didn't want to miss all the fun. Well, hell. Neither did she.

He turned back toward the stairwell. "Watch your step and where you wag that thing," he said, gesturing to her gun.

As if she needed Frankie Vega to give her advice on weapons. Marisela reholstered her LadySmith and slipped through the door into the small kitchen. Chatter came to an abrupt halt and serving spoons dropped in a clatter against the steam tables. Marisela pasted on her best smile and started talking in Spanish.

"I'm looking for my friend," she explained, thinking as quickly as she could. "She came through here, carrying a bag."

Six men and women with dark skin and frightened

eyes all exchanged furtive glances. They'd clearly been instructed not to talk.

"*Por favor,* I have something she needs. She could be . . . hurt," Marisela said, eyeing the door behind her, implying people were after her—and the woman the kitchen staff was oddly protecting.

The confused and clearly torn group remained silent, forcing Marisela to count to ten in order to hold her anger in check. She continued to implore them with her eyes and a pathetic smile, repeating in her mind, Patience, Marisela. Wait for it. They'll trust you. Give them just a few more . . .

"*Sí, sí,*" a man dressed in a white chef's uniform finally answered, grinning broadly, if not guiltily. "Through there."

Marisela smiled and took off, hoping like hell they hadn't led her on a wild-goose chase.

The Houghton House grounds were well lit, glowing with more land, statuary, topiary, and reflective pools than one mansion just minutes from the center of bustling Boston had a right to. In the distance, Marisela could hear the scream of ambulances and twice she saw police dashing through the line of limousines parked along the stone drive far to the west of her, forcing open doors and searching for the shooter.

She and Frankie should back off, she supposed. She hadn't been hired to protect the congressman. But she'd been so close to the shooter when the hit went down.

Maybe she would have noticed the threat sooner if she hadn't been more concerned with her own sexual pleasure than with keeping her eyes and ears open.

Movement to the east of the main house caught her eye. Shadowed movement. If the shooter was hiding in the cars or along the drive, then the cops and security guards would find her. But no one that she could see was moving in this direction, likely because the manpower hadn't yet been deployed. Wouldn't hurt for her to explore a little.

She entered a garden with tall hedges on either side. Only after she was a few steps in did she realize the bushes were shaped into a maze. She stepped back out. She wasn't screwing around with that shit. Making her way around the outer perimeter, she caught sight of a shadowy figure slipping under the portico.

Just up the brick stairs, inside the tall, beveled-glass doors, the invitees to the masquerade soiree were milling around, sucking down cocktails as fast as the waiters could serve them and talking in hushed, horrified tones.

The closest door was slightly ajar.

A nice touch.

Make them think she went back inside. Engage the next few hours in interviewing each and every attendee while the real assassin makes her escape.

Muy engañosa.

But the shooter wasn't the only sneaky female in the house. Marisela bounded up the steps, slammed the door, then hid behind a large urn.

Only a few heartbeats later, Marisela heard fabric rustling on the grass. A second later, a tall, statuesque form folded out of the darkness, looked left, then right, and then dashed toward the sculpted bushes. Marisela took a deep breath and launched herself over the porch railing.

She landed with a thud and a grunt, the wind rushing from her lungs. Marisela snatched and clawed until she had handfuls of the shooter's slim knit dress in her grasp. The shooter fought back, jamming sharp nails in between the bone and sinew at Marisela's wrist.

With a scream, Marisela released her. After taking a split second to regain her equilibrium, she rolled on the ground, landing directly behind the assassin, who stumbled only a few feet away.

With a vicious yank, Marisela tore the flouncy skirt off her own gown, kicked off her *tacones,* assumed a fighting stance and shouted for the woman to stop.

Surprisingly, she did.

The shooter turned slowly, oozing confidence. Elegant in a sleek, full-faced white mask and a soft-black gown that hid the identifiable features of her body, she straightened first, then matched Marisela's crouch.

"Something you want?" the woman asked.

Her Spanish was perfect. Crisp, but chic.

"Just admiring your dress. Did you get that from the set of a horror movie?"

The woman made a sweeping gesture, showing off the dramatic neckline that curved stiffly behind her head. Maybe she didn't realize that Halloween was over a month away. But the choice was clever, since the accessory made her height hard to judge. The bodice was fitted, but the skirt and sleeves flared, making it nearly impossible for Marisela to tell if she'd challenged someone thick, skinny, or even bottom heavy. She was betting, at least, on strong and wily, because her assailant had taken a stance that would only be familiar to someone who knew how to fight.

"Back off," the shooter said, the voice deep and throaty, but decidedly female. And she spoke in English. With no accent at all. "I'm not here for you."

"That makes me feel better. I don't much like imagining myself lying in a pool of my own blood after being shot by a hidden sniper. It's a lot like shooting someone in the back, don't you think?"

The woman's eyes flashed behind her mask. Except for her flowing dark hair, thick and reaching well past her shoulders, Marisela would have no decent description to offer the cops. The assassin was dark-haired, sneaky, and spoke fluent Spanish and completely American English. She might as well have described herself.

"The manner of death doesn't matter; he pays for his crime in blood."

Marisela swallowed thickly. This wasn't murder for hire. This was revenge.

"Who are you?"

"A shadow. An avenging angel. Don't cry for that man, Marisela," she said in Spanish. "He doesn't deserve your pity."

Marisela stepped back, the use of her name catching her off guard. Instantly, the assassin feinted left, then right, but Marisela instinctively mirrored her actions, anticipating her next move so that when the assassin grabbed for Marisela, she spun, prepared to kick the woman to the ground. But before she could complete her rotation, the shooter shot out a foot and tripped Marisela, sending her careening onto the lawn.

The woman turned to flee, but Marisela kicked from the ground, hitting the woman in the small of the back with her heel. She followed through with a second, higher kick, sending the woman sprawling. With powerful arms, the woman crawled forward, but Marisela launched on top of her, attempting to pin her arms behind her.

"Let go of me!" the woman screamed.

The assassin kicked and flailed, sending grass and dirt into Marisela's face. She spit in between her gasps for breath, struggling to keep her grip on the woman's legs. "Not . . . in this . . . lifetime!"

With a twist, Marisela flipped the woman onto her back and propelled herself forward, raising her arm to strike down hard with a hammered fist, but the woman blocked her move. They rolled across the lawn. Seconds ticked by in excruciatingly slow motion, punctuated by scratches, punches, and kicks. When they finally spun to a halt, they both heaved for precious gulps of air.

"This is not your business," the shooter said, pointing her finger at Marisela.

Marisela could hear someone shouting authoritative orders from the other side of the stone wall. The woman's only escape route was over a fence at the far end of the property—and Marisela was blocking her path.

Nearly simultaneously, Marisela and the shooter climbed shakily to their feet. Marisela stood, hands up, palms out, ready to strike. The shooter dipped her hand beneath her mask, which had cracked, but still hid her face well. When her gloved hand emerged, Marisela saw blood smear the white plastic.

"Where's your gun?" the shooter asked.

"Where's yours?" Marisela's thigh holster dangled empty against her leg. Quick glances on the ground told her the weapon was out of sight, so it might as well be out of mind. "Besides, shooting people in cold blood is your MO, not mine."

"*Cómo dulce,*" the shooter commented, her tone dripping with false sweetness. "Why stop me at all? I'm not your concern. Yet."

"I don't know," Marisela replied, her voice laced with sarcasm. "I was just thinking that some people inside might want to talk to you. You know, guys with badges. Maybe the friends of the dead guy you left lying on the floor. Or maybe I just wanted to catch you because I could."

By now, sirens filled the air. Flashes of red and blue lights caught Marisela's peripheral vision. She wondered where Frankie was. Why hadn't he emerged from the house after doubling around to rendezvous with her on the back lawn? But mostly, she tried to figure out what the hell she should do next.

The assailant took two steps back. Marisela matched the move.

"I have no intention of going with you peacefully," the assassin said.

Marisela shrugged. "Violently's been fun so far. No need to change tactics now."

The shooter's first volley of kicks and punches came hard and fast, giving Marisela little time to block. She got in a few good licks, but not before the woman clocked her with a roundhouse kick to the chin. Marisela went down, but managed to grab the woman's ankle on the way, crashing them both to the ground.

The struggle was messy and ugly and hurt like hell. Every move Marisela made was countered, every punch blocked, or at least hampered by the woman's incredible strength and skill. Marisela allowed herself a split second to respect her opponent before she locked onto the woman's arm and twisted. The woman groaned, but broke off the attack by unexpectedly surrendering to Marisela's momentum, catching her offguard.

The shooter's gloves, glossy and slick, slipped from Marisela's grip, but with a determined yank, Marisela ripped the fabric off her opponent's hand.

Bright orange and green flashed from the woman's wrist. The odd shape, clearly a tattoo, mesmerized Marisela just long enough for the woman to break out of her hold.

She held the wrist up proudly. "Take a good look.

Interesting, isn't it? Yours is more *básico,* but we both wear our *tatuaje* where the blood pulses, where the pain is great."

The realization stunned Marisela. In that moment, the shooter kicked out hard. Marisela caught the woman's foot and moved to throw her off balance when she struck Marisela across the back of the neck. Marisela tumbled backward cursing and the assassin, without another word, disappeared into the darkness and shadows.

Marisela scrambled to her feet. Frankie finally emerged from the house and jogged down the steps and across the lawn.

"Holy shit, woman. What happened to you?"

Marisela wiped a drop of blood from the corner of her mouth. "I found the shooter."

"You let her go?"

Marisela took a brief, exhausted look at her ripped dress and scratched and bloodied skin. "Yeah, poor woman. She'd had a tough day. Who was I to stand in the way of her scheduled spa massage?"

"She kicked your ass?" he asked, eyebrow arched in disbelief.

Marisela stalked over to the portico and retrieved her abandoned shoes. The dress, on the other hand, was headed for the trash can. She plodded around the grounds, searching for her gun. "She knew what she was doing. And where the hell were you anyway? Some partner you are, disappearing. Does the word *backup* mean anything to you?"

He smiled coolly and she suddenly noticed he'd lost not only the mask he'd worn earlier, but his tie. He still looked sexy enough to eat. "*Lo siento, vidita.* The cops stopped me on my way through the hall."

She snorted. "Isn't that always your story?"

Three

COCOONED IN THE BACK of a Titan limousine waiting for the police to clear their car for exit, Frankie tugged Marisela's wrist to his lips and kissed the very spot where her tattoo throbbed with the beat of her heart. She was dirty and bloodied and sore—and yet, when a flash of light from outside streaked across Frankie's midnight eyes, so dark with hunger, warmth pooled deep in her belly. And lower.

"Your skin is so soft." He swiped his tongue across her pulse point, blew a heated breath across the moist path, and then smoothed her palm against his cheek.

Pleasure eased over her skin at the touch of his hot breath, but pleasure had cost her a hell of a lot tonight. She yanked her arm back. "What are you talking about?"

Frankie dug into the limousine's built-in bar and mixed her a Cuba Libre. The car even had a stash of fresh lime. He went light on the cola, but heavy on the rum, just the way she liked it. "If you had shot the assassin, you'd likely be in jail right now, *vidita*. Or worse."

She took a sip of the rum and cola. The icy trickle slowed her racing pulse. "There are worse things than jail?"

"Dead is worse. If the cops thought you'd just shot a party guest, I'm thinking they would have returned fire first and asked questions later."

"Even if the party guest I shot just killed some congressman?" she pointed out.

"Could you prove that?"

She skewered him with a sharp look. "I know what I saw. What I heard. Trust me, this woman had one purpose and one purpose only. Revenge."

"For what?"

Marisela slid an ice cube into her mouth. "It wasn't like we were shooting the shit, Frankie. She just said a few things while we were kicking each other's asses." Marisela combed her fingers through her hair, massaging her scalp to appease the headache threatening to split her skull in two. She did love a good fight, but the aftereffects sucked.

Frankie changed seats, moving beside her. Her body ached to lean into him and let his natural heat envelop her, but she resisted. This was exactly why she hated having Frankie around—and exactly why she missed him. He could be a stone wall, surrounding her, protecting her—and that's precisely what she didn't need.

"You're beating yourself up for not shooting her when you had the chance in the garden."

"She wouldn't have gotten away."

"You don't even know for sure if the woman you fought with in the grass was the same woman who fired the shot that hit the congressman."

"Uh-huh," she grunted, doubtful. Who else would fight like that to get away? "I know what I saw."

"What you *saw*," Frankie emphasized, "was the barrel of a rifle through a curtain on a dark balcony. Then you saw some woman in black come out from under the portico."

"You think Boston socialites regularly hang out with the rats under the porch?"

"Depends on who you consider a rat in this town," he quipped.

Marisela didn't want to laugh, but the combination of Frankie's logic, the rum, and the glamorous comfort of the limo inspired her to at least crack a sardonic smile. "I could have fired a warning shot."

"And what if she ignored it? Then, the cops book you for endangerment or some shit. I'm sure threatening rich people gets you a hefty fine around here, if not a twenty-year jail sentence. And let's say you just wound her. And let's say the cops screw up and don't get any physical evidence linking her to the crime. You end up in jail for reckless endangerment or even attempted murder and she goes on to collect her fee. Stop beating yourself up."

He knew her well—too well—which was why she hated how he could sneak into her brain uninvited and figure out the complicated workings of her mind. Half the time, she didn't even understand the crap running through her brain. Ordinarily, she wasn't one to harbor regrets or even look back ten minutes into the past. But all that had changed when she joined Titan.

The limousine finally started to move. They'd crawled about twenty feet away from the house when it jerked to a stop, splashing the contents of Marisela's drink across her chest and lap. She screamed, and as she let lose a string of curses, the door wrenched open.

Frankie turned, his arm stretched protectively in front of her. "What the hell?"

"I'm so sorry," said the man who climbed gingerly inside the limo, uninvited. "My security guards can jump the gun when I'm anxious. One of the reasons why I hired your outfit in the first place."

His annoyed grumble belied his smooth exterior. His black tuxedo contrasted starkly with his thick white hair and pale blue eyes, but when he looked up and smiled, Marisela felt her anger diminish.

"Ms. Morales, your dress is ruined. I insist you

send the tattered remains to me immediately so I can have it replaced." He pulled a silk handkerchief from his pocket, offering it to her. "You looked so stunning tonight."

She arched a brow. "Do I know you?"

He didn't answer until she accepted the cloth, which she used to mop her drink off her cleavage.

"Leo Devlin," he said, his voice deep and arresting. "We hadn't yet been formally introduced, but every man at the masquerade noticed you, I'm quite certain. I was your host this evening."

Marisela waved the sopping rag at him. "Great party. We'll have to do it again sometime."

Frankie sat back against the seat. "Marisela, Mr Delvin is *also* our client."

Marisela frowned. "Oh. No one's jewels got swiped, did they?" She'd never made it to her shift on diamond patrol. She'd been too busy messing around with Frankie, and then, trying to avert an assassination.

Devlin's smile reached his eyes. For an *hombre de poder y dinero* who owned a house that could double for a small town, he seemed incredibly comfortable talking to "the help."

"Everyone's jewelry was perfectly safe, thanks to Titan. But the police informed me that you may have tangled with the person who shot the senator. Is this true?"

Marisela exchanged glances with Frankie. She'd given the police a report, but she hadn't exactly told them everything. Old habits died hard. And she wasn't sure she should talk to anyone else before she'd been debriefed by Titan. She'd learned the procedures recently enough that she actually remembered them. However, Devlin was the client. Or had been up until the time when the party came to a bloody end.

"I confronted a woman who seemed intent on leaving the party in a hurry," Marisela offered.

Devlin's eyes widened. "A woman?"

She quirked a grin. "We can be very dangerous."

Devlin chuckled, shaking his head. "Apparently so. I don't wish to impede the investigation in any way, but this shooting happened at my event and in my house. Congressman Bennett and I weren't on the same page politically, but the idea of him dying in my house . . . you can see how I'd want to make sure the perpetrator is brought to justice as quickly as possible."

Marisela shrugged. The man wasn't talking out of his ass. If he were a political rival, he'd likely rush to the top of the suspect list.

"Talk to the police, then," she offered.

"You didn't hire us to protect your perimeter," Frankie reminded him.

"Perhaps I should have," Devlin said ruefully. "Is there anything else you can tell me?"

Marisela shook her head and returned his soiled handkerchief.

Devlin's eyes twinkled and his smile reflected the kind of humor that looked good on a man who was richer than God. "You will send me the dress?"

Cool and cocky, this one. He was three times her age, she figured, but he was still flirting.

"I don't have much use for ball gowns," she concluded.

With a nod, Devlin said good night and exited the limousine. Moments later, the car was released and they sped off to rendezvous, Frankie told her, with Ian Blake. She was tired and sore and now damp and sticky. He was so the last man she wanted to see.

Fifteen minutes later, the limousine pulled to a stop behind a large white building with stark brick architecture and institutional iron doors. A tall, blond, tuxedoed man emerged from the back seat of the limo parked ahead of theirs and started toward her and Frankie. Ian Blake opened the door and leaned inside, looking cool and contained and, damn him, delicious.

"Don't you look . . . spiffy," she said, admiring Ian in his tuxedo, a classic Giorgio Armani with slim satin lapels that emphasized the broadness of his shoulders and the golden hue of his tan. His dark blond hair was close-cropped, but with fashionable spikes that defied conservative expectations—which made sense, since the man defied just about everything, including Marisela's instinctual need to hate his guts.

Under the dim dome light, he gave her a quick once-over. "You, on the other hand, have looked better."

She gave him the finger. The first time they'd met, she'd been bruised and bloodied. They were starting to establish a pattern. "No thanks to you. Makes me wonder if you don't get your rocks off when I'm in pain."

He held out his hand gallantly. "Sadism really isn't my preferred fetish, truth be told."

His accent was a mix of urbane British and pure American snark. She cast a glance at Frankie, who plunged out of the car, forcing Ian to move out of the way. The coast cleared, Marisela climbed out after him. She might be stiff and sore, but she didn't need her boss's help to get out of the car. Especially when that help involved touching him. Last time she'd done that, they'd almost ended up in bed together.

"In case you're wondering," she said, "I don't ever want to know your *preferred fetish*."

Ian's pale blue eyes twinkled as his generous mouth struggled to contain a smile. "You say that now, but things change."

Frankie grabbed Marisela's elbow possessively. "Some things never change, Blake."

"Like your predictable personality, perhaps?" Blake replied.

Marisela yanked her elbow free, rolled her eyes at both of them, and marched into the building. Nothing propelled her out of a situation faster than excess testosterone. Only after she'd walked a good ten paces down the hallway did she realize she was in a hospital. She spun around to retreat when Blake blocked her path, Frankie close behind.

"I don't need a hospital," she said, crossing her arms tightly over her chest. "I hate hospitals."

Images flashed in her brain. She'd wanted out of the gang so bad, she'd opted to beat out. A roll of the dice had determined the number of homegirls she'd had to take on. She had to fight them and live in order to be allowed to leave *las Reinas*. She couldn't remember now how many she'd rolled. Five? Six? Seven? All she knew was that she'd won.

She'd suffered cracked ribs, a punctured lung, a torn scalp, destroyed spleen, and permanent scars. But as the saying went, "you should have seen the other guy."

Ian slid his hands coolly into his pockets. "Few people like hospitals, but our client is here, so you'll have to make do. I won't make you see a doctor. However, if you pass out, you're on your own."

She narrowed her gaze. She was sore and cut up, but hadn't experienced anywhere near the damage it would take to force her to seek medical help. "We just left our client back at the museum."

"The party at Houghton House is over and so is that assignment," Ian informed them. "We have a new objective now. You and Frankie are now charged with finding out who tried to kill Congressman Craig Bennett."

"You mean they didn't succeed?" Marisela asked. She'd seen the man lying on the ballroom floor, though admittedly, she'd been high above him at the time and hadn't stuck around long enough to see if he was moving.

"Thankfully, your intervention drew the bullet astray," Ian confirmed, glancing back and forth between Marisela and Frankie. "But that's not exactly common knowledge and it could be in our best interests to keep it that way for as long as possible."

"You think she'll try again?" Marisela asked.

Ian stared at her intently. "You spoke with the assassin. What do you think?"

Marisela turned and proceeded down the hall. This wasn't over. Not for the congressman. And obviously, not for her.

After a short debriefing in an unoccupied hospital room, Ian shuttled Marisela and Frankie through hallways and up stairs until they stopped outside the chapel, or so Marisela guessed from the cross on the door. Frankie shrugged out of his tuxedo jacket and offered it to her; she accepted appreciatively. The torn and tattered state of her dress hadn't mattered much until she was inches from entering a house of God. Or at least, His tiny sublet apartment.

Ian leaned in close, his voice a whisper. "Craig Bennett's wife is inside."

"Where's her husband?" Frankie asked.

Ian glanced at his watch. "More than likely, still in surgery. I posted Max at the operating room door. In case our assassin tries to finish the job."

Marisela shifted her weight, her eyes locked on the cross on the door. It had no corpus, no body of Jesus, but the symbol was still powerful. Funny how Catholic school imprints on the brain, even when she'd spent the majority of her time there with the nuns in detention. She could stare down murderers and go hand-to-hand with a trained assassin, but put a crucifix in front of her when she was still lamenting the fact that she hadn't shot the killer and she quaked.

She cleared her throat, trying to push away the thought that if she'd simply killed the shooter when she had a chance, their client's husband wouldn't still be in danger. Commandments were fine and everything, but where did justice come in?

Marisela wiped a smear of blood off her chin. "So we've been hired to provide protection for the congressman?"

"Partly, yes. He has private security, but they did little good tonight. Max is now the lead agent on that assignment."

"Was there any reason to think the congressman would be a target at the party?" Frankie inquired.

"The shooter said revenge," Marisela injected, though she'd just recounted her brief conversation with the shooter to both of them minutes before.

"Revenge for what? And besides, we don't know if she was lying, trying to throw us off." Ian shook his head. "Until we have more proof, we must assume that Bennett wasn't a target any more than the other politicians in attendance. But the congressman's wife asked us to investigate further. Her name is Denise. She's extremely distraught," he said, directing the tidbit of information at Marisela.

Her mouth dropped open in shock. "I can be nice."

"That's not been my experience," Ian contested.

"I wonder why," she shot back. Ian Blake had been nothing more than a high-class bully since the first time they'd met, and with the exception of a few brief acts of compassion on his part, neither one of them had tried very hard to hide their antagonism. The only thing Marisela succeeded in masking was her innate and, frankly, damned annoying attraction to the guy.

Ian opened the chapel door gingerly, then led his agents inside. Marisela shook off the chill and focused on the woman sitting hunched over in the front pew, a rosary dangling from her fingers. A police officer guarded the door on the inside and a man wearing a tuxedo sat beside her, his arm around her shoulder.

"Mrs. Bennett?" Ian said softly.

Frankie and Marisela hung a few steps behind.

The woman looked up. Her wavy caramel hair, streaked with wisps of blond, hung limp over cheeks that had been washed of makeup by rivulets of tears. Her eyes, a soft green, were surrounded by skin at once bruised and puffy from the kind of crying a woman did when her world was ripped out from under her feet.

"Mr. Blake?" The woman held out her hand, which quivered until Ian took it firmly in his. "The doctors are hopeful. The bullet missed a major artery in his neck, but did serious damage to his windpipe. He'll be on a respirator . . . when,"—she forced the word out—"*when* he wakes up. I don't understand how someone could . . . "

She dissolved into tears again and Marisela looked away. She didn't blame the woman for losing it, but she didn't exactly like watching, either.

"Perhaps you can come back later," the man beside Denise Bennett suggested.

Marisela pursed her lips. Though he was clearly close to the victim's wife, this man held his emotions firmly in check. No signs of tears or worry lines, just classic sleek cheekbones and a lift at the end of his nose that had rich written all over it. His crisp brown eyes flicked warily over Marisela and Frankie, and then returned to Denise as he tightened his hold on her shoulder.

Ian stood straighter and matched arrogant privilege to arrogant privilege. "And you are?"

"Evan Cole. Congressman Bennett is my closest friend and I won't have his wife exploited when she's so vulnerable."

Marisela glanced at Frankie, who shared her incredulous expression. Was it her imagination or did she sense Evan Cole had solid gold bars shoved up his ass?

"Please, Evan," Denise said, her voice no more than a weary sigh. "I sent for Mr. Blake. He runs Titan International."

The distrustful look on Evan Cole's face bloomed to full dislike. "The investigation firm?"

Ian grinned. "Our reputation precedes us."

Evan's reply was dismissive. "You did corporate work for one of my subsidiaries a few years ago."

"I trust our work was up to snuff," Ian replied, nonplussed.

Evan Cole didn't respond, just gave a curt nod.

Marisela glanced over her shoulder toward the

tiny window in the chapel door. Nurses and techs in scrubs flashed by in a rainbow of colors. She didn't see one single hint of institutional green, which made her breathing a little easier. Still, echoes of the past rang in her ears. Doctors talking in hushed tones, unaware or unconcerned that she could hear their grave diagnosis. Her mother's weeping. Her father's whispered prayers.

"And this is Marisela Morales," Ian said, snapping Marisela out of her reverie and beckoning her over.

Marisela held out her hand, which she just noticed was smudged with dirt from the fight. She rubbed it on what was left of her skirt, which did very little to remove the grime.

Denise Bennett took Marisela's hand without hesitation and cupped it with care. "You fought with the person who shot my husband?" the woman asked, her eyes wide with what looked suspiciously like hope.

"Yes, I did."

The corners of her mouth quivered as they folded down in a frown. "But your representative," she said, speaking to Ian though she hadn't broken contact with Marisela. "Max, I believe. He said you had no proof she was actually the shooter?"

Marisela shook her head. She had the killer's admission of guilt, but Marisela guessed that telling Denise Bennett that a highly trained professional killer believed her husband deserved to die for some past transgression was not the wisest move at the moment.

"The police recovered very little physical evidence from the crime scene," Ian said. "They may find more in the daylight. You may not need us at all, Mrs. Bennett."

Denise Bennett shook her head furiously and Marisela's hand was released in the tempest. "No, no! I won't rely on the police to investigate this thoroughly. They've never treated him with the respect he deserves. Never."

An odd look passed between Evan Cole and Denise Bennett, one that only Marisela seemed to think was weird judging by the practiced professionalism on Ian's face and Frankie's bored indifference.

"Titan International is a top-notch organization," Ian assured her. "We have contacts within the police department, but we can be discreet."

"You aren't obligated to share what you've learned with the police?" Denise asked, her voice quivering.

The question caused Frankie to step in closer.

Ian eyed both his agents, then glanced to the cop at the door. "State law dictates that unless the information is vetted through you, we have no obligation to reveal what we find out to any state or federal agency. Unless we're subpoenaed, and even then we've fought that battle before and won. You are the client, Mrs. Bennett."

She nodded, then patted Evan's hand. "Evan, please go get an update on Craig for me."

Evan's eyes narrowed. "The doctor knows where you are, Denise. I'm quite certain they'll come find you—"

"Please."

Just as polite, but even more forceful. Evan stood, gave Ian a particularly cagey look, then disappeared out the door. With a nod from Ian, Frankie followed. Ian approached the police officer and chatted with the man quietly. The officer nodded curtly, then took up his post outside the door, leaving the three of them alone.

Marisela smoothed her hands down her tattered skirt, not entirely sure what she was supposed to do in this situation. So far, her training hadn't included client interactions, and judging by her last case, interviewing clients without pissing them off was the area where she needed the most improvement.

Ian helped her out by gesturing to the pew behind Denise. She slid in, not surprised when Denise turned to her with wildly desperate eyes. "You didn't see anything that could help us identify the woman who shot my husband?"

Ian snatched the question before Marisela could formulate a wise response. "Why don't we focus on what you know, Mrs. Bennett? I promise that once your husband is out of surgery and I've had proper time to debrief my agents, I'll give you a full and complete report of our progress."

A look passed over Denise's face, and for a moment, Marisela thought she'd press for more information. Instead, she nodded her head in agreement.

"Who would want to kill your husband?" he asked.

Denise's shoulders drooped. "Who doesn't? He's a politician, Mr. Blake. He's been harassed since he was first elected to office."

"Anything recent?"

She leaned forward, her forehead cradled in her

hands. "He's been working on prescription drug reform, but except for the pharmaceutical lobby, the bill is insanely popular."

Marisela ran her hand through her hair, discovering a new batch of grass blades and a tendril of moss. She hugged Frankie's coat closer around her and focused her eyes on Mrs. Bennett's face.

"Pharmaceuticals?" Ian asked. "Leo Devlin was the host of tonight's fund-raiser."

"Yes," Denise verified. "He's been an outspoken opponent to my husband's plan, but he's done quite a bit to reach out to the politicians supporting the bill, trying to find compromise so companies like his won't go bankrupt. My husband doesn't want to ruin American industry, he just wants a level playing field. Leo Devlin invited both sides to the fund-raiser tonight, and to be honest, he never once brought the topic up. Not when I was there, anyway. I can't imagine . . ."

Ian's expression transmitted directly to Marisela. Mrs. Bennett couldn't imagine Leo Devlin doing her husband harm, but apparently, Ian could. Marisela had little opinion on the matter since she'd only met the man briefly, but in her experience, she'd yet to meet anyone who wasn't capable of extreme violence if the circumstances were right.

"You realize," Ian explained, "that the police aren't even certain your husband was the target tonight? The assassin might have been gunning for any one of the politicians and celebrities at the party."

Denise took a deep breath. "I can't afford to assume

that my husband is safe. As popular as his current platform is, Craig has seen his share of troubles, Mr. Blake. I won't let him die for them."

Denise reached across Ian's lap and retrieved her purse. Marisela expected her to extract a tissue, but instead, she pulled out a small slip of paper. She tossed the beaded handbag carelessly aside and clutched the square tightly in her hands.

Marisela watched as Ian slid his hand over Denise Bennett's shoulder. His blue eyes melted into pools of concern, sympathy, and even encouragement. Damn, he was good. Seconds later, Denise pressed the note into his hand.

He didn't open it right away. "Where did you get this?"

Denise's stare remained glued to the note. "Someone handed it to Craig as we were arriving at the party. People do that all the time. Requests for interviews or meetings with lobbyists in a back corner. Sometimes he shoves them in his pockets. Sometimes he hands them to an aide. Tonight, I was closest, so I simply took it from him and put it in my purse."

Ian waited a few sympathetic seconds, then slowly opened the folded paper.

"You didn't see who gave it to him?"

She shook her head, her lips quivering.

Ian's mouth drew into a tight line. He refolded the note, then handed it to Marisela.

She opened it quickly.

Remember Rebecca Manning.

She flipped the paper over. That was it? But no, that wasn't it. Drawn in the corner in pale colored pencils was a shape. A flower? An odd flower. Tubular, scarlet, with sharp star points around the edges and green leaves.

She gasped.

Ian glared at her and she recovered with a shake of her head and a surrender of the note back to Ian. "Who's Rebecca Manning?"

Denise whimpered. Ian instantly produced a handkerchief, which the woman used with as much delicacy as a woman with a runny nose and eyes could.

"She's the girl who's nearly ruined my husband's life."

The spite was sharp and raw. Marisela sat up straighter. "A girl?"

"He was a boy, then. It was a long time ago. Long before I ever came to Boston. You don't know about it? I thought everyone in Massachusetts knew the whole sordid tale."

With his eyes, Ian encouraged Marisela to speak. She got the impression he already knew what Denise was talking about, but with Marisela in the dark, she could push the questions a little further, perhaps learn something new.

Marisela leaned forward, her hands gripping the pew directly behind Denise. "I'm not from Massachusetts. I've only been here since this morning."

"What a welcome to our fair state." Denise chuckled with no humor. "Rebecca Manning died. Fifteen years ago."

"Then why would someone send a message like this now? Was she related to him or something?"

Denise's eyes instantly blazed with defiance. When she spoke, her chin jutted sharply, as if she'd been asked this question many times before and her reaction was instinctual and instantaneous. "Or something," Denise responded. "You see, he killed her. Or so everyone in this state seems to believe."

Four

FRANKIE WATCHED EVAN COLE pace outside the operating room, his hands pressed hard into the pockets of his jacket. His lips twitched as if he needed a hit of something, whether caffeine or coke or nicotine, Frankie couldn't tell. So cool when they were in the chapel, Craig Bennett's friend now stalked around like an innocent man on death row. Or a guilty man pretending to be innocent.

"Want to go outside for a smoke?" Frankie offered. "I'll stick around, bring you news."

Evan's eyes transmitted pure disgust, with a heavy

dose of mistrust thrown in. Not that Frankie wasn't used to the look, especially from rich *maricóns* who thought their shit didn't stink, but he'd never get used to having to control his reaction to them. Took a lot of effort to remind himself that one punch in the wrong man's face, and he'd end up back in the joint. And that wasn't going to happen.

"No. Thank you."

Manners over emotion. Must be a lesson taught in the prep schools in this part of the country, judging by how both Evan Cole and Ian Blake seemed to have mastered the skill.

Frankie wandered nearer the doors to surgery, where Max stood, arms crossed, expression stoic.

"Any word?" Frankie asked.

Max shook his head. Frankie wandered back to Cole.

"You know Craig Bennett long?" Frankie asked. Might as well do his job for a little while. He was, after all, still enjoying that ripe Titan paycheck in his bank account every week. For now.

Evan Cole eyed him suspiciously. "I didn't try to have him killed if that's what you're asking."

Frankie took a step back and raised a hand in surrender. "No, man, that wasn't what I was asking, but thanks for clearing that up. I'm sure the police will appreciate crossing you off the list."

"I don't abide sarcasm," Evan snapped.

Frankie leaned in close. "I live off it."

"Think you can at least save it for when my best friend isn't dying in the adjacent room?"

Frankie smirked. Yeah, he guessed he could make this one exception. "So, how long have you known him?"

"Since prep school, not that it is any of your business."

"Oh, it's my business," Frankie assured him. "Mrs. Bennett hired us to find out who tried to kill her husband. I'm just doing my job, man. If you're really his *best* friend, then you'll help me out."

Cole eyed Frankie from head to toe, clearly assessing whether the agent had the right stuff. He gave Max a brief glance, then nodded, his frown belying the approval flashing in his eyes.

"I'll help in any way I can, of course."

Evan wandered back to the door beside Max, and then stared through the window for a long while. Frankie hung back, waited. He didn't like the idea of Marisela being alone with Ian in the chapel, but not for the reasons she'd probably expect. On Marisela's first case, Ian had misled Marisela about the client and her motives. Frankie didn't figure Denise Bennett had the same twisted intentions, but he preferred to stick close. Keep Marisela out of trouble.

As if that were possible.

Seconds later, Evan Cole stalked toward Frankie, his eyes wild with barely checked fury. His gaze alternated between Frankie and Max, as if he wanted to ask a question but wasn't sure which operative he should address.

Max broke eye contact, leaving only Frankie.

"You guys really any good?"

"Word on the street is we're the best," Frankie assured him.

Cole dug into his pocket and extracted a gold money clip straining from the layers of hundreds folded inside. He took the entire stash and pressed the Ben Franklins into Frankie's palm. "When you find who did this, I want to know first, got it? Before Denise. Before the police."

There had been a time not too long ago when the smell of easy money would have tempted Frankie into a deal with the devil without a second thought. It wasn't as if he'd grown ethics in prison or anything, but if Titan had taken money from Denise Bennett, he couldn't jeopardize the case by indulging Evan Cole's thirst for . . . what? Revenge?

Besides, Max had seen everything. Cool as the guy was, he was still Blake's right hand.

"Keep your money, Mr. Cole," Frankie said, slipping him back the bills. "You cooperate with us and we'll find out who tried to kill your *compadre*. Stay in the loop, and you'll know what you need to know."

Max gave Frankie an approving nod, but Frankie only shook his head and wandered a few feet down the hall. Life had been so fine when lining his pockets had been his only motivation.

Well, that was how he liked to remember it. Thinking about Marisela down the hall with Ian Blake probably drooling over her canceled out the nostalgia. With his decision ten years ago to hang with his boys and embrace the *Toros* quest for stolen wealth, he'd lost Marisela for a decade. Now, thanks to his own big mouth, they were working together again. Since their reunion, she'd slipped under his skin like a splinter, except the pain she brought was as cruel as it was intoxicating. She'd screw around with him like she did on the balcony tonight, and they'd likely engage in some hot sex real soon, but she'd erected a wall between them—a wall he knew would take a lot more than sex to break down.

Not that sex wasn't a great way to start the process.

Cole paced around the waiting area for a few more minutes, then headed back toward the chapel. Frankie followed, giving the man a few feet of distance. Watching a friend nearly die was a life-changing experience—and one that gave Frankie a few ideas on how to deal with Marisela when the time came.

And it would come. Very, very soon.

Marisela emerged from the chapel, followed by Ian, who led Denise Bennett out with his hand supporting her elbow. Once Evan Cole saw they were on the move, he jogged to meet them.

"What do you want to do now, sweetheart?" Evan asked Denise. He cast suspicious glares at all of them.

Oh, yeah, this guy had something to hide.

Denise looked up at him with weary, bloodshot eyes. "I just want to wait for Craig."

Evan nodded sympathetically and led her down

the hall. When they were out of sight, Ian turned to Marisela. "Well done, Ms. Morales."

"Shouldn't I be Aphrodite again?"

Ian quirked a grin. "No need for covert ops and code names just yet. Fill Frank in on the new information. I'm heading up to surgery to relieve Max. I want him to get his team started on investigating Rebecca Manning."

Frankie leaned back on his heels. "You doing grunt work? This I'd like to see."

Ian sneered. "You doing any work is something I'd like to see. Stick with Marisela. She'll fill you in."

Marisela looked down at her feet and tried not to laugh. Not that Ian's quip had been particularly funny, but Frankie hated being bossed around, by Marisela more than anyone else. She started toward the end of the hall, but Frankie stopped her before she could open the door, grabbing her hand and swinging her around until her back was against the wall and he was looming over her with those hungry dark eyes of his.

Her ribs ached, but she wasn't going to show her pain to anyone.

"Blake says you'll fill me in, huh?"

"Someone has to bring you . . . up to speed," she countered, easily twisting her words into a tease. Came so easy with Frankie. They could get each other hot reciting recipes.

"I was thinking we could get in the back of that limo and I could be the one doing the filling, if you know what I mean."

She licked her lips, trying to ignore how her nipples pearled at the crude but enticing invitation. "I know exactly what you mean, *cabrón,* but we're on the job. How about we put the client's needs above our own?"

"I guess there's a first time for everything," he replied.

Marisela rolled her eyes, grabbed Frankie by the bolo tie he'd worn with his tux, and led him out the door. When they opened the back of the limo, they discovered that the decision to work rather than play had been taken out of their hands. Max sat in the center of the seat, a laptop engaged and operating, while two other units sat across from him, clearly waiting for their arrival.

Once they were both inside, the door was locked and Max typed in the codes to bring the information they needed to the screen.

The first image was of a newspaper headline, dated 1991.

BEACON HILL BOYS SUSPECTED IN MURDER.

"That about says it all," Marisela said, her eyes wide.

She read the first few paragraphs quickly. Rebecca Manning, seventeen at the time, had indeed been killed fifteen years ago, her body found two months after her disappearance in a marsh on Peddock's Island, a national park campsite just a few minutes by boat out of Boston Harbor. The Manning fam-

ily, which included a younger sister, Tracy, claimed
that Rebecca told them earlier in the evening that
she was going to meet her boyfriend, high school
football star, Bradley Hightower. Hightower, who'd
been camping with his younger brother, Raymond,
and best friend, Craig Bennett, son of a state senator,
denied seeing Rebecca at any time during the cold
winter evening.

The police found no hard evidence linking the
boys to the crime and no witnesses that placed Rebecca on the island or near the marina, though a stolen dinghy with Rebecca's scarf caught on the railing
was recovered a few days later in the harbor. But there
was no evidence of any struggle and no fingerprints
at all.

The next article revealed that despite public outcry
that the rich Boston boys had exploited their money
and influence to intimidate prosecutors, the boys were
never charged, not even after the body was discovered
not far from their campsite. The detectives assigned to
the case had protested that the prep school students
knew more than they were admitting, but had been
unable to come up with hard proof. The Hightower
boys, who'd been whisked away to Europe by their father, had never even been questioned by the police.

"Talk about getting away with murder," Marisela
said.

Frankie leaned back in the seat and sighed heavily.
"If they'd come from our neighborhood, they'd still be
in prison."

"Nah," Marisela contradicted. "Electric chair. Do you have the electric chair in Massachusetts?" she asked Max, curious.

Max looked up from his laptop, his gray eyes stoic. "Are we back to the case or are we still making jokes about your misspent childhoods?"

Marisela smirked. "Sorry, it's just that after talking to Denise Bennett and reading all this, I can't help but guess that these guys are guilty as sin."

Frankie clucked his tongue. "Evidence is circumstantial."

She couldn't believe her ears. "You're taking the side of the defense?"

Frankie tapped a few keys. "There was no defense. The guys were never charged. Besides, innocent or guilty makes no difference to me. I met both in prison, and under most circumstances, one wasn't any better than the other."

"We aren't concerned at this point with their guilt or innocence," Max said. "We need to piece together exactly what happened that night. Right now, the note is our only clue, so that's where we start."

"Why didn't Bennett's wife turn the note over to the police?" Frankie asked.

"She doesn't trust the cops," Marisela answered. "Claims they tried to railroad her husband all those years ago."

"The cold case squad of the Boston police department recently started investigating the case again," Max informed them. "The inquiries caused a public relations nightmare for the good congressman. Probably turned Denise Bennett's life into a living hell."

"She doesn't know what happened back then?" Frankie asked.

Marisela pursed her lips. "Before we left the chapel, she claimed her husband told her exactly what he told the police at the time. He'd been camping with his buddies and none of them saw Rebecca that night."

Frankie frowned. "What about Evan Cole?"

Marisela looked at Max.

He shook his head. "So far, there's nothing in my initial research that links him to the incident at all. I don't think he was there."

"He told me he was Craig Bennett's best friend," Frankie informed them. "If the guys all went out for a night in the woods, why wouldn't he go along?"

Max nodded appreciatively. "Good question. Another avenue for us to pursue."

Marisela pressed her hand to her forehead. She was starting to get a headache, though whether from excessive thinking, exhaustion, or a combination of both, she couldn't be sure.

"Did that new task force dig up anything new?" Marisela asked.

"No," Max replied. "My sources tell me the case is just as dead in the water, if you'll pardon my pun, as it was fifteen years ago."

"Any political influence to reopen the case?" Frankie asked.

Marisela and Max both eyed Frankie with surprise.

"What?"

Normally, Frankie was more muscle than brains, but Marisela should have learned a long time ago not to underestimate her ex.

Max cleared his throat. "I find it hard to believe that a congressman who is making serious waves in Washington, D.C., with his new prescription-plan initiatives isn't ruffling feathers somewhere. The D.C. crowd doesn't like upstarts. He's in the news quite a bit with a new prescription-drug proposal. I'll keep checking with my police sources, but in the meantime, we need to come up with a list of probable suspects and start checking them out."

"We should start with Leo Devlin," Marisela said.

Max typed the name into the computer. "He certainly has a reason to want the congressman out of the way. I'll put a few agents on him. I want the two of you exclusively on the Manning murder."

"What about Bennett's friends? Aren't they in danger, too?" Marisela asked.

"Good chance," Max answered. "If the assassin can't get at Bennett while we're protecting him, she might move on to the others, if revenge is truly her motive and if the note is connected to her."

"It is," Marisela insisted.

She described the flower on the note and the possible resemblance to the tattoo the assassin had on her wrist.

Max nodded. "I'm sending a message to the office right now. I'll put agents on scoping out the locations of the Hightower boys. In the meantime, let's look at who we have right here in Boston."

Marisela scanned the news article Max had transferred to their screens. "Parker Manning."

"Victim's father?" Frankie asked.

"Victim's brother," she replied. "Father's dead. The brother lives here, in Boston. He's a reporter. Declined to comment for this article about the case, though."

Frankie flipped the lid closed on his computer and turned Marisela's laptop toward him. "A reporter declining to comment?"

"That's weird, I think," Marisela decided.

Max's grin implied that he agreed. "Seems like a good place to start. Frankie, take the other car and head back to the office. Find this Manning guy. Ian ordered both of you to get some rest, but tomorrow, you can pay Mr. Manning a visit, see if you can change his mind about the no-comment thing. Marisela, check in with Ian. I'll be right behind you."

Frankie and Marisela exited the car. She headed to the hospital door, but Frankie grabbed her hand.

"Meet me at the office?"

"What office?" she said with a chortle. "I flew in, went shopping, got dressed, and then went to the party. The only place I'm going is to my hotel room."

Frankie eased closer so the rough texture of his slim beard sparked against the skin on her cheek. "I'll meet you there, then."

Tempting as the offer was, Marisela wasn't in the mood for sex. Her muscles protested every step she took and between jet lag and exhaustion and the beating she'd endured, all she wanted to do was sleep.

Well, it wasn't *all* she wanted to do. But it was clearly priority one. However, she could be convinced. By the right guy.

"We'll see," she replied, then entered the hospital without looking back.

Perfect timing.

Yizenia stored the flip chart in the case outside a patient's door and checked to make sure that the badge she'd created was clipped in plain view. She patted her auburn hair and blinked rapidly, ensuring that her hazel contact lenses were in place beneath her glasses. The sweatbands she'd used to cover her tattoo were snuggly in place beneath her long-sleeved scrubs, bubble-gum pink with cupids on the pants. Thankfully, American hospital workers reveled in the tacky. Patterns like this grabbed attention. If anyone needed to describe her later, they'd likely say the redhead in the Valentine's Day pants. Which, of course, would no longer describe her once she left and ditched the disguise in the nearby trash bin.

But until then, she had information to gather—and the perfect source just a few steps away.

"Excuse me."

Yizenia affected her best Southern accent, one of her favorites to emulate, with the twangs and elongated vowels oddly similar to a British accent, but with more rhythm.

From her perch leaning against a stark white wall, arms crossed, Marisela Morales stood out like a splash of color. Her dark hair, eyes, and skin contrasted against the purple of her dress, now torn and bloodied, but still caressing curves that Yizenia couldn't help but admire. That shapely body had provided quite the challenge. If she didn't have this role to play, Yizenia guessed she'd be back in her apartment with ice packs and painkillers.

"Excuse me?" she asked again.

This time, Marisela skewered her with a suspicious, wary glare. "I'm waiting for someone."

Marisela stood up straighter and dropped her crossed arms to her side. Always ready for a fight, this one. Perpetually prepared to defend herself. Could she do the same for others, especially those who no longer had the capacity to defend themselves?

"You look pretty beat up," Yizenia commented. She'd taught this young one a valuable, painful lesson about underestimating an opponent. Could she teach her more?

Marisela returned to her defensive stance—arms crossed, scowl steady, eyes trained on the door across from her, one foot braced on the wall behind her in case she needed to launch herself into the line of fire. "I'm fine."

Yizenia pointed to a slash of blood marring the girl's face.

Marisela slapped her hand aside.

Taking on the persona of a strong-willed nurse,

Yizenia fisted her hands on her hips. "Your lip is bleeding."

Marisela gracelessly swiped at the blood coagulating at the corner of her mouth. "It's just blood."

Yizenia glanced at the door Marisela seemed so intent on watching. The congressman had been moved there not twenty minutes ago, and through the slit of a window, she could see a large man blocking the only way in and out of the windowless room. One guard inside. And clearly, one guard outside.

"A little ointment could keep away an infection," Yizenia said brightly, returning her attention to Marisela. "Why don't I take you down to emergency . . . "

The wild, trapped look in Marisela's deep brown eyes caught Yizenia off guard. Interesting. The young woman was brazen and bold, but she had the good sense to experience fear. Fear of medical treatment wasn't exactly on the top of Yizenia's list of acceptable phobias, but she figured the kid had her reasons.

"Look, I'm going to be fine. I just gotta wait for my boss and then I'm out of here. Two minutes with a first aid kit and I'll be good to go."

Ah, her boss. Yizenia had experienced an odd little thrill when she'd seen Ian Blake standing guard outside Congressman Bennett's operating room. The man had been a more than adequate lover even when drunk beyond reason. She could only imagine the sensual skill he'd display when stone-cold sober. Too bad she'd likely never have a chance to find out.

She doubted he'd recognize her again, even without her disguise. He likely wanted to forget the entire incident. In the throes of bourbon-induced delirium, he'd called out Marisela Morales's name, and the knowledge that Ian wanted his new agent had nurtured an idea.

An idea sparked by Ian's sister, Brynn, who had also mentioned the Cuban-American agent in passing, during Yizenia's biannual rendezvous with Titan's chief executive in Barcelona for *tapas* at the little bar overlooking the Mediterranean Sea.

It was fate. A young woman half a world away, a young woman who was strikingly familiar. Marisela and Yizenia shared similar tattoos, both imprinted on the inside of their wrists. They both possessed the will and skill to fight hand-to-hand, a talent usually reserved for men. And both of them had blood spawned in Yizenia's native Spain. Who was she to ignore what higher powers were forcing her to see?

The torch could be passed.

She'd once considered tapping Brynn to take her place, but Brynn was well past thirty, set in her ways, already seduced by the power of running Titan. Yizenia needed someone fresh. Someone she could mold into a crusader.

Someone like Marisela Morales.

Pretending to bow to Marisela's desire to be left alone, Yizenia wandered over to the nurse's station. She'd timed her appearance to coincide with hospital rounds so she was able to slip in and retrieve a basic first-aid kit unchallenged.

She made a big show of looking superior when she presented the cocky agent with the kit.

Marisela sneered and kept her arms tightly crossed. "I said I could wait."

"I'm a nurse. Sue me."

Funny, that expression. Wouldn't work in any other country in the world except the *Estados Unidos*.

Marisela glared at her, but the expression must have cost her because she winced, then snatched the kit, popped it open, and pulled out an individual dosage of antibiotic ointment.

"Don't you have any real sick people to harass?" she asked.

Yizenia chuckled, her humor genuine. "I'm on my break."

Marisela tore the small package open, smeared the cream on her fingertip and applied it gingerly to the cut on her mouth. From experience, Yizenia knew the injury would heal quickly, but it would hurt like hell until it did.

"Happy now?"

"Ecstatic," Yizenia answered, glancing at the congressman's door.

"Don't let me keep you if you have work to do," Marisela offered.

"They're not letting any nurses inside the room," Yizenia replied. "Just the nursing supervisor and the chief of surgery. I've been told they're in a meeting to discuss added security right now."

"Smart," Marisela responded.

Yizenia decided to push this interview a little further. How did Marisela view her client? Did she even know he was a murderer?

"I suppose," she said wearily. "Guy like that doesn't deserve to live, if you ask me."

Marisela shot her a disgusted glare. "I didn't ask you, but remind me never to be admitted here."

"Do you know who he is?" Yizenia asked, trying to sound scandalized.

"Congressman Craig Bennett."

"Do you know what he did?"

"I don't have a head for politics," Marisela replied. "I'm not even sure what a president does."

"Not his job! What he did to that girl."

Perhaps she'd pushed too far. Marisela's gaze sharpened. "How do you know what he did?"

"It was in all the papers."

Marisela stepped forward, leaned in close, and turned on the full force of her silent intimidation tactics, which, admittedly, were impressive. Stiff jaw. Controlled tone. Eyes that could slice you open with a glance.

"What else do you know?"

Yizenia pasted on a nervous look. "Just that the police think he and his friends got away with murder."

Marisela allowed the comment to hang in the air without responding, which impressed Yizenia. Clearly, Marisela Morales could control her emotions when the mood struck her. She'd obviously reserved judgment regarding her clients—clearly not entirely

convinced they hadn't committed a heinous crime all
those years ago.

Yes, this was promising. She didn't need Marisela
to take her side against these *monstruos* who killed
Rebecca Manning, but an ally never hurt. Never hurt
at all.

Five

BY THE TIME MARISELA SLIPPED INTO HER hotel at about five o'clock in the morning, the only thing on her mind was sleep. She yawned widely as she trudged through the deserted lobby toward the elevator. Her instincts had shut off hours ago, so she wasn't surprised when Frankie slid into the lift just as the doors closed.

"And where do you think you're going?" she asked, her voice raspy with exhaustion as she punched the button to her floor.

"With you," he said, sliding his hands around her

waist and tugging her tight against him. "We have a lot of lost time to make up for."

Marisela's muscles ached, her chest hurt from her bruised ribs, and her eyes felt like she'd applied sandpaper contacts, but she mustered enough of a second wind to send him flying against the opposite wall just as the elevator doors sliced open on her floor.

She'd caught him off guard, which wasn't so hard to do when he was so full of his sexy self.

"I need sleep," she said, pointing her finger at him.

"You need more than sleep," he claimed, stepping through the doors before they closed again.

Her annoyance swelled as he licked his lips and raked his hand through his long, glossy black hair.

Man, it looked like silk. Next to crawling into bed alone and sleeping for the next three days, the thought of feeling the sleek strands against her bare skin taunted her to near madness. She'd never made love to a long-haired man before. But she'd made love with Frankie before and she knew that the experience wouldn't be quick or easy.

Not anymore.

It was one thing to flirt with him on the dance floor or steal a few sensual moments in the balcony. But now that she'd spent the last hour watching a desperate wife pray over the broken body of her husband, she wasn't in the mood to fool around. Hadn't she prayed over his broken body just three months ago? Then, only a few weeks into his recovery, she'd left him to continue her training with Titan. She hadn't realized until right now how little had changed while they'd been apart. She still cared about him.

Dammit.

He closed in on her until his scent, so spiced and male, invaded her senses. "You dealt with a lot of shit tonight, *vidita*. Blood. Fear. Death. All the crap we can't control. But you and me," he said, easing his fingers up the side of her dress, "we lose control in the good way, *verdad*?"

And how much had stayed exactly the same.

She swiped her hotel key through the lock and entered her room, with Frankie right behind her. She might have tried locking him out, but he'd only find a way to break in while she slept. Not that she minded a good invasion fantasy, but with her luck, she'd expect Frankie and end up face-to-face with someone trying to kill her for fucking up a secret conspiracy to murder the congressman.

Ian had given them half a day to catch up on their zs. While she'd waited at the hospital exchanging small talk with the wily nurse on duty, Frankie had reportedly dug up an address on Parker Manning, Rebecca Manning's brother. Ian, after debriefing Marisela one last time on the exact details of her run-in with the assassin, had had his driver deposit her at her hotel.

"Aren't you supposed to be watching Parker Manning?"

Frankie's grin oozed sensuality. "One of the night shift guys is keeping him in sight. We've been assigned as partners. Where you go, I go, *vidita*. Ain't that how that works?"

So they had at least eight good hours without any responsibilities.

Frankie secured the dead bolt on the door with a loud click.

This was not a good idea.

Marisela found the zipper hidden in the side seam of her dress and released the material, determined to take a hot shower and dive into bed. Alone. Yet when she saw the hunger in Frankie's hazel eyes, flashing in the flecks of jade green that had been melting her insides since age ten, she nearly stumbled. She turned her back to him and yanked her feet out of her sandals.

"Stop looking at me like that," she ordered, padding barefoot to her suitcase where she snatched the Tijuana T-shirt Brynn had bought her in Mexico as a joke. ONE TEQUILA, TWO TEQUILA, THREE TEQUILA, FLOOR. Man, could she go for a shot of the strong agave blend right about now.

"Like how?" he asked, as if he didn't know.

She glared at him from over her shoulder. "Like you want to devour me."

"I do want to devour you."

Her mouth watered, but she jumped and writhed out of her dress, trying to deny how her body instantly reacted to Frankie's sensual suggestion. Her muscles ached in protest, but other than a tiny yelp, she kept the pain to herself.

"Too bad, because I'm not in the mood," she insisted.

Liar. Liar, liar, liar.

In one great and crazy act of defiance, she whipped off her thong, allowing her bare breasts and throbbing *concha* to torture the man for the split second it took her to toss the lingerie on the floor and then drag the sleep shirt over her head. Screw the shower. She was going to bed. Without him.

Unfortunately, standing nearly naked in front of Frankie again, watching his eyes blaze with pure lust, caused an instantaneous stirring that rushed straight to her nipples.

When she yanked at the hem of her shirt, her breasts poked at the material, hard and tight. His gaze dropped, lingering first on the indisputable twin signs of her arousal, then sliding lower. Just a sweep of his stare and a throb bloomed to pure torture.

"You so sure you don't want something to soothe that ache?" he asked.

She slinked closer to him, feeding off the warmth she could feel sluicing off his body. Yeah, she wanted him. But he wanted her right back.

"I was just at the hospital. Remember? With Ian? Maybe I already had my aches taken care of."

He captured her arm and swung her back to him, as if they'd taken the dance floor again. Pressed close against him, her body ignited. Her breath came in shallow rasps.

"You don't give a shit about Ian Blake," Frankie whispered, dipping his mouth close to her ear. "Not when you can practically feel my lips on you."

The heat from his flesh burned into hers, taunting her with the possibilities of pleasures to come if she could just let go. Surrender. Take what he offered, what she wanted with every fiber of her soul.

"Let me go," she said softly.

"No," he replied.

"I can make you."

"You won't."

She tried to relax, but her body thrummed to the familiar tango she and Frankie danced, kicking out for power, swaying for control.

"Only because I'm exhausted," she conceded.

"The shooter gave you a workout," he said, slipping his hand up her arm until he could curve his fingers around her shoulder. "I know you could use a rub-down."

"I'll call a masseuse."

"No one knows your body like I do, *vidita*."

She allowed him to prove his point, unable to resist the pleasure kneading into her body from his. He drew both hands against her shoulders, rubbing, caressing, coaxing out the stress that had tightened her to such tautness, she feared she might snap.

She spun around, locked her arms around Frankie's neck, and pushed him back. Not away from her. Oh, no. She kept him tight in her possession, her mouth locked with his, her body pressed fully against him so that every curve of her body, every aching muscle, every nerve ending flamed with want. His hands were instantly under her loose shirt, roaming and touching and pleasuring. When they fell back against the door, she whipped the nightshirt over her head and yanked the elastic tie from her hair.

Frankie tore out of his clothes in record time, and without another word they clashed together. Lips roamed. Hands dipped and parted flesh. He used the door to balance their bodies, the leverage crucial as the delirium of passion overtook them. Marisela grabbed at the slick surface of the door, desperate to find something to clutch onto, finally settling on Frankie's hair. She climbed and clawed, hot to have him inside her. When he finally pushed inside, deep and hard, her sex melted around his and her breath released in a steamy hiss.

Marisela didn't think, didn't speak, didn't try to manage more than moans of pleasure as she soaked up the sensations of his body linked to hers. They came in rapid succession, each spilling the others name into the thick, humid air.

In a clumsy stagger, Frankie pushed away from the door. Marisela crossed her legs around his waist, hanging on as the delirium ebbed. By the time they splayed onto the bed, naked and sweaty and spent, she could barely breathe, much less keep her eyes open.

"I don't know why you thought this was a bad idea."

She stirred up enough energy to smile. "For you, sex is never a bad idea."

Frankie drew lazy loop-de-loops across her backside with his fingertip. "And it is for you?"

She took a deep breath, inhaling as much of his

scent as she could. In case she didn't indulge again for a while. In case she found the means to resist. "Just because it feels good doesn't mean it's good for you."

He chuckled. "You sound like my mother."

Marisela yanked the comforter away from the edge of the bed, covering them against the air-conditioned chill. "Well, that's one way to kill the mood."

Frankie laughed. "As if our mothers didn't try to kill that a long time ago. Accept it. We're meant to be together. Like coffee and milk," he said, kissing the curve of her breast. "*Guayaba* and cheese," he continued, lowering his lips until he could flick her nipple with his tongue. "*Arroz y* . . ."

"Hungry?" she asked, twisting out of his reach.

He chuckled. "Not for food."

Marisela eased into the comforter, tucking the fabric between them and leaving him in the cold. She'd played long enough. Now, she needed sleep. And distance. Lots and lots of distance.

"Too bad," she said with a yawn, snuggling deeper into the mattress and allowing her eyes to close. "Because food's all you're going to get. If you call room service. From *your* room."

She expected an argument. Some sort of protest. Instead, when she peeked an eye open, she caught one last glimpse of his gorgeous *culo* before he put on his pants, grabbed his shirt, and turned to leave the room.

When she sensed he'd swung back in her direction, she closed her eyes and feigned sleep. She heard his chuckle as his face descended toward hers and he brushed a soft, sensual kiss across her lips. If she'd had the energy, she might have slapped the smug expression she knew he wore right off his face. Or surrendered to the overwhelming urges coursing through her to drag him back to bed.

But luckily for both of them, she was too damned tired to do anything more than fall asleep.

From his customized chair behind the antique mahogany desk that had once belonged to his father, Ian listened, eyes shut, to the sounds of Titan International an hour after dawn. Computers beeped and buzzed. The smack of files flying from one in-box to another broke up the sound of employee chitchat. The strong scent of coffee sneaked under the doorway and tempted Ian to wake up and face the day. Not that he was hiding. He was simply exhausted—and as such, he couldn't grab hold of a thought, an idea, a painful truth connected to this case buried deep within his psyche.

He opened his eyes, leaned forward, and reexamined the note Denise Bennett had provided.

Remember Rebecca Manning.

Coupled with what the assassin had said to Marisela about revenge, the message was simple enough to interpret. That wasn't what plagued him.

He flipped the tiny square over, to the drawing. He'd seen this flower before. Only not done in pastels, but in bold colors. But where?

His door opened and he quickly flipped the note over.

"Brynn," he said, watching as his twin eased into the room as if she owned the place. Which, technically, she did.

"It's a tomb in here," she announced, flipping on the light. He squinted, but didn't complain. It was too early and he was too tired for an argument over something so trivial. And if ever siblings had perfected the art of fighting over minutiae, it was he and Brynn.

"Good morning," he said, standing. "The Mexican sun looks good on you," he commented.

He wasn't offering the compliment without cause. His sister's red hair gleamed with blond streaks, and despite the fact that he knew she was militant about using sunscreen, UV rays had pinkened the skin on her flawless cheeks and the tip of her nose. She looked carefree. Friendly. Charming.

"Well, the Boston sun isn't doing a damned thing for you," she concluded.

Looks could be so deceiving.

He retrieved his coat from the back of his chair and shrugged into it. "I've been up all night."

"I heard," she replied. "Did you know Craig Bennett from school?"

Ian shook his head. "I was a few years ahead and at Oxford when the whole scandal broke."

"Didn't Father work on the case in some capacity?"

"Indirectly."

She shed her sunglasses and scarf, worn more for their stylishness than for protection against the mild summer weather. "Checked his notes?"

Their father had kept copious diaries, files, and dossiers on all his cases, all encrypted, of course. And all decoded on an as-needed basis by either Brynn or Ian. Immediately after his return from the hospital last night, Ian had consulted the records and archives. "He met with Bradley Hightower's father, but only to give his advice regarding relocation. The entire Hightower family moved to Paris only a few weeks after the state attorney opted not to press charges."

Brynn's nose crinkled the way it always did when she was thinking hard. "I didn't know the girls, either, but I don't suppose that's any surprise, considering their background."

"The Manning father once worked as the Bennetts' yacht captain. He was harbormaster for some time, as well."

"The mother?"

"Housewife. They did not, as we should say politely, run in our circles."

"Funny," Brynn said with a chuckle. "When we lived here as children, Boston always felt so very small compared to London. Now I realize how many separate worlds exist here."

A soft knock at the door announced Max's arrival. He came in with two steaming mugs of coffee. While Ian was eternally grateful for the caffeine jolt, he'd hoped to see Max balancing three cups. With one for himself, he'd be more inclined to stay.

"I'm headed back to the hospital," Max explained. "The next shift of hospital employees comes on in twenty minutes. I want to make sure our bases are covered."

Brynn accepted the coffee and rewarded Max's generosity with a kiss to his cheek. "Good to see you, Max."

Max smiled rather uncomfortably and backed out of the room. "Enjoy your visit, you two. Try not to kill one another while I'm gone."

Ian arched a brow as Max shut the door behind him.

"Bring me up to speed," Brynn ordered.

"I have the case under control, Brynn." Ian shifted in his seat. He didn't want to pick a fight, but he also didn't need his sister interfering in his investigation.

Brynn sipped her coffee, her eyes locked with his over the rim of her mug.

"I didn't mean to imply you didn't, Ian. I seem to recall a time when you and I could at least discuss work without invading the other's turf."

Ian tapped his finger on the file hiding the note. "That all changed when you returned to the States. You had Europe, I had North America. Seemed a fair enough arrangement."

"You're still smarting about Marisela?"

"Hard not to when I have to stare her in the face every day."

"You shouldn't have fired her. If you'd been thinking more clearly, I wouldn't have had to intervene. Besides, I've had her with me for the past two and a half months," Brynn reminded him. "You're the one who recalled her for the fund-raiser at Houghton House."

"I needed a female agent," he answered simply.

"And you got one who's already tangled with the shooter and lived to provide us the only information we have. Look, Ian, I'm sorry I had to step in during Marisela's first case, but you left her . . . and me . . . no choice."

Ian took a hearty swig of his coffee. He'd made mistakes on that former case—mistakes he would not make again. "Let's move on to the case at hand."

Brynn cocked an eyebrow, but capitulated to his suggestion. "Here's what I know so far. An assassin took a shot at Craig Bennett during the fund-raiser, but Marisela spotted the barrel of the gun and fired."

"She likely caused the shot meant for Bennett to go wild," Ian added. "He was seriously injured, but he'll live."

"He still has his brain matter, so I'm sure he considers himself lucky."

"He will when he wakes up. But he won't be able to speak and his ability to communicate under the influence of painkillers is an unknown. We can't depend on him for information."

Brynn nodded in agreement. "So his wife hired us to find out who ordered the hit?"

"She doesn't trust the police. She thinks the cops have been trying to railroad her husband for the Rebecca Manning murder for years."

"Funny how perception colors things. Other than the Boston elite, of which we are members, the entire community thinks those boys got away with murder."

On his computer, Ian pulled up the outline of information they'd gathered. "The guilt or innocence of Bennett and his friends is not our concern—what we need is to determine who might be using Rebecca Manning's death as reason for revenge. The police had nothing more than circumstantial evidence linking Bennett and the two Hightower boys to Rebecca's murder. They admitted they were on the harbor island, but not in the bog where the body was recovered. There were campers near the boys who reported hearing a loud argument, but otherwise, not a shred of proof linked them to her killing. And the body was badly decomposed by the time she was dragged out of the marsh. For all we know, she died of natural causes."

"And threw herself in a marsh?" Brynn asked skeptically. "Wasn't she dating one of the Hightowers?"

"Bradley, the oldest," he replied, "but they'd reportedly broken up a month earlier. The archival police report notes that her classmates reported that Rebecca wouldn't let go."

"Fatal attraction?"

"For her, clearly. But the boys insisted they never saw her that night and no one could prove she didn't go over to the island on her own searching for Hightower, got lost, and died in the marsh."

"And yet suspicion lingers after all these years," Brynn noted. "Why?"

Ian shrugged. "I suppose that's our job, to find out why. Frankie and Marisela will interview Parker Manning, the girl's brother, later today."

Brynn nodded decisively. "What about political enemies?" she asked.

"He has several, including the host of last night's party."

"Leo Devlin?"

"You know him?"

Brynn ran her hand through her hair. "I seem to believe I met him once. You?"

"He hired us directly to protect the jewelry several designers loaned to his guests for the party last night."

"Have you interviewed him since the shooting?"

"He came to the hospital to pay his respects this morning just before I left. I made arrangements to see him this afternoon."

"And the shooter?"

Ah, the shooter. "Marisela identified her as female, five seven to five nine, slender, excellent in a fight."

"That's not much to go on."

"There can't be that many female assassins in the world," Ian said.

Brynn arched a brow. "You'd be surprised. She didn't catch a glimpse of any identifying marks?"

"The woman wore a mask. Hair was dark, but she could have colored it or worn a wig. She did report," he said, consulting the notes from Marisela's interview with the police, "seeing something red on her wrist."

Something red on her wrist . . .

An image flashed in Ian's mind. A woman. Dark haired. On top of him. Rocking into him. Deep-throated groans. Nails digging into his skin. His kiss on the inside of her wrist as her hand smoothed under his chin.

A tattoo.

The memories existed in a fog, but were suddenly clearing. He remembered fantasizing that the mark he'd seen on his lover's arm had been a purple crown tipped with dots of ruby-red blood, the brand Marisela had imprinted on her arm as a sign of her loyalty and lifetime commitment to *las Reinas*.

Now he realized, there had been no purple. Red, yes, but in the shape of a tubular flower, cradled by green.

He retrieved the note. Yes, that had to be what he had seen that night.

Brynn stood up and snatched the square of paper from his hand.

"Good God," she said with a deep, shocked breath.

Ian's gaze snapped up to hers.

"What?" he asked.

"I know this symbol. It . . . can't be."

"What is it?" Ian asked sharply. "What do you know about this flower?"

"Did Marisela see it on the woman's wrist?"

"She said she saw something red. Elongated. She didn't know what it was, but dammit, she reacted oddly when she saw this on the note. Why didn't I put it together?"

"Call her in," Brynn demanded. "I need to know if she could have seen this image tattooed on the woman's wrist."

Her voice deepened, just as it always did when she was upset.

"What is it, Brynn?" he asked, forcing his own tone to be calm even while his chest tightened with a sick sensation.

Brynn tore her gaze away from the note, her lips drawn in a tight line. "This is a pomegranate flower. It's the national flower of Spain."

"Marisela did say the woman spoke with a completely authentic Spanish accent. Old school, she called it."

Brynn nodded gravely. "This can't be a coincidence."

"Brynn, I swear on our father's grave that if you don't tell me everything you know right this instant—"

"I'm sorry," she said. "I was taken off guard."

"Who is she?"

Brynn took a deep breath and exhaled slowly. "Her name is Yizenia Santiago. She's one of the deadliest assassins in the world, but she doesn't just work for money. She believes in justice. Punishing the unpunished."

Ian dropped into his chair. "How do you know this?" he asked.

Brynn clutched the note tightly. "Because I know *her*."

"You know her?"

His sister nodded slowly, as if the shock hadn't quite released her yet. "We've been . . . friends . . . for years."

"What do you mean, *friends*?"

Brynn leaned closer, gripping the edge of the desk so tightly, her knuckles turned white. "She murdered the men who killed our mother."

Ian's heart dropped. "What?"

"Father hired her, years ago, to avenge our mother's death. She's deadly, Ian. A master of disguise. An expert with accents and she speaks, I don't know, twenty languages. And when she's on a job, she's incommunicado for as long as it takes to succeed. If we're going to protect our clients, we need to find her. And stop her. Fast."

Yes, they needed to find her. And unfortunately, he knew just where to look.

Six

"WHAT THE HELL DO YOU WANT?"

Marisela slid her sunglasses down her nose and leaned her shoulder on the threshold of Parker Manning's apartment door, eyeing the man who glared at her.

"Is that any way to greet a guest?" she asked, her voice a seductive purr.

"Gue—?" Manning paused mid-bark, cigarette hanging precariously out of the corner of his mouth, his ratty Harvard T-shirt sporting a wicked collection of condiment stains, including but not limited to, mustard, ketchup, and, from the smell, sauerkraut.

Marisela arched her back and let her tight, scoop-necked, jewel-encrusted *chica* T-shirt weave its magic.

He straightened, grabbed the top of the doorjamb and leaned forward, like he was frickin' Rocky Balboa or something. He probably meant the pose to be sexy.

Fat chance.

At one time, Parker Manning might have pulled off Stallone, but now his muscles sagged, he reeked of cigarette smoke and booze, and while he was probably only in his late thirties, he had the crags, wrinkles, and lines of a much older man. The only thing he had in common with the Italian Stallion was that he'd gone into the ring and got the shit kicked out of him.

Still, she needed information from him, so she moved in closer. "So are you going to invite me in, or what?" she whispered.

"Funny," he said with a vulgar chuckle. "I don't remember calling 1–800-HOOKERS ARE US."

The hell with seductive. Marisela slammed the door open with her shoulder, knocking Parker Manning hard against the arm. But she didn't walk inside. Last thing she wanted was this jerk having her arrested for trespassing. Assault would be enough, thanks.

The guy's bellow sent Frankie scrambling from where he was waiting down the hall.

"What did you do?" he demanded.

She stared at Frankie with complete innocence. "You know these doors nowadays. Hinges are too loose. Just like this asshole's lips."

"She nearly fucking killed me!"

Crybaby.

"Accidents happen," Frankie said to Manning, who was glaring at both of them now. "I apologize for my associate," Frankie continued, his voice calm, friendly, and so Ian-like that Marisela nearly lost her breakfast. "She can be . . . unpredictable. We'll have no need for more violence, if you ask us inside."

"For what?" Manning demanded.

Frankie's *el diablo* beard and moustache lent power to his sharp reply. "We have business to discuss."

Manning sneered, but not without a skitter of fear in his eyes. Frankie had clearly copied the polite routine from their boss, but the intimidation factor was all Frankie, all the time.

"Who the hell are you?" Manning rubbed his shoulder furiously and eyed Marisela with acidic spite, but he made no move to block the door.

And without a definitive *no* to stop him, Frankie strolled past him, then turned to Marisela so she'd follow. "We're investigating the shooting of Congressman Craig Bennett."

"You aren't cops," Manning spat.

Marisela rolled her eyes. "Do you see us flashing badges?"

"What I see are a couple of thugs coming into my

apartment. You got a business card or something? I could call the police."

Frankie slid a card from his pocket and flicked it within Parker's reach. "The police will be here soon enough without your call."

Manning didn't react to Frankie's comment, but instead kept his eyes glued on the card. "Titan International? You're private dicks."

Marisela chuckled. "He can actually be a really public dick when he puts his mind to it," she said, thumbing in Frankie's direction.

With a snicker, Manning nodded his head toward what Marisela suspected was his living room. Overflowing with piles of paperwork, worn furniture, half-empty bottles of scotch and discarded beer cans that littered the brown pile rug, the apartment reflected a man who didn't get out much—a detail verified by Manning's rough beard, pasty skin, and bleary eyes.

"What would the cops want with me?" he asked finally, handing the card back to Frankie.

Frankie remained near Parker—and near the door—while Marisela casually looked around. Newspapers littered nearly every flat surface and legal pads filled with illegible scribbles were stacked in several piles, each one threatening to topple if anyone so much as brushed by them.

Yet somehow, Marisela suspected this work was important, probably by the way Manning never took his eyes off her as she surveyed the room.

"Congressman Bennett wasn't exactly a friend of yours," Marisela said.

"Yeah, well, we didn't run in the same social circles," Manning quipped.

"And still, your sister managed to hang around with him pretty regularly," Frankie pointed out, drawing Manning's attention.

Color rose in the man's neck, but his tone remained balanced. "That was a lifetime ago. My family doesn't have a damned thing to do with those people anymore. We haven't since Rebecca died. Now if you don't mind, I've got a lot of shit to do today."

Marisela sensed strong iron walls shooting up around Parker Manning. He was, for the time being, Titan's prime suspect in the plot to assassinate Craig Bennett. According to their briefing at Titan's home office before they'd headed over here, Parker Manning had been an inconsolable grieving brother fifteen years ago. He'd pushed the hardest for indictments against Bennett and the Hightower boys in his sister's death, if for no other reason than to force an investigation. He'd haunted the police station, written pleading letters to the prosecutor's office, even picketed the Hightowers' Back Bay mansion until he'd been arrested for harassment and trespass.

Then suddenly, he'd stopped.

No more phone calls to detectives or prosecutors. No more letters to the editor. No more bad-mouthing the Hightower family to any tabloid reporter willing to listen. He'd simply focused on his work as a freelance journalist, covering the crime beat mostly, with a special emphasis on organized crime.

And with reported mob connections stemming from a series of articles he published about criminal families moving into Boston (thus gaining the gratitude of the homegrown mob), Titan couldn't help suspect that at the very least, those ties provided him access to a professional killer.

Parker Manning's motive for wanting Craig Bennett dead had festered a very long time.

"You know," Marisela offered. "We could come back at a better time. You could pencil us in to your social calendar." She picked up a date book on his desk from 1997, replete with condensation rings, pizza sauce, and if she wasn't mistaken, little tiny red mouse tracks. "Give you some time to hire a new housekeeper, because the one you have now sucks."

With a disgusted cough, Manning slammed the door shut. Either he was stupid, curious, or completely numb to the reality that he'd just let two perfect strangers into his home. Or maybe he just wanted to clear his name.

"I've never even met Craig Bennett."

Frankie slipped his hands into the pockets of his jeans and remained near the door. "You really want to start with a lie? We've checked you out. You think the congressman had something to do with your sister's death."

Manning paced the room. "So did the Boston police. You interviewing any of them as potential suspects?"

Marisela used the least-chewed pencil she could find on the desk to lift a stained pair of boxer shorts off a chair. With a grimace, she threw them aside. "Our boss has that covered."

"Well, you can tell your boss to fuck off. I have nothing to say to either one of you."

"Then why'd you let us in?" Marisela asked.

Manning sniffed, rubbed his runny nose. "Thought you might give me an inside scoop. Can't help but wonder why a corporate giant like Titan International is working a political case. Is Bennett dead?"

"Nearly," Frankie replied. Titan had hoped to keep the congressman's condition under wraps, but the local television station had already reported that the politician hadn't yet expired, though he was unable to communicate. "Clearly, the man isn't as easy to kill as someone might have thought."

"Kind of like a cockroach," Manning muttered as he moved toward the kitchen.

"Sounds exactly like something a guy who might order a hit would say," Marisela noted, following him into the place where he cooked his meals—or more accurately, where he tossed his takeout containers. Chinese, Italian, pizza, subs. She counted at least five bags from McDonald's. Either he was a recluse, he was hiding out, or his junk food addiction required professional help.

Parker took a long toke on his cigarette and blew the smoke in Marisela's direction. "I won't pretend I didn't hate the bastard. But I didn't buy any fucking hit."

"Says you?" Marisela challenged.

"Yeah, says me. Look around. Do I look like I have cash to spare? Anyone who checks out my bank accounts knows I don't have the dough to hire a professional."

"What about your parents?" she pressed.

The vein in his neck pulsed. "My father died six years ago with no life insurance. My mother lives with my aunt out in Illinois. Check it out. You'll find that the Mannings aren't exactly the retribution types."

While Marisela sparred with Manning in the kitchen, she spied Frankie looking around the living room. He worked slowly, methodically, covering much of what she'd already perused and, like her, finding nothing of interest.

"You live like *un puerco*," Frankie assessed.

"I live however the hell I want," Manning replied. "Look, if you find out who did order the hit, tell him I owe him a beer."

"We just might," Marisela said, "if you tell us what happened that night."

"I wasn't there. I was here all night, working."

"Not last night," Marisela said. "Guy like you on that guest list? Please. I'm talking about the night your sister died."

His mouth seemed to constrict even as he pushed out the words. "I was away at school."

"But according to our sources, you came home right away and talked to a lot of people. Rumor has it you were a hotshot journalism student then. And you knew all of Rebecca's friends. What did they think happened?"

Manning tossed his cigarette into the sink. "Those creeps camped out on that island all the time."

"Which creeps?" Marisela asked.

"Hightower, both of them. Cole and Bennett, too. It was their getaway from all that money, privilege, bodyguards and nannies. They drank, smoked, fucked around. Whatever."

"Does that *whatever* include bringing their girlfriends out with them for a little tent action?" Marisela asked.

With a disgusted sneer, Manning shook his head. "Those boys didn't invite anyone along on their trips. Kids were salivating to get asked to go to the island. Fucking social event of the season. But no one copped to ever going. Just Bennett, the Hightower boys, and that Cole asshole. Summer, spring, fall. Once a month, they took a boat from the marina and hit the trail."

"So they knew the place pretty well?"

"Well enough to know where to stash my sister's body so she wouldn't be found for two months, if that's what you're asking."

Marisela watched regret and anger play on Manning's face.

"Why was your sister there, then?"

Manning reluctantly shook his head. "They *said* they never brought girls out there and I couldn't prove otherwise. Doesn't mean she didn't go out there on her own and they were pissed off about it."

"You think they killed her because she crashed their private party?" Marisela asked, doubtful.

He patted his shirt in search, she guessed, of more nicotine. "I don't know what to think. All I know is that my sister was wild for that Bradley Hightower jerk and she ended up dead just yards from where he was camping out. To me, the math is pretty simple."

Marisela looked for Frankie, who'd slinked out of sight. Probably checking out the rest of the apartment while Marisela kept Manning occupied in the kitchen.

"Tell me about Brad Hightower."

"Big fucking bastard," Manning said, removing the last cigarette from the pack in his pocket. "He could easily have snapped her neck."

"Didn't she die from blunt trauma to the back of the head?" Marisela asked.

Manning skewered her with a disgusted look as he wiggled in his chair while extracting a lighter from his pants. "You read the autopsy?"

"That surprises you?"

"Nah, guess not. Look, Bradley Hightower was Boston's golden boy. Honor roll. Quarterback. Drove a Porsche. Used to put the top down even when it was snowing. Girls used to cream over him down at the marina."

"That's where your sister met him?"

Manning nodded. "Becca actually thought the son of a yacht owner would fall in love with the daughter of the guy who cleaned his boat. She and Tracy started hanging out at the docks weekends, scoring invitations on board those million-dollar floaters. Mom told me they even took the bus from school to watch football practice at the fancy private academy those assholes went to. It was pathetic."

Marisela watched Manning carefully, noting the perspiration gathering along the collar of his shirt. She'd attributed his shaking hands to DTs, but what if he was nervous? Afraid of what they might find out? He was telling them quite a bit, but he wasn't revealing anything they couldn't find out through other sources. Why, then, did he look so uncomfortable?

Marisela guessed that discussing the situation wasn't exactly easy. His sister had died in a horrific way.

"What about Tracy?" Marisela asked. They'd read next to nothing about her in the police reports, but Marisela figured a brother who'd lost one sister would be extra protective of the other. "How did she play into all this?"

Amazing self-control kept Marisela from breaking Parker Manning's finger when he jabbed it close to her face. "You keep Tracy out of all this. Becca's death nearly destroyed her. She's never been the same."

Marisela stared at his grimy fingernail until he lowered it. "They were close, then?"

"Only a year apart," he replied. "Becca was seventeen when she died. Tracy was just about to turn sixteen. Of course they were close."

Now that was a big fat lie, or at least a huge misconception. Marisela was only two years older than her sister, Belinda, and they hardly spoke to each other during their childhood. Of course, special circumstances played into their poor relationship—circumstances she'd rather not think about. Not now. Not ever.

"Did Tracy see Rebecca that night?" she asked.

"She was home with my parents. Asleep in her room."

"Did she share the room with Rebecca?"

"What the fuck does that have to do with anything?"

"The police report said Tracy didn't notice her sister missing until the next morning."

Parker narrowed his eyes and the shaking in his hands increased so that little flickers of ash were flying over the newspapers, threatening to ignite the kindling at any moment. "Tracy didn't see anything. That Hightower asshole was using her. He probably just wanted to piss Becca off, so he started fucking around with Tracy. She was a kid, okay?"

Marisela held up her hands, processing the new information. Brad Hightower had dumped one sister for the other?

Interesting.

"Okay, I got it. She was your little sister. You're protective."

"You have no idea," he grumbled.

"Then let's go back to Rebecca," she suggested. "How do you think she ended up on the island that night if the guys didn't invite her?"

Parker Manning blew more cigarette smoke into the haze gathering around his head. "For whatever fucking reason, she thought she loved that asshole. She'd pinned her future on marrying Bradley Hightower and becoming the lady of the fucking manor. Rebecca wasn't stupid, but she knew she didn't have much book smarts, and frankly, she was lazy. Always wanted the easy way. She wasn't going to get out of our parents' house by going off to college like I did. She had to marry her way out."

"She couldn't just get a job?"

The question was out before Marisela could call it back and the hatred burning through Parker Manning's eyes nearly singed her hair. "Sorry," she said, her apology genuine. "I just never could understand women who were willing to pin all their hopes on some guy."

She flicked a look over at Frankie, who'd returned and was now quietly chuckling at her comment.

"I wish she hadn't, but she did," Manning replied. "I don't know how or why she was at that island if they didn't take her. The night she disappeared, Becca had told my parents and some friends that she was looking for Bradley. The police searched the island, but they didn't find any sign of her. Few days later, a fisherman towed in an old maintenance boat he'd caught floating near Grape Island, just southeast of where the jerks were camping. The marina manager figured someone had gone out joyriding with it and dumped it. Happened every so often. He showed my dad, who found Becca's scarf."

"But there was no other sign of her anywhere?"

"Not until a month and a half later," Manning replied, his voice choked. "Winter had set in. Rangers found her body in the marsh on Peddack Island. If there'd been any physical evidence of a crime, it was long gone."

Frankie came around the corner and leaned against the doorjamb between the living room and the kitchen. "Then why blame the guys? You had no proof."

Manning slammed his hand on the table. "The Hightower family couldn't get their silver-spoon sons to Europe fast enough. Police never even interviewed them. And Bennett? He gave a statement written by his rich father's attorney and then clammed up tighter than a drum. Even changed prep schools to one in Newburyport for the rest of his senior year. They acted guilty. They were rich and privileged and thought they could get away with murder. And obviously, they did."

"What about Evan Cole?" Frankie asked.

Dismissively, Manning inhaled half his cigarette, then ground out the filter on a plate. "He wasn't there."

"You know this for sure?"

Manning shot up from his chair. "Look, you don't think I checked into every dirty little secret those creeps had? You think I didn't do my best to find out who killed my sister? Girls her age don't steal boats and then walk into a nearly frozen marsh, bang their head on a tree, and die alone, okay? Whether on purpose or because they were fucking with her mind, they lured her there. She died because she couldn't let go of Brad Hightower or his lifestyle."

He took a deep breath, which instigated a coughing fit. "But the past is the past," he said once he'd regained his ability to speak. "Leave it be."

Manning slumped back into his chair, defeated. Marisela could easily guess what he was feeling. He hadn't been there to protect his sister. He hadn't been able to give her justice. Now, he seemed to have just given up. On a lot of things, including himself. Or else he'd turned the dirty work over to someone else who could get the job done.

Marisela stood, figuring they couldn't get much more out of him right now. Their next step would be to find Brad and Raymond Hightower and find out their side of the story.

"One more thing," Frankie said just as Marisela brushed past him. "Where can we find your sister, Tracy? We'll chat with her next, see what she can share."

In the flash of movement that followed, Manning launched forward and grabbed Frankie by the collar.

Marisela moved to intervene, but Frankie already had the man in a headlock, his forearm tight against the guy's throat and his arm twisted behind him.

"Get . . . off . . . me," Manning ordered, failing to execute a decent head-butt thanks to Frankie's iron grip.

"Calm down first, *maricón*," Marisela spat out, knowing if the jerk didn't comply, he might be nursing a broken arm in the next few seconds.

Manning gulped huge breaths of air and held his

hands out, as if to show he had no further urge to attack. Once satisfied that the man had recognized the error of his ways, Frankie tossed him toward Marisela, who broke his fall.

Frankie stood in front of them, arms crossed, eyes cool. "You don't want to push us, Mr. Manning."

Manning heaved, his face red and skin splotchy. "Stay the fuck away from my sister!"

Marisela struggled to contain the man. He was out of shape, but his rage imbued him with unpredictable power. He'd gone from calm to out of control in seconds. Question was, was Manning so hot to protect his sister because of what she'd suffered in the past—or because of what he'd done in the present, like hire a hit on a congressman?

Or maybe the wallet behind the hit belonged to Tracy? Maybe Parker Manning didn't have the cash on hand to pay an assassin, but perhaps, despite her sad past, Tracy Manning did.

"Something you want to tell us about Tracy?" Marisela asked. "Something you're hiding?"

Manning just shook his head.

"Leave her alone. She's been through enough."

"Which makes her all the more likely to want Bennett dead," Frankie offered.

"Tracy's been to hell and back. You don't know. You don't have a fucking clue. She doesn't want—she *can't* relive that night again. I won't have you harassing her. I swear to God, if you go anywhere near her, I'll make you pay."

Frankie allowed the threat to hang in the air, then smoothly moved to the door, gesturing for Marisela to follow. "We'll make a note. Thanks for your . . . cooperation."

"Fuck you."

"Where do we go next?" Marisela asked as she slid into the cab of the custom truck Frankie'd pulled out of the Titan garage. At first, she didn't think the vehicle suited him. For her, he'd always be a souped-up *El Dorado* kind of *hombre*. But witnessing him wrestle all the horsepower of this top-of-the-line F150 really turned her on.

Not that it took much for Frankie to push her buttons.

"Next up is Tracy Manning," he replied. "Her brother might be protecting her for a reason."

She nodded. If some dickhead had not only fucked with her heart, but murdered her sister and then jetted off to Europe looking guilty as sin, she imagined she'd have all the motivation she needed to hire an assassin to off the guy, money or not. Actually, she'd likely just do the job herself. But fifteen years later? What had stirred up the pot? And why was Bennett the first to go, instead of Bradley Hightower? He was the one who'd pitted sister against sister.

"What about the Hightower brothers?" she asked. "The police reports said Tracy was home in bed when her sister disappeared. I mean, she can't tell us anything more than her brother did about what happened that night. But I'm betting Brad Hightower could."

Marisela undid her ponytail, ran her hand through her hair, and then refastened the tie. The pulse at her temples was starting to pound. "We've got to find Brad Hightower before we can interview him."

"Does he have a motive to have his own friend killed?" Frankie asked.

"How do we know if they're still friends? The Hightowers left the country, and so far as anyone knows, they never came back."

"Max has a team checking on that," he reminded her. "Give the office a buzz and tell them to pull us an address for Tracy Manning, too. And financial records, if they can find them. With any luck, we'll get this taken care of quickly."

Marisela whipped out her cell phone, wondering about Frankie's dismissive tone. He'd made no secret of his dissatisfaction with working for Titan, but after he'd survived his bullet to the gut three months ago, he hadn't said anything more about leaving. Marisela guessed he'd been sticking around for her, and the fact that he was still restless caused a pit in her stomach. Damn if she wasn't getting used to having him around.

Before she could press the speed-dial link to the home office, the device vibrated, signaling an incoming call. The caller ID read, *"Private."*

"Marisela," she greeted.

"Good, I'm glad I caught you."

"Brynn?"

"Yes, I'm with Ian and we have a lead on the shooter. Is your interview with Peter Manning complete?"

Marisela activated the speakerphone and slid the phone into a holder on the dashboard. "We're just leaving his place. He gave us the 411 on what he knew about his sister's death, but so far, we have nothing to connect him to our anonymous shooter."

"Well, that's the thing," Brynn said, a chuckle in her voice causing Marisela and Frankie to exchange curious glances. "She's not anonymous anymore."

Seven

MARISELA FOUND IAN sitting on the edge of a queen-size bed in a Jamaica Plain apartment that from a cursory glance, was about ten steps down from the luxury her boss was used to. The place was clean and sparsely furnished, but the stale smell in the elevator and the worn carpets beneath her boots made this place much more her world than his. And from the way he sat with his head cradled in his hands, she guessed he wasn't taking the culture shock very well.

"You rang, boss?"

He looked up, worry etched on his face.

"Where's Frank?"

"Brynn caught us on the way up," she explained. "She wanted Frankie to go with her to interview the guy who hosted the fund-raiser last night."

Marisela dug her hands into the pockets of her jacket, feeling a chill that had more to do with Ian's mood than the temperature.

"She said something about you and I needing to talk."

His frown deepened. "She did, did she? What else did my dear sister say to you?"

Nothing as interesting as what Ian clearly didn't want her to know.

"Said the interview with the fund-raiser guy would be a waste of time and that I'd better get my ass up here. Made a crack about my being Catholic and needing to hear your confession. What the hell is going on? Whose apartment is this?"

Ian stood, and she noticed that while he had changed clothes from the tuxedo he'd worn last night, his pants weren't as perfectly creased as they normally were and the knot of his tie was off center by half an inch. He looked tired. Any sleep he'd gotten had not been enough.

"Are you okay?" She didn't want to care, but couldn't bite back the instinct.

He ignored her. "This apartment was used a week ago by the assassin who shot Craig Bennett."

The apartment, with its fading paint and outdated furniture, looked like a standard hotel or motel room after housekeeping had done their work. If there were any clues about the last tenant, she certainly didn't see them.

"And you know she was here how?"

Ian glanced aside. "I was here with her."

Not the answer Marisela expected.

And judging by the uncomfortable look that skittered over Ian's face, he wasn't thrilled about telling her the ugly truth.

She smiled broadly. "Oh, this is going to be good, isn't it? Should I sit down?" She grabbed the nearest chair, which had been shoved beneath a small desk. "You give me all the sordid details, *mijo*. You'll feel better once it's all out in the open."

His steely glare told her he was not amused.

"The entire situation will be more than amusing to you, I'm sure." he said. "I nearly had to provide my dear sister with a respirator."

She couldn't be this lucky, could she? Had he slept with the killer? Why else would he have been with her in her apartment? Okay, there were lots of other reasons why he might have been here, but judging by the crimson skin just above his collar, his sin was obvious. She spun the chair around and sat backward, her arms braced on the back. "So . . . spill. Don't spare the details, either. I've been around the block. I can take it."

She wasn't sure, but she thought she heard a growl vibrating in the back of his throat.

"Her name is Yizenia Santiago," he replied tersely.

"You've known her name the whole time?"

"I wasn't informed of her identity until this morning when Brynn examined the note given to Denise Bennett. She recognized the flower."

"The flower that was like the tattoo I saw on the shooter?"

"Precisely," he replied curtly, but with a sense of relief. He probably thought Marisela was going to let the sordid stuff drop. They hadn't known each other long, but he didn't seriously think she'd let this go, did he? She was just biding her time.

"What can you tell me about her that's not X-rated?" she asked, her expression serious.

"Yizenia Santiago is a relatively well-known killer for hire based out of Madrid. She has a tattoo of a pomegranate flower on her left wrist."

Marisela leaned on one hand, exaggerating her interest with a wag of her eyebrows. "Any other tattoos in less conspicuous places that I should know about?"

The color rose on his neck. "None that I recall."

She nodded. "Right. Still, I have this tattoo on my—."

"I think it's best that we discuss only the details that are relevant to the case."

"Okay," she agreed reluctantly, "but I think how you met her is damned relevant. Can't be a coincidence."

He frowned, but answered. "Not likely. I met her at a bar. We came back here. When I woke up the next morning, she was gone."

Marisela stared at the bed and tried not to conjure

images of Ian making love to the *perra* she'd fought in the garden. She shouldn't give a rat's ass who he screwed around with. She *didn't* give a rat's ass. She'd just thought he'd have better taste.

"Did she ask you about the job at Houghton House?" Marisela asked, trying to make a connection between the assassin and Titan that applied to the case they were working.

He shook his head. "We hadn't been hired yet."

"So she wasn't trying to pump you for information."

Ian raised his eyebrows. Okay, so maybe *pump* wasn't exactly the right word. Then again, maybe it was.

"Then if sex was all she wanted, I guess she got it," she concluded.

He stood up straighter and that arrogant grin she'd come to expect from him returned. "And then some."

"Cocky, are we?"

"Merely stating a fact."

Suddenly, she wasn't so curious about his rendez-vous with the killer.

"Why didn't you put two and two together about the tattoo and the killer the night Craig Bennett was shot?"

"I didn't remember seeing any marking on her wrist the night I met her in the bar, so I could not make the connection. Brynn, however, identified the tattoo this morning when she saw the note."

"Brynn?"

Ian crossed his arms tight and his lips drew together

in a thin line. "Yizenia Santiago has . . . ties to our family," he replied. "Ties I knew nothing about until this morning."

The bitterness lacing his tone was not lost on her, but Marisela didn't know whether or not to push. Finally, Ian was talking to her as an agent and not just an employee.

"So it's no coincidence that you and she met at a bar just a few days before she shot a guy who ended up becoming our client?"

His frown deepened. "Not likely."

Marisela reached over and patted the seat of an ottoman. He gave a doubtful chuckle, then leaned on the desk instead. Probably didn't want to sit anywhere other than above her.

"So she set you up?" she guessed.

"Possibly, but for what reason, I have no idea. We had no ties to Craig Bennett then. No plan with Houghton House. Leo Devlin hired us at the last minute after the security he'd previously arranged reported they were stretched too thin. We were backup and only required to protect the borrowed jewels."

"Where was Max?" she asked.

He eyed her oddly. "What do you mean?"

"The night she met you. I always thought Max followed you around everywhere. Kept you out of trouble."

"I'm more than capable of keeping myself . . . "

His denial died a painful death. He rolled his eyes. "He had the night off."

"Do you always go drinking at that bar?"

Ian nodded curtly. "It's a place I frequently visit, yes."

"So she probably went looking for you." Marisela toyed with her gold hoop earring. "How does Brynn know her?"

"They met in Europe," he replied briskly.

The hair on the back of Marisela's neck prickled. "I had no idea she regularly hung out with assassins. I didn't think they'd be the social types."

Ian crossed his arms, the sleeves of his jacket tugging tight across his biceps, but said nothing.

"Look, boss, I know I'm not your favorite person," Marisela said. The fact that she was still employed at Titan after she'd defied Ian's orders on her first mission testified only to Marisela's quick thinking and her ability to manipulate situations to her advantage. "But you've picked me to find this woman, right? To do that, I'm going to have to outthink her. And to do that, I'll need all the information you have, even if it sucks that you have to tell me."

Ian's jaw clenched, square and unmovable, as if he were fighting the urge to speak. "Yizenia Santiago is not your standard-model assassin."

Marisela shook her head, confused. "They come in deluxe editions?"

"Some are better than others, but that's not what I'm talking about. Yizenia Santiago has her own signature. She doesn't work just for the money, though her price is exorbitant. Yizenia believes in retribution. According to Brynn, she's fashioned herself into a sort of avenging angel, taking on only cases where the cruel and the criminal escaped punishment."

Marisela blew out a self-satisfied whistle. "So revenge is her thing."

"Exclusively. If no horrific deed has gone unpunished, then Yizenia turns down the assignment. No exceptions."

"Well," Marisela decided, "now I know why Brynn thought that meeting with that fund-raiser guy was a waste of time. That note given to Denise Bennett pointed us to Rebecca Manning."

Ian shook his head. "Leo Devlin only arrived in Boston a few years ago and his ties to Craig Bennett are exclusively political. Still, we can't leave that stone unturned. Hopefully by the time Brynn returns from her meeting with him, he'll have been eliminated as a suspect and we can concentrate solely on the Manning connection."

"But you still haven't explained exactly how Brynn knows her."

Ian pushed away from the desk and paced from one side of the room to the other, his arms still crossed, his gait clipped and tight. Marisela watched him, tapping into the full store of her patience. Whatever secret the man was considering revealing, it had to be good.

"Did Brynn ever tell you anything about our mother?"

Marisela considered his question. In the months

she'd spent with Ian's twin, they'd talked about a lot. She knew that their mother had died when Brynn and Ian were kids, but now that she thought about it, she didn't know why or how.

"Was she sick?" she guessed.

Ian frowned. "She was the picture of health until the day three Soviet traitors kidnapped her. Our father was a spy who worked for British Intelligence, even after he'd moved to the States and started Titan. Apparently, he'd been a key operative on a case that ended with several Soviet double agents being revealed to their government. Four died during their capture. Three survived their prison terms and decided upon their release to take our mother as retribution."

Marisela moved to stand, but Ian directed her to remain still with a simple hand gesture. A flat palm, forcefully presented. She didn't move.

"My father called in every contact he had to find her, but these men were ruthless. They had nothing to lose. Titan was merely a start-up at the time. Father paid the ransom they demanded, but the kidnappers didn't live up to their end of the bargain. Our mother died in the muddy hole they'd shoved her in. She was buried alive."

Marisela clutched at her sleeves, trying to keep her hands from reaching out to this man who was struggling to contain emotions Marisela couldn't begin to comprehend. She stared down at the ratty rug on the floor, then glanced out the window, not knowing where to look or what to say.

She took a deep breath and faced him squarely. "Ian, I—"

He cut her off. "I know."

She nodded. Of course he knew. Anyone with a heart would feel for what Ian had gone through. And Brynn. And their father. Over the past few decades, they'd likely heard others offer their sympathy one time too often.

"The kidnappers were able to escape the United States and prosecution for their crime, even though my father did gather enough evidence to prove their guilt. He was a very strong man. Ingenious, really. Top of his field. But he had children at home and a business to save and from what my sister explained to me just a few hours ago, he opted to pay for his revenge rather than mete it out himself."

"So he hired Yizenia?"

Ian gave a curt nod. "She was younger then, clearly, but just as expert. Brynn discovered this information when she read one of our father's journals a few years ago."

"And she didn't tell you?"

Ian's jaw clenched. "My sister was born a few minutes before I was. She seems to think that in addition to the fact that our father chose to give her majority stock in the company, her birth order gives her the right to provide family information to me on a need-to-know basis. Since I'd slept with the woman who not only avenged our mother's death, but who also attempted to murder the husband of our client, she finally decided I needed to know."

Marisela whistled again. "So where do we go from here?"

"We find her."

Marisela twisted so she could look Ian in the eye. "What are you going to do, start hanging out in the bar and hope she'll pick you up again?"

"It's not unreasonable to think she'd enjoy a second go-around with me," he intoned, "but no, that doesn't seem like a wise course of action. By *we*, I mean Titan. Chances are she'll avoid any further interaction with me or Brynn, although apparently, she and my sister are friendly. Brynn and I need to step back from any dealings with Yizenia, at least on the front line. She'll see us coming a mile away. It'll be up to you and Frankie to smoke her out."

Marisela nodded, the idea growing more appealing as she considered the implications. Yizenia Santiago had been more than a worthy opponent. And now Marisela realized that the assassin's actions that night and even before had been calculated and working toward some greater end. But what? Was revenge for Rebecca Manning's death all she wanted? Why sleep with Ian, then? Why get to know Brynn? And who had paid her fee?

"Have you warned the other men involved in Rebecca Manning's death?"

"*Allegedly* involved," he clarified. "Or did you learn anything from Parker Manning that proves our client's husband was guilty in Rebecca Manning's death?"

Marisela shook her head. "The only thing Parker Manning can prove is that Craig Bennett and his friends could be assholes. They fucked around with some poor girls with stars in their eyes. Nothing new or original there. Manning verified that the High-tower brothers left Boston years ago and he claims to have no idea where they went. But he's superprotec-tive of the sister he has left. Frankie wants to look her up."

Ian pulled out his cell phone and started writing a text message. "We'll try and get a lock on her. In the meantime, you and Frank are going to spend some time casing this neighborhood. If we find Yizenia, we might be able to use our family history to convince her to reveal who paid her to take a shot at Craig Bennett."

"What makes you think she's still around here?"

"The building manager saw her last week, or else he thinks he saw her, hanging out on the main strip, Cen-tre Street. This neighborhood is called Jamaica Plain. It's been primarily Hispanic for decades. Makes sense that she'd stick around since she can blend in. My sister informs me that Yizenia enjoys culture, arts, and food. If she wants a taste of home, this is where she'd be most likely to get it."

"What else do we know about her?"

"She's deadly. She has to be stopped."

"What does she look like?" Marisela asked.

Ian suddenly looked at her deeply, as if seeing her for the first time. She couldn't help looking down at her chest to make sure a boob wasn't popping out of her T-shirt.

"What?"

With a sniff, Ian turned away. "She's a master of disguise."

His answer came too quick.

"Okay, then what did she look like the night she picked you up in the bar?"

He shoved his phone in his pocket and stood up straighter. "She looked like you."

Ian gestured toward the door, but when Marisela didn't immediately follow, he left alone. She stood there, stunned for a second, and then figured he was just fucking around with her. Ian may have come on to her once in a vulnerable moment during her first case, and even now, they enjoyed a weird flirtation based on the fact that he was hot and she was hot, and well, there wasn't much more to it.

Though she had to admit, if what he said was true, a whole new window had opened up into Ian's inner workings. Was he saying he was still hot for her? Or was he simply messing with her mind?

Marisela jogged to catch up to him at the elevator. She had her finger on the call button when Ian's phone trilled.

She'd already pushed the down arrow when Ian's chitchat with the Titan receptionist shifted from polite to serious.

"Put him on and record the call," he instructed. He pressed his thumb over the mouthpiece and spoke to Marisela. "Evan Cole wants to speak with me."

"You? Why?" she asked.

Ian walked toward a window at the end of the hall
for clearer reception. "We'll soon find out."

Marisela ignored the elevator as it opened and followed Ian down the hall. She hopped up on the sill and
waited, kicking her heels against the paneling until Ian's
hand on her knee forced her to stop. As he waited for
the receptionist to make the connection and engage the
surveillance equipment, he paid no attention to how he
was touching her. She tried not to pay attention to it.
But the warmth of his skin pressed against her knee, so
casually, so naturally, nearly made her squirm. Instead,
she lifted one of his fingers and bent it backward to the
near breaking point.

He stared daggers at her, but didn't verbally protest.
As if pain meant nothing, he slowly twisted out of her
grip.

Her heart wasn't in it, anyway. What was up with
that?

"Mr. Cole? Yes, this is Ian Blake. Excuse me?"

Marisela leaned forward, attempting to hear the
tiny voice buzzing from next to Ian's ear.

"Where?" Ian asked. "Yes, I know where it is. We're
just a few minutes away. Should we meet at the entrance?"

Whatever Evan Cole answered caused Ian's eyebrows to shoot up high on his head. "Absolutely. We'll
find it."

He clicked the phone shut, but didn't say anything
for a few very long seconds, even as he mindlessly
rubbed the hand Marisela had assaulted.

"Bennett okay?" she asked.

"Max is at the hospital, so we'll know of any changes to his condition likely before anyone else."

"Then what did Cole want?"

Ian gave a casual but confused shrug. "Evan Cole wants to meet with us at Forest Hills Cemetery."

Marisela scrunched up her nose and hopped off the sill. "A cemetery? That's so sick. His friend isn't even dead yet."

Ian shook his head. "I don't think he's planning anyone's funeral. I think we're about to hear a confession. He wants to meet us at Rebecca Manning's grave."

As they passed through the stone-hewn archway at the entrance to Forest Hills Cemetery, Marisela wondered if they did everything different in Boston. In her Tampa neighborhood, tombstones, mostly square and gray, were set only a few feet apart. Rocks bleached white by the sun marked the patch of earth holding a dearly departed, while weeds battled with overgrown palmetto bushes and faded plastic flowers for the attention of mourners. From her own grandmother's graveside, Marisela remembered being able to watch the cars go in and out of the gas station across the street, while the sounds of traffic battled with the scent from the churro man's truck parked around the block. Three more Hail Marys and she'd get her treat for good behavior. Only the promise of fried dough dusted with sugar could tempt her into the decrepit cemetery.

This place, however, was like paradise. Acres of manicured lawns, winding roads, and gravestones that resembled museum-quality art dotted the landscape. She nearly gasped when she witnessed a flock of swans landing like seaplanes on the glossy black surface of a lily-free pond. Some of the mausoleums looked like minicathedrals, complete with stained glass and statues of saints guarding the entrances. Saints with all their appendages and stained glass not broken by teenagers with nothing to do on a Friday night.

"Are only rich people buried here?" she asked, wondering how Rebecca Manning made the cut.

Ian quirked a grin. "Rumor has it."

"Any of your peeps?"

"A few."

His face froze in a stoic stare and she winced. *Dios mio*! What if his mother was buried here? Good thing Marisela had a big mouth or she wouldn't have room for her size-nine foot.

"It's beautiful," she said quickly. "Peaceful."

Ian arched a brow. "Too bad the dead can't appreciate the view."

An amazing display of sculptures dotted the green landscape. Bronze angels perched on marble columns. Pine trees wrapped with willowy dresses that fluttered in the breeze like ghosts. A gold door suspended from the branch. Crypts that reminded her of Disney's Haunted Mansion. She opened her mouth to ask Ian what was up with all the funky art when he stopped the car and pointed to a grave beside a mournful willow.

"There's Rebecca Manning."

They exited the car in silence. Marisela shoved her hands into her pockets, but when that didn't work to chase off the chill, she crossed her arms tightly over her chest, fisting her hands to keep from making a telltale sign of the cross.

"Don't like cemeteries?" Ian asked.

"Oh, no. I love hanging out with the dead," she replied, careful not to tread on any ground that might, six feet under, contain a decaying body.

Ian chuckled. "Marisela Morales afraid of a bone yard? It is daylight, you know. The zombies don't come out until at least sunset."

She cursed at him in Spanish. "I don't believe in that zombie shit. *Santería* is not my deal."

He stopped, just a foot from Rebecca's headstone. "Then what do you believe in?"

She glanced around, noting the cross-shaped headstone just a few yards away. "I believe this is consecrated ground, okay? Show some respect."

Surprisingly, Ian glanced down at his shoes. Marisela arched a brow. Either he was acting all contrite for her benefit, or he was mocking her. Probably the second one. But he remained quiet as they examined Rebecca's final resting place. It was small, but pretty, with a sailboat etched into the granite of her headstone and her name, followed by "loving daughter."

Marisela knelt down and touched the petals of the roses curling out of the bronze vase permanently screwed into the ground.

"These look fresh," she noted. "Maybe two days old."

Ian squatted beside her. "Her brother probably pays his respects every so often. Maybe her benefactor. Someone had to exert influence to have her interred here."

Marisela tried to imagine Parker Manning respecting anything. She couldn't conjure an image. And flowers? They'd probably wilt in his hands. She moved to stand, then noticed a flash of red much bolder and brighter than the dark crimson of the roses. She dug down and found a different flower.

Bright red-orange. Shaped like a trumpet.

Marisela pulled it out so Ian could see. Instantly, he yanked out his cell phone. Yizenia had been here. This could be a trap.

After a few seconds, he shook his head and flipped the phone shut. "Cole doesn't answer."

The next few minutes moved like hours, until screeching tires alerted them to a dark blue sports car careening around the corner. They heard a crack, then the shattering of glass. The sports car swerved, then headed toward them, barely missing the back bumper of Ian's sedan as it leapt off the road and onto the lawn. Ian grabbed Marisela's arm and together they sprinted to the right, diving behind a tall marble crypt. The car smashed into a six-foot-high stone wall twenty feet to their left.

Marisela's muscles constricted with the sound of crunching metal. Marisela dashed toward the wreck, the stench of gasoline and burning tires assaulting her from within a thick, black cloud of smoke.

"Is it Evan?" Ian shouted.

Marisela tried to wave away the smoke as she attempted to peer through the shattered glass. Ian grabbed the driver's side door handle and yanked, with no luck. Marisela ran around to the passenger side, which wasn't as damaged, but that door wouldn't yield, either. She kicked in the window, reached in and popped the lock.

She moved to slide in, but Ian pulled her back.

"Don't. He's dead."

He pointed to a bullet wound oozing from the back of the driver's neck, blood slicking down the buttery leather seats. The driver's face was turned away from them, but one glance at the passenger seat identified him instantly. An envelope sat undisturbed beneath a shower of glass, the name EVAN COLE printed in bold block letters—the same letters used to write the note delivered to Craig Bennett.

"Holy shit," Marisela said, snatching the stationery. She pulled out the paper inside and read with a mixture of confusion and anger. Damn. Damn, damn, damn. She and Ian knew Evan Cole was on the brink of confessing something major to them. Now that fucking whore assassin had gotten to him before he had a chance to talk.

Ian led Marisela away from the wreck, his eyes scanning the horizon.

"She could still be out there."

"She has no reason to kill us, remember?" Marisela

spat, though the thought of choking the life out of the murderous bitch gave her comfort.

Behind them, the car creaked and hissed. Glass continued to pop from the frame. The airbags deflated and Evan Cole's body, without a seat belt to hold him in place, slumped to the side. His sightless eyes stared upward through his sunroof into the cloudless sky.

Marisela looked at the letter again.

"Let me guess," Ian said, "'Remember Rebecca Manning'?"

She flashed the paper at him, her thumb below the warning he'd just dictated word for word. Just to the left of the sinister advice was a drawing of the pomegranate flower, just like the one now crushed in her hand. "I thought he said he wasn't there that night."

"Clearly," Ian replied, his tone cold and emotionless, "he lied."

Eight

MARISELA SHARED A SEAT with a trio of stone cherubs, carvings on a bench that she hoped like hell wasn't some funky headstone. The longer she stayed in the cemetery, the more she was certain that when her time came, she wanted to be cremated and scattered. She'd instruct her best friend, Lia, to spread her ashes at Clearwater Beach. She didn't think Theresa, the owner of their favorite bar, would appreciate having burned pieces of Marisela smearing her dance floor. But Lia could have the memorial there. Preferably on salsa night.

Ian was in deep confab with the cops, who'd arrived minutes after Ian phoned them, along with paramedics and now the coroner's van. Marisela had already done a walk around the perimeter and saw no sign of Yizenia Santiago. Fact was, she could have shot from anywhere. Hills, embankments, tall trees, and buildings marked the landscape all around them. She could still be there, sitting pretty, watching as the bloodied body of her latest victim was dragged from the wrecked car and zipped into a body bag.

But how did she know Evan was heading here? Had she bugged his phone? Had she been following him? And why kill Evan Cole anyway? Even Parker Manning had insisted the man hadn't been at the campsite the night Rebecca died. Marisela could understand his friends protecting him, but Manning? Why?

"Hell of a mess," muttered a wizened old woman in overalls, flannel shirt, and work boots who tramped across the gravesites as if they were stepping-stones.

Marisela fisted her hands, fighting the urge to make multiple signs of the cross to ward off the bad luck the woman was invoking all around her.

"You work here?" Marisela asked.

The woman's gray ponytail flicked across her shoulders when she turned. "Who's asking?"

Her accent was thick and Bostonian in the way Marisela had expected everyone to talk here, though so far, nobody had.

"I was visiting Rebecca Manning's grave when that car came crashing toward us," Marisela told her.

"You okay?"

Marisela shrugged.

"Damned shock, huh, paying your respects? Nearly getting mowed down?"

Marisela sighed with an exaggerated shiver. "I'm already spooked just being here."

The woman grinned, revealing teeth that likely needed professional attention, but the twinkle in her eyes was warm and genuine. "Dead people can't hurt you, honey."

"Tell that to the stiff who nearly ran me down with his car."

"He was dead before the crash?"

Marisela nodded.

"That's freakish," the woman said. "You know him?"

"Met him once," Marisela answered.

"Figured, since you said you were visiting the Manning girl. Died tragic fifteen years ago, that one."

Marisela scooted forward on the bench and the woman strolled over. "You remember her?"

"Oh, yeah. Didn't know her myself, though. But someone pulled big strings to get her buried here."

"Do you remember who?"

The woman shook her head. "Nah. My husband was a caretaker back then, but we didn't get involved in that. Just did our jobs. He died ten years back, my Will, but I've kept on here. I'm used to the place. It can be downright peaceful sometimes. You'd be surprised how many people come here right regular. Like that guy who nearly ran you down. Saw him here all the time. Recognized the car."

Marisela stood, slid her hands casually into the pockets of her jacket. "Really? How often?"

The woman rubbed her chin vigorously. "Don't quite know. Started coming after my husband was already dead, that much I remember. Sometimes I wouldn't see him for months. Sometimes two, three times a week. Always dressed nice. Driving a nice car."

"Did he bring flowers?"

"Every once in a while. Never stayed long. Always seemed to be looking over his shoulder. I just figured he was one of those rich boys everybody thought had done her in, but it weren't my business if his guilty conscience was getting to him."

"He won't have to worry about that anymore," Marisela said.

"Nah," the woman agreed. "Guessing he won't."

Marisela asked the woman's name, and after she thanked her, she programmed the name into her cell phone for future reference. She then dialed Frankie's number.

"Where are you?" she asked immediately after he answered.

"You missing me, baby? I'll make it up to you to-night, I promise."

She rolled her eyes. "Evan Cole is dead. Score one more for the shooter."

"Cole? When? How?"

She explained what happened, right down to the

pomegranate flower in the planter and the note in Evan Cole's car. In the background, she could hear he was on the road. "Where are you headed?"

"Back to the office."

"What happened with that Devlin guy?"

"He never showed," Frankie informed. "Got tied up in a meeting or some shit. I think he was blowing us off. Brynn wanted to wait around, so we did, but after an hour, we took off."

"Is Brynn suspicious?"

"She claims wealthy dudes like Devlin blow people off all the time. Doesn't make them guilty of anything."

"Or innocent."

"Exactly," Frankie agreed.

Ian walked up just as she was disconnecting the call.

"We need to find Tracy Manning," she concluded. "Maybe she knows how Evan Cole was dragged into this."

"Perhaps. We should have something on her today. But I believe the Hightower brothers are more likely to give us the information we need. And their lives are clearly in danger."

"Any word on where to find them?"

He shook his head.

"What about Bennett?"

"According to Max, our client remains in stable but serious condition. He can't talk."

"Can he write?" she asked. Bennett had almost

died. If revealing his part in Rebecca Mannings death increased his chances of living, then she thought he might be motivated to tell them the whole story.

Unfortunately, Ian shook his head again. "He's too weak. He's barely conscious with all the medication they're pumping into him. We don't even know if he has any brain damage. We can't look to him for answers just yet."

If ever.

Ian gestured toward the car. "Max's team has a lead on Bradley Hightower, but nothing that's panned out. Let's rendezvous at the office and plan our next move. Cole's body is going to the coroner's for autopsy, but they found the bullet lodged in his dashboard. I'm betting it matches the one that downed Craig Bennett."

"Doesn't take a Harvard degree to figure that out," she quipped as Ian gestured toward the car.

"Oxford, dear, Oxford."

She snickered. She'd never put much stock in the value of a college degree, but two days in Boston had alerted her that the rest of the world, as usual, thought differently. "Is Oxford better?"

It was Ian's turn to roll his eyes as he headed down the grassy hill toward the car. "Consider the difference between Cole Haan and Bruno Magli," he replied, bringing the comparison down to something she could understand—expensive men's shoes.

"You're a fucking snob, you know that?" she commented, glancing down at Ian's footwear. He probably had Magli's entire new fall collection in his closet, as well as his latest thousand-dollar loafers on his feet.

"Tell me something I don't know," he answered coolly.

Marisela smiled as she opened the passenger door and slid inside. "Okay," she agreed once he was tucked in the driver's seat. "Evan Cole visited Rebecca Manning's grave on a regular basis."

Ian arched a brow. "That is something I didn't know."

Her grin widened. "That's why I'm the agent and you just sign the checks."

"I should be insulted," Ian replied, humor lacing his voice. "But right now, I'm just going to remember that I'm the brilliant one who hired you."

"And fired me," she reminded him.

"All men make mistakes once."

Marisela chuckled. All the men she knew, with the possible exception of her father, usually made the same mistakes over and over and over again. It was up to the women in their lives to figure out how to stop the madness. Trouble was, in this Manning case, the people they were trying to protect were men and the killer after them was a woman.

If Marisela didn't get a jump on her, those guys didn't stand a chance.

Yizenia walked into the tiny boutique hotel where she was staying under the name Lourdes Concepción, a nod to Bernadette, one of Yizenia's favorite saints. Not that she communed much with her faith since she'd become a gun for hire, but the lessons of childhood were hard to dismiss. The cemetery, so overwhelming with religious imagery, churned up the deep-seated dogma of her youth. Still, the woman who'd watched her family cut down by Franco's death squad hadn't had much choice in the direction of her future. She trusted that when she met *El Señor* someday, he'd understand. She may have denied the peaceful ways of his Son, but she'd embraced the old traditions. An eye for an eye.

Mía es la venganza; yo pagaré, dice el Señor.

She just made sure those who deserved vengeance got to the Lord a little quicker. She wondered if Marisela Morales could embrace her vocation with the same dedication.

Watching her potential protégée at the cemetery had been a gift Yizenia had not expected and what she'd seen concerned her. She'd watched Marisela through her scope, noting her unease among the dead. She'd watched her react to Evan Cole's crashing car. She'd tried to rescue him. If Yizenia hadn't done her own checking into the woman's past and seen for herself the long list of crimes Marisela had committed prior to her employment with Titan, Yizenia might have thought she'd been mistaken about the girl entirely.

Perhaps she was.

Yizenia needed to find out for sure. If the seeds of retribution were buried in the young woman's gut, with the right nurturing, they could take root. Grow. Blossom. Yizenia glanced at her tattoo, the symbol of her country, the symbol of her pain. Could Marisela share her devotion to her cause?

She should be moving on. Craig Bennett and Evan Cole were taken care of, relatively speaking. She'd watched both men for weeks. Marking their habits. Watching their pain. At least, Cole's pain. His habit of visiting Rebecca Manning's grave had touched her. Momentarily. Clearly, he lived with the knowledge of what he'd done every day.

Bennett, on the other hand, lived as if he'd never known Rebecca Manning, as if his actions had not contributed to her death. He smiled at the crowds, gladhanded his fellow politicians, took interviews with the press that dressed him up as a hero rather than a killer. He'd needed to be stopped and his death had been a challenge. And a triumph. A man surrounded by security almost every day, gunned down in a room full of elegant people who hadn't a clue that the public servant they fawned over had been a coldhearted, gutless killer in his misspent youth.

As she jogged up the stairs to her third-floor room, Yizenia felt the rage building inside her.

"Señora, señora!"

Yizenia spun around, pasting on a smile as her landlord, a squat, doe-eyed man named Juan Ramos, chased up behind her. "*Sí, Señor Ramos?*"

"I thought you would like this," he said, handing her a hot-pink sheet of paper.

She scanned the flyer. The Jamaica Plain neighborhood was hosting a festival celebrating their Hispanic heritage in just a few days.

"*Gracias, señor.* This looks like quite the party."

"I could show you around," he offered.

Maybe thirty years ago when she wasn't so particular about who fulfilled her sexual needs. Now, she was entirely more selective.

"You're sweet," she purred to him in Spanish. "But I don't think your wife would appreciate your hospitality."

She turned and strutted her way up the stairs, knowing he was drooling over the swing of her ass and not caring one way or another. Reveling in her sensual power bored her now, though she didn't take her natural assets for granted, either. She'd used her talents to lure Ian Blake into bed, to taste a bit of the son of the man who'd so impressed her with his loyalty to his wife.

She wondered . . . did Marisela Morales understand the spell she could cast over men? Did she know how she'd ensnared Ian Blake or did she think his aloof attitude was genuine? Yizenia knew the child treasured her physical prowess, but she'd need to value so much more if she was to move in the shadows and take up the mantle of revenge.

Yizenia unlocked her door, ignoring the rather shabby state of the room. Like the place she'd stayed before, it was clean and functional. It would do until her employer provided her with a location for the fourth and final target—and the payment that would ensure her next long holiday.

❖

Frankie kicked his heels up onto Ian's desk, drawing a glare from Brynn.

"Show some respect," she snapped.

Frankie smirked. "Why?"

"He's your boss."

"And you're his boss. Should I bow down and kiss your feet or something?"

She smirked. "Wouldn't be the first time," she reminded him.

"I said kiss your feet, not suck your toes."

After looking shocked for a split second, she broke into a peal of laughter. The sound reminded him of the woman he'd first met years ago, when running Titan and lording her power over her brother wasn't as important to her as diving into a case, forcing their opponent into a corner, then swooping in for the kill. Frankie hadn't been able to resist Brynn's hunger for success, her devotion to grabbing what she could from every situation and milking it to fill her own needs. Their affair had been brief, but memorable. That they'd remained friends afterward still freaked him out. Things never worked that way for him.

Well, almost never.

As if on cue, Marisela sauntered into the office in step with Ian. Their conversation halted the minute they realized they were not alone.

What the hell?

Ian cleared his throat. "You're up to speed, then?" he asked Marisela as he approached his chair, giving Frankie's boots only a cursory glance.

"Completely," she replied.

Was her voice suddenly softer? Or was Frankie imagining things?

Marisela knocked him in the arm playfully as she took the seat beside him. He felt his expression coil into a scowl. She and Ian looked mighty cozy on their way in. Had they bonded over Cole's dead body?

Brynn, however, seemed less interested in the camaraderie between her brother and her protégée. "So if we assume Yizenia did the hit, then we can also assume that Evan Cole had something to do with Rebecca Manning's death."

"Cole claimed he wasn't there," Frankie reminded them.

"He lied," Marisela said decisively. "And something made him finally want to confess his part. But what?"

"The note with his name on it?" Ian offered.

"Perhaps," Brynn replied. "He didn't know about Craig Bennett's note, did he?"

Marisela shook her head. "Denise Bennett sent him out of the room before she showed it to us. I talked to this caretaker lady at the cemetery. She said Cole visited Rebecca's grave regularly."

Brynn's eyebrows shot up. "Interesting. Unfortunately, we've literally a dead end on our hands. Didn't the police report list an alibi for Evan Cole?"

Frank nodded. "Party on his parents' yacht. Even Manning believed Cole was in the clear."

"Maybe Yizenia made a mistake," Marisela offered. "Maybe she just assumed—"

"Yizenia never assumes," Brynn assured them, sliding her slim backside onto the corner of Ian's desk. A split second later, Marisela slapped him on the arm. Must have caught him looking.

Leaning forward, Marisela eyed Brynn with suspicion. Not the accusatory kind, but with enough distrust to get Brynn's hackles up.

Frankie winced. Not a smart move, *vidita*.

"Just how did you get to know Yizenia so well?" Marisela asked.

Brynn cast a glance at her brother.

"I told her about our mother," Ian conceded, his eyes darting to his computer monitor, which had just pinged with an incoming message.

Brynn swallowed thickly. Frankie knew the story. Had heard it a long time ago, and frankly, it wasn't the kind of story a guy forgets. He could imagine that if anyone touched one permanent-curled, dyed hair on his mother's head, he'd easily and without regret cut the heart out of the person responsible. And if he'd do the job himself.

Brynn, on the other hand, seemed to harbor guilt over her relationship with Yizenia Santiago, judging by the shadow darkening her eyes. "I made it a mission of mine to find her once I realized what she'd done for my father, for my family. I didn't expect to like her, to be intrigued by her, to be fascinated by someone who is almost fanatical about seeking revenge. But once you meet her, you'll understand."

"I've met her," Marisela said. "I'm not so impressed.

Pero, she did you a service. But now she's the enemy. Am I the only one who remembers that?"

Frankie chuckled. Marisela as the voice of reason? That was a new one.

Brynn gave Marisela a sly grin. "No, you don't have to remind either of us. I know this woman well enough to realize that Yizenia's choice to"—she lowered her voice—"*contact* my brother, suggests she has some ulterior motive that could affect us all. We need to find her. We have two ways to go about doing that. One is to search the neighborhood where she's been spotted. The other is to find out who hired her and track her through that avenue."

Frankie clucked his tongue. "There's no guarantee she'll contact the person who hired her until after the job is done. Cole is dead and Bennett is too well guarded. My bet is she'll go after the Hightower boys next."

"She already has," Ian said. He typed on his keyboard, bringing the large, flat-screen monitor behind his desk to life. A large scan of a newspaper article appeared on the screen.

"Switzerland?" Brynn asked, standing and turning to see the article close up. "What's this?"

Ian frowned. "Raymond Hightower's obituary. He died a month ago. Ski accident."

"They're sure?" Marisela asked.

Ian's fingers flew over his keyboard. "Took several days to recover the body. He went over a cliff. An autopsy was performed, but the results are pending.""

"Yizenia strikes again," Frankie said.

"Actually, that would make him the first of the guys to go," Marisela assessed.

"He was in Europe," Brynn said. "Yizenia's home base is Spain. She could have hit him first because he was closest."

"Then Bennett, now Cole here in the States. We don't know where Brad Hightower is. Maybe she doesn't, either," Marisela suggested.

"Or else he's already dead," Ian said. "The team has nothing solid on him yet, though Max discovered that ten years ago, when the parents died in a yachting accident in the Greek islands, he showed up for the funeral and then promptly disappeared. No one seems to have heard from him since."

"What about the will?" Brynn asked. "To whom did the Hightowers leave all their money?"

Ian arched a brow. "Good question."

He typed again, more than likely sending a request to his research team. Sounded like a simple question with a complicated answer.

"Always follow the money," Brynn reminded them. "Unfortunately, Yizenia uses untraceable offshore accounts."

"So where do we go next?" Frankie asked. The case was confusing and, in his estimation, pointless. They'd been hired to protect Craig Bennett. That was fine, but they couldn't do it forever. Once he was out of the hospital and on the mend, he'd be a sitting duck.

To find Yizenia fast, they needed to pursue the one

solid clue they had—she preferred hanging out in Jamaica Plain, which wasn't exactly a small area. So far, his money was on Parker Manning as the one who'd hired her. He was the only one with a personal score to settle. But why kill Evan Cole? He'd had an alibi and even Parker Manning claimed to believe the guy had no part in his sister's murder. Or had that simply been a ruse to throw suspicion off him when Cole turned up dead?

"I think we need to go back to Parker Manning," Frankie suggested.

Marisela shook her head. "I don't trust him. And I don't think Evan Cole was as squeaky clean as he wanted us to believe. A rich guy doesn't hang out at some chick's grave just to be nice. He was there that night."

"He had an alibi," Ian argued. "The police have witness statements that place Evan Cole on his father's yacht in Boston Harbor, attending his parents' anniversary party, on the night Rebecca went missing."

"He was on a yacht in the same harbor as the island where Rebecca's body was found?" Marisela asked, incredulous. "That can't be a coincidence."

"She's got a point," Frankie agreed. "He might have been on the yacht at some point, but he could have left. A yacht that size would have lifeboats, *verdad*?"

Ian and Brynn nodded. They'd both spent a hell of a lot more time on yachts than either he or Marisela, but on their last mission, they'd been on at least three floating palaces. All of them had had dinghies and tenders and even lifeboat rafts. Hell, Titan's own yacht had a two-seater helicopter.

Ian nodded as Frankie's suggested scenario started to make sense. "If Evan was there, what was his part in Rebecca's death?"

"The only person left who could tell us is Bradley Hightower. *If* he's still alive," Brynn said.

"Evan Cole claimed he wasn't there," Marisela mused, "but he must have been because someone had proof enough to convince Yizenia of his involvement. What if Evan wasn't the only one who lied about not being there?" Marisela asked.

"You mean Parker?" Frankie asked.

She shook her head. "No, we know he was away at school. I'm talking about Tracy. She was Bradley's current girlfriend. Apparently, Bradley dumped Rebecca and took up with Tracy. If you think about it, she had more reason to be on that island that night than her older sister. What if Bradley Hightower brought his new little girlfriend camping with him and her older sister wasn't happy about it and went to bring her back?"

"But then why would Tracy not tell the police if she saw her sister get murdered?"

Marisela shrugged. "I don't know. Maybe she didn't see anything. We don't know until we ask her. She was only fifteen. Maybe she kept quiet to cover her own ass. Can't imagine her parents would have allowed her to go out to some island with her boyfriend and his friends. Look, I'm just supposing, but Parker Manning said his sister was really screwed up. Maybe her troubles aren't so much that her sister died, but that she was murdered and Tracy never said a word."

"So you think Tracy hired Yizenia?" Ian asked.

Frankie bristled, the intense connection between Marisela and Ian spiking the hairs on the back of his neck. The boss wanted her opinion. All of a sudden, he respected her observations?

"We won't know if she's angry enough to hire a killer until we check Tracy out," Marisela replied. "But we have two people left who were involved that night—Bradley Hightower, who we can't find, and Tracy Manning."

"We can't find her, either," Brynn pointed out.

Marisela stood, slapped Frankie's thigh, and jerked her thumb toward the door. "Parker Manning knows where she is."

Frankie wondered exactly what his ex had in mind. The guy hadn't been exactly cooperative before. "You want to rough him up?"

"Ew, and touch him? Only if he's showered. No, I was thinking something a little more . . . *engañosa*."

Deceitful? Better than being bored, he supposed.

"Do whatever it takes," Ian said, his gaze locked with Marisela's.

Again, Frankie fought off a chill. Those were the kind of words a man could live to regret.

Nine

MARISELA'S BRAIN TINGLED WITH IDEAS on how to smoke out Tracy Manning—some of them legal, some of them not so much. The chance of engaging in a little larcenous activity for a good cause put an added swing in her step, which Frankie clearly noticed. As soon as they were out of Ian's office, he slapped her on the ass and whistled like a construction worker. The feel of his hot hand across her backside sparked another list of possibilities to form in her brain—none of which had anything to do with finding missing women or breaking laws. Well, not in most states, anyway.

"You can't keep your hands off me, can you?" she teased.

Oddly, he didn't return her smile. "I'm not the only one."

She stopped, her hands on her hips. "You've never been the only one, *cabrón*."

She'd meant the jibe to be a joke, but Frankie wasn't laughing.

"What the hell is wrong with you?" she asked, annoyed. He tried to look casual when he crossed his arms, but she wasn't buying it.

"What was up with you and Ian back there?" he asked, his jaw a little tighter than necessary for such a casual question.

Damn, he was so transparent.

She played innocent, drawing her hand dramatically to her chest. "I don't know what you're talking about. We were just working, same as you and Brynn. I noticed you checking out her *culo*, by the way. It's nice. A little on the skinny side, but she's a rich girl, so you've gotta cut her some slack."

She turned and laughed, but once again, Frankie didn't find her comment amusing. He grabbed her arm. "I'm serious, *vidita*. You can't let that guy get under your skin. He's a snake."

"He's our boss," she replied over her shoulder, nonchalantly glancing at his hand. He'd started to squeeze her arm, but she doubted he was aware of it.

"For now," Frankie snapped back, releasing her.

He quickened his pace down the hall, but she didn't

follow. She knew Frankie chafed under Ian's rule, even before the Titan chief had used Frankie's life to manipulate Marisela. But after Frankie recovered, he'd hated Blake no more—and no less than he had before. She always figured Frankie's machismo attitude simply didn't mix with Ian's overbearing managerial style. But now she suspected that whatever anger ran between them stemmed from more than just excess testosterone and went back further in time than just three months.

Ian could be a self-absorbed, smug prick half the time, so she usually understood why he pissed Frankie off. But today, Ian hadn't been so bad. Despite how it made him look like a fool, he'd confessed to his tryst with Yizenia. He'd come clean to his sister and then to Marisela. He'd discussed every aspect of the case with her, and back in his office, he'd listened to both her and Frankie's suggestions during the debriefing. Hell, he'd not only told her some depressing shit from his childhood, but they'd also nearly gotten run over together in the cemetery. So she wasn't feeling so annoyed with him at the moment. Didn't mean Frankie had to go acting all betrayed.

Or worse, jealous.

She caught up to Frankie at the ornate, wrought-iron and marble staircase that angled down to the main floor of the Titan International home office. To anyone casually strolling inside—not that anyone was ever allowed to do that—the building looked like a high-priced law practice or renovated Boston home. Behind the locked doors of the offices, however, hummed the inner workings of a highly technical, covert organization peopled with the best private investigators and security specialists money could buy. Marisela hadn't had much time to explore the inner workings yet, but she was about to make her first requisition.

"What's your problem with him, anyway?"

"Look, Marisela. Ian Blake was my way out of the joint. He pulled the strings that got me released."

"That's why you went to work for him?"

"Working for him was a condition of my release."

"For the rest of your life?"

Frankie laughed, but the sound vibrated more with defiance than humor. "What do you think?"

"I think you're like a caged animal here. I think you've stayed because of me. You were going to leave before Blake hired me, weren't you?"

He didn't have to answer. She knew the truth.

"I can take care of myself, Frankie."

"Can you?"

His question wasn't cocky or challenging—just a question, plain and simple, one she wasn't quite ready to answer.

He waited for her reply, and when he didn't get one, he headed toward the stairs, but she stopped him. Maybe she should drop this conversation for now, because while she knew Frankie was chafing under Ian's rule, she didn't want Frankie to go. He might be a royal pain in the ass, but he watched her back. Not to mention other parts of her body that appreciated male attention.

"I want to stop by the gadget room," she said.

"Titan doesn't stock the kind of toys you need," Frankie said, flashing a cocky smile. "But I know this place on Tremont Street that might interest you."

She gritted her teeth. She wanted to slug him, but damned if his little jealous act didn't warm her insides. "You've got sex on the brain."

"You better requisition a compass, because my sex comes from a place a whole lot lower than my head."

"You're crude," she snapped, and twisted away from him. Frankie was notorious for his sexually charged flirtations, but he'd never been so crass before. Or maybe she just hadn't cared? Either way, she wasn't in the mood. If he was trying to turn her on, then he was the one who needed a compass because he was definitely working her from the wrong direction.

He grabbed her arm again, this time yanking her up close. "Yeah, I'm crude. That's who I am. I'm no college-educated rich boy with a dead mother you can weep over."

Without thinking, Marisela thrust upward with her elbow and jammed Frankie in the jaw. He released her with a curse.

"I can't believe you're protecting him," Frankie said through clenched teeth.

"He doesn't need protecting," she seethed, rubbing her elbow. "What are you? Ten? And you don't have to talk shit to get my attention, you *pendejo*."

He stood up straighter and wiped a single drop of blood from the corner of his lip with the pad of his thumb. "Last night, you liked when I talked shit to you."

"Yeah, and I hope you enjoyed yourself," she said, "because that fuck is going to have to last you a hell of a long time."

Marisela spun around, nearly knocking into Max, who had appeared from nowhere. She blasted out a curse, much cruder than the one Frankie had uttered moments before.

"Testy, testy," Max said.

"Stop sneaking up on me!"

Max glared at Frankie with his spooky gray eyes. "What did you do to piss her off so much she wants to kill *me*?"

Frankie muttered something unintelligible, spun around, and headed down the stairs without another word. The minute he was gone, Marisela felt her entire body relax. After a second, Max released her.

"Sorry," she said, straightening her T-shirt.

"I don't see why the two of you don't just hit each other when you're mad and leave the rest of us out of it."

"I did hit him," she said, massaging her elbow. "Hurt like a bitch."

Max gestured for her to follow him up the stairs, away from Frankie. The man was a born peace broker.

"How's Bennett?" she asked.

"Improving, but still uncommunicative. His wife ordered me back here for an in-person update on the search for the shooter."

Marisela winced. "That must have been fun."

He shrugged as they reached the top of the stairs. "She's a desperate woman in love with a man marked for death. I can see where her manners might not be important to her right now."

He led her down the hall and Marisela wasn't surprised to see that he was leading her exactly where she wanted to go. Though they'd first met under shaky circumstances, Marisela and Max had developed a comfortable working relationship. Nothing she did or said ever seemed to shock him, whereas he got an honest-to-God kick out of scaring the shit out of her every time he popped in out of nowhere. Max was not only Ian's right-hand man, but he was an incredible investigator—and he wasn't half bad in a fight, either.

"Listen, I think I know how to track down Tracy Manning," she said as they approached the gadget room, officially called Technical Services on the Titan directory.

"She's a hard woman to find," Max commented, typing a code into a panel beside a door. "Between her and Bradley Hightower, my team is threatening to mutiny."

"If your team doesn't mind, I have an idea."

The door clicked open, revealing an office literally humming with electronics. A trio of technicians, each wearing wireless headsets, concentrated on the half-dozen flat-screen monitors glimmering in front of them. The sound of one-sided chatter added to the urgency zinging through the room. Steel shelves and locked cabinets overflowed with wires, key pads, optical scopes, and LCD screens. This was where Titan technicians created their electronic magic.

"Have you run this plan by Ian?" Max asked as he picked up an electronic clipboard and paged through the reports with a touch of the screen.

Marisela grinned sheepishly. "Not exactly. I wanted to see if my idea worked first. He told me to do whatever I had to."

Max stopped walking, turned, and arched a brow.

"He gave you carte blanche?"

"Isn't that a credit card?"

"The kind with no limit. What's your idea?"

Max matched her smile. Interest sparkled in his enigmatic gray eyes, accentuating the crinkle of skin at his temples. Max couldn't possibly be old . . . but honestly, Marisela couldn't begin to guess what age he was. However many years he'd been in this world, he'd used them all very well.

Marisela led Max to the nearest console and asked him to obtain cell phone records for Parker Manning.

"My agents already explored this avenue. There's no number assigned to Tracy Manning."

Marisela rolled her eyes. "Of course there isn't. Parker Manning might be a slob, but he's not stupid. He's trying to hide his sister, remember?"

Max nodded and retrieved the records his team had pulled earlier in the day. Didn't take more than a cursory glance to figure out what numbers Manning called most frequently.

All but three were landlines, easily identifiable as originating to and from Manning's editor, a neighbor, his favorite takeout places, and a friend in New York City. The other listings were cell phones number—two attached to names of friends. The third cell phone—the one he called the most—piqued Marisela's interest. The calls came from a phone registered under Parker Manning's own cell plan.

"What about that one?"

"Lots of reporters have more than one phone."

"This reporter isn't on anyone's payroll. He's freelance."

Max dug a little deeper. "They share the same area code. If Tracy has the second phone, we still don't have her location."

Marisela memorized the number. "It's a place to start. We have no address, but if we call it, we can pull an E911 reverse signal location and pinpoint her that way."

Max's eyebrows shot up in surprise.

Marisela glared at him. "I listen during training."

"Apparently," Max replied.

"So if we call her and she answers," Marisela speculated, "we just trace the signal?"

"That's the easiest plan I've heard all day."

Marisela paced in a tight circle while Max set up the technological trap, then on his order dialed the number from a blocked Titan phone. When Tracy answered, Max's team would follow the signal as it bounced from cell tower to cell tower and then finally landed on Parker Manning's AWOL sister.

After the eighth ring, Marisela pressed the phone into the cradle. "She's not answering."

"Any voice mail?" Max asked.

She shook her head.

"She probably has caller ID," he surmised. "Maybe she won't pick up an unidentified call, which is how we come through."

"Can we disguise our phone as Parker's? Clearly, she picks up when he calls."

Max looked down at the geeky tech guy who'd been tracing the call. "We could," the guy answered, "but it'll take a while. Be easier to swipe the guy's phone and just call the number yourself."

Marisela smiled, her stomach warming at the prospect. That's the sort of plan she could embrace.

Unfortunately, Parker Manning had other plans. The agent who'd been watching him at Frankie and Marisela's request reported that he'd left half an hour before. Fortunately, the agent who had been following him reported that he'd just parked his car on a side street in Jamaica Plain.

"Coincidence?" Marisela asked. Jamaica Plain was, they still believed, Yizenia Santiago's base of operations.

"I think not," Max replied. "While you're there, keep a lookout for her. We find her and we don't need either Tracy Manning or her brother."

"That's if she'll cooperate."

"We'll leave that to Brynn," Max said. Clearly, he'd been brought entirely up to date on the current situation, which didn't surprise Marisela at all.

"I'll need a car and a map," Marisela said as they headed down the stairs. "Unless you'd like to come along and fracture a few laws with me?"

For a split second, Max looked tempted. With a reluctant frown, he shook his head. "Frank has a car and he knows his way to JP."

"Frank has an attitude and I don't want to deal with him right now," she groused.

Max clucked his tongue. "He's your partner on this case."

"Yeah," she said, her voice rising. "And how exactly did that happen again? You'd think Ian would have learned his lesson by now."

"Maybe it's a racial thing," he teased.

"Latino is not a race," she corrected. "It's a culture."

"A culture very prevalent in Jamaica Plain," Max pointed out. "Frank's waiting outside. My tech team will be ready once you have Manning's phone. But try to get it back to him before he notices it missing, okay? I'm really not in the mood to have to bail you out of jail for petty theft."

"You sound just like my father," she quipped.

"God help the man."

Complaining to herself all the way through the lobby, Marisela realized that no matter how annoyed she was with her Frankie, she had no choice but to work with him to finish out this case. With a curse that made the towheaded receptionist jump out of her seat, Marisela tore out of the Titan office to find Frankie leaning against the hood of the truck, sucking on a cigarette as if he didn't have a care in the world. That was his problem, wasn't it? He didn't give a shit about anyone or anything beyond himself. He didn't get all protective over her because he gave a shit, but because he couldn't stand anyone else having influence over her. He could care less what Ian and Brynn had gone through with their mother's murder or what conflicts they faced while searching out the killer who'd avenged her death.

Of course, the fact that Marisela cared too much struck her like a slap in the face. Her emotions got the best of her on a regular basis. And Frankie, knowing her like the back of his hand, never hesitated to use that against her, especially to further his own agenda.

Without a word, she opened the passenger door and climbed inside the truck. When Frankie made no move to join her, she leaned across and pressed hard on the horn. He jumped, then turned and glared at her.

She smiled sweetly and tapped on her watch.

He took one last toke on his cig, then smashed it under his heel and came around to the driver's side of the car.

"What am I now, your fucking chauffeur?"

She snickered. "If the car key fits."

"What're our orders?"

"I'll tell you once we get to Jamaica Plain."

Frankie shoved the key into the ignition. "Why don't

you just tell me now and put me out of my misery."

"There's an idea," she sniped.

Knowing things would work more smoothly if she concentrated on the case, Marisela filled Frankie in on the plan she'd devised with Max. As he drove onto the highway, she opened her bag and checked her weapon, which she switched to a shoulder holster she could wear under her jacket.

"You expecting trouble?" Frankie asked, his voice tight.

"I'm always expecting trouble."

"If that's true, you wouldn't be letting your guard down with Blake."

She turned in the seat, watching Frankie's sharp profile as the streetlights and neon signs drew flashes of color across his dark skin. The sun had set while they were inside the Titan offices and Marisela tried not to think about how long a day this had been. How much she'd learned. How much she'd possibly lose.

"What is your problem with Blake?"

Frankie spared her a quick glance. "Do you forget that he almost let me die three months ago? That he used my life to blackmail you?"

Marisela frowned. No, she hadn't forgotten. But she also knew that the animosity between the two men had existed long before Marisela joined Titan. "*Mira,* just because I cut him some slack today doesn't mean I trust him. But I've got to work with the man, and while it might be fun to yank his chain all the time, that's not the way for me to get anywhere."

Frankie pulled up to a stoplight and turned to face her. "Why not? You've already proved you're good at this shit, *vidita*. You've learned a lot. Why do you have to stay with Titan, anyway?"

"Why do you?"

"You know why."

"Frankie, *escúchame*—don't stick around here because of me. I can do this on my own."

"So anxious to get rid of me?" he asked, his voice teasing.

Her ire with him dipped to a manageable level. "If I really wanted to get rid of you, I would have by now and you know it. But man, it's not cool for you to put your life on hold because of me."

He maneuvered onto the highway, chuckling. "Sometimes you give yourself too much credit. Sometimes, not enough."

"What is that supposed to mean?"

"You don't need Ian Blake or Titan. You could work for anyone now."

Marisela snorted. "Yeah, right. You forget that the only reason I'm able to carry this gun is because Titan worked it so the suspension of my license to carry miraculously disappeared. They also don't seem to mind that pesky criminal record of mine. Think other private investigators would be so forgiving?"

"You could work for yourself," he said.

The idea appealed to her on many levels, but Marisela had to admit the truth. "I'm not ready and you know it."

He arched a brow. "Where's all your *machisma, vidita*? The *gringos* already breaking you down?"

She narrowed her gaze. "My *machisma* is fine, okay? But I'm not stupid no more, Frankie. I know when I still have shit to learn and Brynn, *gringa* or no, wants to teach me. I can't walk away from this just because you and the boss can't go five seconds without having some sort of pissing match."

"My dick is longer. I'd win," he said cockily.

"And you measured him, when?"

That shut Frankie up. They rode the rest of the way in silence, chatting only to review their plan. With the help of the agent assigned to tail Manning, they were going to locate the reporter, swipe his cell phone, and use it to call his sister while Titan's experts triangulated a location for Tracy. They might not get her position right on the money, but they'd be a damned sight closer than they were now.

Once they were in Jamaica Plain, Marisela called in to the agent tailing Parker Manning. She repeated his location to Frankie, who consulted the GPS module on the truck.

Parking half a block from where Manning was sitting at a bar, Frankie turned off the engine. Marisela stepped out of the truck, instantly reconnecting with the sights and sounds all around her. This morning, they'd been in too much of a rush to look around, but now, even in the dark, Jamaica Plain rocked with a rhythm that lured her. One of the largest neighborhoods in the city of Boston, JP was as diverse as it was large. Murals starring citizens from every ethnic background imaginable graced the walls of hair salons, restaurants, and a bakery. Motorcycles were parked outside taverns while women with baby strollers maneuvered on the sidewalks. The music was loud, the talk was louder. And to Marisela, the vibe was pure heaven.

Finding Parker Manning would be a snap. But Yizenia?

"Needle in a haystack," Marisela said, looking around.

Frankie slammed his door shut and clicked on the security system. "Gotta start somewhere."

The Titan agent who'd been tailing Parker Manning caught up with them almost immediately. He directed them to a tavern a few doors down from where they'd parked.

"He went in about half an hour ago," he reported. "Once you spot him, I'm out of here, right?"

Marisela smirked at the blond-haired, blue-eyed agent in his slick polo shirt and khaki pants. "Got a hot date or are you just afraid someone will jump you and steal your iPod?"

With a sneer, he crossed his arms tight over his chest. "I have better things to do with my time than keep tabs on your suspects."

Frankie stepped forward, and though her ex didn't quite reach six feet, he managed to make the taller, although skinnier guy take a shaky step back. "We've got it from here. Why don't you blow?"

With a quick glance at Marisela, who mockingly blew him a kiss, the agent left.

Marisela turned to Frankie. "Let's go."

Through the tinted window crowded with beer signs and painted advertisements for twenty-five-cent wings, Marisela and Frankie spotted Parker Manning sitting at the bar, surrounded mostly by men glued to the television sets mounted from the ceiling. Parker's gaze, however, hardly strayed from the door for more than a minute. Frankie had a hell of a time entering through the front door without Manning noticing, but Marisela figured he had a better chance than she did to blend in. She circled around to the back door, waited for a guy in a white apron to exit with the trash for the Dumpster, then slipped inside.

The place was hazy with smoke from the barbecue in the kitchen. The crowd stood three deep at the bar, where the main libation seemed to be beer on tap, though the mirrored cabinets glittered with half-empty bottles of cheap rum, scotch, whiskey, and bourbon. Two televisions in each corner blared with high-stakes soccer action, the players blurring by in bright greens, blues, and reds. After a goal, the commentary in, if Marisela wasn't mistaken, Portuguese, stirred the sports fans to near hysteria, giving her a chance to slither through the throng until she was directly behind Parker Manning, whose eyes kept darting toward the door.

Who was he waiting for? Or who was he afraid would find him?

All around him, faces with complexions that ranged from light caramel to deepest ebony ensured that Parker Manning stood out like a beacon with his graying brown hair and ruddy skin. Marisela couldn't see Frankie, but she knew he was close by. Funny how she could sense that. When they were in sync, they were a pair to be reckoned with. Tonight's job was a relatively simple one, but she couldn't discount the comfort of working with someone she could rely on.

She sidled up to Parker Manning and in a quick move she'd perfected at age fourteen, checked his jacket pockets for his phone.

Nothing.

Plan B.

She took a deep, fortifying breath, leaned forward and blew in his ear.

Manning spun around. "What the—?"

The phone was on his belt.

"Hey, there," she purred, pretending that her once-over of his body was sexual and not professional. "Did you come here looking for me or is this just my lucky night?"

Whatever leftover curses were lingering on his tongue dissolved in a puddle of drool.

"What a weird coincidence," he said, his frown deep.

"Maybe it's just destiny."

God, she couldn't believe she'd just said that. Out loud.

"What? You live around here?" he asked, not so

subtly scraping his gaze down her body, lingering on her breasts long enough to make her stomach turn.

"Nah, I'm new to town," she said. "But Jamaica Plain is my speed. What's a gringo like you doing around here, anyway?"

Manning smirked. "I like the beer and *pasteles fritos*."

His New England accent chopped the words up until they were nearly unrecognizable, but she took the opening anyway.

"Then we have something in common."

He eyed her skeptically. "Is this a setup? 'Cause I told you everything you need to know earlier. I'm not telling you one damned thing about my sister."

Marisela smiled softly and shook her head. "Just like a man to have a one-track mind. I'm off the clock." She leaned across him, snagged his beer and took a sip. "Everyone has to wind down, right?"

The man wasn't a fool. Though he grinned at her sensual move, his shoulders remained tight and he'd kicked the bar stool slightly behind him so he could bolt if the situation warranted. She had to move fast. Pulling the sexy, hot-for-you act would only get her so far.

The crowd seemed to swell as the players on the television went in for another forward rush. Marisela felt someone press against her, but before she react, she heard Frankie whisper, "When they score."

All the eyes in the place were drawn to the televisions, including Manning's. The minute the forward

in the green striped shirt kicked the ball into the
net, the crowd erupted. Frankie pushed back, pro-
pelling Marisela into Manning. She stole his phone,
slipped it behind her back, where Frankie retrieved
it and tunneled through the cheering crowd until he
was gone.

Marisela spun to follow, but Parker Manning
stopped her, his hand tight around her upper arm.
"Where do you think you're going, sweetheart?"

Ten

MANNING'S GRIP WAS TIGHT, painful. She figured their run-in earlier would have taught him about pissing her off, but she decided to put her disgust aside and concentrate on the case. She had what she wanted and he didn't have a fucking clue. And nauseating as the prospect was, she might need him again. So she wouldn't kick his ass. Yet.

"Little *chicas'* room," she replied sweetly, her eyes darting to the back where she assumed the bathrooms were. With her prettiest pout, she leaned forward until his breath, a putrid combination of nicotine and beer, assailed her nostrils. "Will you miss me?"

His expression was uncertain, but with a nod, he let her go. Smart man.

She rendezvoused with Frankie in the alley.

"Got it?" she asked anxiously, wiping at the spot where Manning had grabbed her.

Frankie frowned. "Yes, and no."

"What do you mean, no? That was some of my best work. He didn't even know I'd touched him," she insisted, shaking her hand as if it were saturated with stinky-man smell.

Frankie nodded in the other direction, so they took off before Manning discovered he'd had his phone lifted and came after them. If they had any luck at all, he'd think he lost it in the crowd. Once they had what they wanted, they'd break into his car and shove it between the seats so he'd never be the wiser.

Once they were at the end of the street, Frankie stopped. He held up the phone, an older-model flip phone with no special features—no camera, no video, and apparently . . .

"No signal?" she asked, unable to read the LCD in the relative darkness.

"Worse. No power."

"You've got to be kidding me! He didn't charge his phone? What an asshole."

Frankie shook his head, unruffled. "Max's team is tracking down a universal charger. Said to check back with him in an hour. Apparently, Manning's phone is a dinosaur."

"So what do we do until then?"

The number of people walking down and around Centre Street had swelled as the night wore on. Even if she could muster up the enthusiasm to search for Yizenia, she didn't have the energy.

Frankie pocketed the phone, then surveyed the street around them, inhaling deeply. Marisela couldn't help but do the same. The minute the savory scents hit her, her stomach growled. She hadn't eaten all day.

"Hungry?" he asked.

"Who wouldn't be in this neighborhood?"

He smiled. "*Bien*. It's been too long since we've had a taste of home."

They grazed their way down Centre Street, chowing down on fish tacos at a local *taquería*, checking out the *pastelitos de carne* at a bustling Salvadoran cafeteria, and then trying, for the first time, Guatemalan *rellenitos* for dessert from a glorious-smelling stand set up on a corner where Centre Street ran into Ballard. Marisela was so enthralled by the sweet fried *platanos* filled with savory refried black beans, dusted with sugar and dipped in sour cream that she nearly forgot why she was in Jamaica Plain in the first place.

They managed to avoid seeing Parker Manning again, and when they checked, his car was no longer in its parking space.

"He's gone," Marisela grumbled. "Now how will we get the phone back?"

Frankie shrugged. "We'll slide by his apartment later."

Seemed easy enough, though she couldn't remember ever breaking into a car to return something. "Okay, then, I'm full. Let's get the hell out of here," Marisela said.

Frankie whipped an old, grainy photograph out of his jacket. "It's early. Let's see if anyone's seen our favorite assassin."

No one they spoke with had seen or heard of anyone fitting Yizenia's sketchy description. After a while, Marisela got tired of asking and decided to simply enjoy the sights and sounds. Hearing Spanish spoken all around her, from the shopkeepers to the children to the DJs spinning tunes at the club they strolled by, filled her with a warm comfort that made her, for a minute, long for home.

Unfortunately, Frankie wasn't so quick to give up the search.

"You see this woman around here?" Frankie asked a guy selling tickets for the upcoming festival after he made change for a twenty. Frankie gestured for the man to keep half the money, then whipped out the fuzzy picture of Yizenia, the only one the research team could dig up.

The man looked at him as if he'd sprouted a second head.

Marisela dazzled the man with her best smile. "She's *mi hermana*," she lied, watching her charm and cleavage do the work as the man looked again at the picture with much more serious consideration.

"We were supposed to meet her here," Frankie added.

The man shook his head. It wasn't a very good shot—and didn't much look like the kind of family photograph you'd shove in a wallet. More like the result of computerized enhancement from a shot taken by a long-distance security camera.

"That was helpful," Marisela quipped once they'd walked out of earshot.

"Never hurts to try," Frankie replied, popping the last of his *rellenitos* into his mouth and sucking the remnants of sugar and sour cream off his fingertips.

Marisela forced her eyes forward as they walked back toward their truck. They'd wasted enough time here. Tomorrow's objective was to find Tracy Manning and they couldn't do that until they deciphered her location, which meant getting back to Max and charging the damned phone.

"Well, other than finally pushing me over the edge into a size ten," she said, tugging at her waistband, "tonight was a big fat waste of time."

"We've got the phone. Once we find Tracy Manning, we'll know if she hired Yizenia Santiago. Seems so *loca*."

"What?"

"A chick hiring a cold-blooded killer for something that happened so long ago."

"What's crazy? That she's a chick or that she hired a killer?"

"All of it," Frankie said.

"Doesn't seem crazy to me at all," Marisela decided. "If those rich boys did that girl, then they deserve to die."

Frankie eyed her skeptically. "*Mierda*, Marisela. You're not going to freak out again and screw the client, are you, just because you don't think he deserves to live?"

She stopped dead. In all the time that had passed since their last mission together in Puerto Rico, she and Frankie hadn't really discussed how the case had ended. He'd been too busy fighting for his life and recovering from his wounds.

When she'd first learned that Frankie had opted to stay with Titan after she'd gone off with Brynn to Mexico, she'd been shocked as hell. Frankie had hated Ian before their boss had nearly sacrificed Frankie's life for a client. At least when he'd been with the *Toros*, his boys cared if he died—at least, they would have to the point of avenging his murder. Ian Blake, on the other hand, had used Frankie's injury as a bargaining chip—a way to keep Marisela in line.

"I did what I thought was right," Marisela told him. "Doesn't mean I'll do it again."

He didn't look half as unnerved by this conversation as she felt. "I don't want to risk my *culo* trying to catch a killer if you're going to turn around and let her win because you think she should."

His words hung in the air between them, amid the highpitched trumpets of a mariachi band playing on the terrace of a restaurant above them and the thrumming bass from hip-hop riffs blasting from a nearby car. Marisela had no argument. He was right.

"We were hired to find the assassin, discover who

paid her, and stop her from killing again," she concluded. "That's what I intend to do."

Frankie nodded. Her promise was all he needed.

They continued down the street, watching out for somewhere to pick up a cold drink before they headed back to the hotel. About a block from where they'd parked the truck, they jaywalked across the street, leaping over the unused streetcar tracks that ran down the middle of the road.

"Do you think she'll give up?" Marisela asked.

"She's not done."

"She can't get to Craig Bennett," Marisela reasoned.

"There's still Bradley Hightower."

"If she hasn't already killed him."

"Then she'll stick around here to finish her job. Brynn insists she won't quit until she has them all."

Inside the *bodega,* they bought a pair of Havana Colas, the next best thing to a *Cuba Libre* without the rum, popped open the tops with a bottle opener the owners kept tied with a string to the cash register, and exchanged some small talk with the cashier. This time, Frankie didn't flash the picture, but he asked if anyone had seen a woman, a stranger, who fit Yizenia's description—including her tattoo. The owner's wife had a field day speculating on why anyone would mar their skin that way, causing Marisela to slip her hand into the pocket of her jacket. She hadn't traveled thirteen hundred miles from Tampa to get a lecture she'd already heard from her own mother.

They left, with no more knowledge than before.

As they closed in on their truck, Frankie suddenly grabbed her arm. What was up with everyone pawing her today? She would have complained, but she saw a man dressed in dark clothes lingering near the front end of their F150, his movements jittery. Marisela quickly downed a swig of soda, then tipped the bottle so the rest poured free. She hated losing her delicious drink, but she wasn't going to pull her gun just because someone was acting weird. A tall glass bottle made a great weapon in a pinch.

Frankie stuck his hand beneath his jacket, and pushing her slightly behind him, shouted to the guy near the car.

The guy took off running. Marisela hurried to the truck only to see wires and cables hanging from beneath the chassis. Without hesitation, Frankie and Marisela took off after the guy in black, following him down an alley that skirted a playground. Marisela hopped the fence, running beside the jungle gym which loomed like a multicolored monster among the deserted concrete and fencing. She pumped her arms hard. Ever since she'd lost the battle with Yizenia, she'd been itching for a fight.

Now she had one.

Frankie caught the guy, no more than a kid, before he slid into a dark alley on the other side of the playground. The brick apartment buildings on either side captured the sound of Frankie's voice and echoed back his anger. "What the hell were you doing to my truck?"

Marisela skidded to a stop a few feet away. She opened her mouth to announce her presence when she was rushed from both sides.

The attacker on her left was skinny, not much of a challenge. The guy on her right, however, easily weighed two-seventy and smelled like pepperoni. She managed to elbow the lankier attacker in the chin, but the other, easily double her size and weight, cold-cocked her across the jaw.

While she was dazed, they each took her by an arm. The skinny guy grabbed her hair and yanked her head back so that Frankie could see the carved-handle knife he held across her neck. The fat one then reached under her jacket and removed her 9 mm from its holster.

"Let him go!" *Gordo* demanded of Frankie, his bulbous arm jiggling as he aimed her weapon at Frankie's skull. "Drop your gun or he'll cut her fucking head off."

Marisela swallowed, the action painful as the movement caused her skin to slice against the sharpened blade.

Frankie pushed the kid away so that he crashed against the wall. Seconds later, the kid ran out of the alley as if his pants were on fire, leaving two against two. Only she'd been disarmed. And while Frankie's gun remained heavy in his hand, his eyes wide and wild, she knew his hesitation on her account would cost them.

The fat guy jabbed Marisela's gun into her side, a cruel punctuation to his threat. The skinny one didn't move, the blade ice against her skin. Frankie dropped his weapon.

"Kick it over here," the fat guy ordered. "Do it!" He bounced on the balls of his feet, shifting his considerable weight. Marisela could feel his impatience vibrating off him.

Frankie kept his hands out, his fingers outstretched—the closest thing these assholes were going to see from him in terms of surrender. His eyes flashed at Marisela and she held her breath. He moved his leg to punt the gun, at the last minute kicking up with enough force to bash the cojones of the guy with the knife. Marisela slackened her body, ignoring the painful pull the fat guy still had on her hair. Once on the ground, she executed a spinning kick that dropped the fat guy to his knees.

He dragged her down with him, the gun still jabbing into her side. "You're not going anywhere, bitch," he prophesied.

"Wanna bet?"

She grabbed his gun wrist and twisted. His fingers, caught in the trigger, snapped. He howled and dropped the rest of the way to the ground. Marisela spun to aim at Frankie's opponent when she realized the guy Frankie fought might not have weighed more than a flea, but he was keenly effective with a knife.

Slashed across the chest, Frankie's white T-shirt flapped, tiny red drops of blood marring his dark skin. Marisela sucked in a breath, resolved to fire the minute the man circled around and gave her a clear shot.

A noise to her side caught her attention, so she swung right just as the fat guy rolled toward her. She fired, but he knocked the barrel sideways, deflecting the shot. He dragged her down and tackled her, his putrid flesh enveloping her in sweaty anger.

"Get the fuck off me!" she shouted, pushing fruitlessly at his blubbery body.

He grunted and cursed, trying to grab her gun. Unable to fire again without risking shooting herself, she used the 9 mm like iron knuckles, wrapping her hand tightly around the grip and pounding into his temple with her reinforced fist. He pushed away, but the glint of his knife caught her eye just before he sliced open her brand-new leather jacket.

"Fucking son of a bitch," she muttered, rising to her feet and roundhouse-kicking him square in the cheek with the heel of her boot. Bones crunched. He fell forward, the gash across his face oozing bright red.

Behind her, Frankie went in for the kill. Even as the skinny guy's knife tore across Frankie's arm, he threw a succession of heel-palmed punches that splattered the skinny guy's nose and dropped him to his knees. Frankie grabbed the knife and pressed it against his assailant's neck.

"Why'd you jump us?" Frankie demanded.

He sputtered, blood coating his teeth, mouth, and lips. "Fuck you."

Marisela slid to Frankie's other side and pressed the barrel of her gun to the skinny guy's temple. She cocked the hammer. The guy flinched and terror sped across his eyes.

"Try again," she ordered. "Why did you jump us?"

"Paid to," he croaked.

"By who?"

"Don't know. Danny did the deal."

His gaze darted to the fat guy on the ground, only he wasn't horizontal anymore. He held Frankie's recovered Glock in his hands. Marisela jerked to aim and fire, but a shot popped in her ears seconds before hers rent the air.

Danny's body jerked, vibrated, then collapsed.

On shaky legs, Marisela stepped closer and saw the bullet hole in the back of the fat guy's neck, clearly slicing straight through his spine.

The work was unmistakable.

She slammed up against the nearest wall, her gaze scanning the buildings across from them. "Sniper!"

The skinny guy on the ground scrambled like a crab until he was out of sight. Frankie retrieved his gun. Lights in the building across the open courtyard flashed on and someone yanked up a creaky window and screamed.

"Help! Police!"

Frankie grabbed Marisela's hand and yanked her farther into the inky alley. An iron gate stopped their direct escape route, but Frankie launched himself to the top, then pulled Marisela over with him.

"What the hell was that about?" he asked, panting, once they were on the other side.

"I don't know," Marisela said, her equilibrium still wavering. "But I think Yizenia may have just saved our lives."

Eleven

FRANKIE EYED MARISELA with utter disbelief. "Have you lost your mind?"

Marisela stalked away from him, her entire body shaking with adrenaline. Breathlessly, she paced circles in the dim lighting from a busted streetlamp, only half listening to the scream echoing from the courtyard near the alley. The body had been found.

Yet Frankie looked like he'd just strolled off the dance floor—heated, but cool.

Marisela, with blood still smeared on her face, blended into the shadows near the stoop of a walk-up brownstone while Frankie phoned Max.

The police roared past them, and yet, for the split second that the blue and red lights flashed over Marisela's skin, her breath caught in her throat. They needed to get the hell out of here.

The Titan cavalry arrived in a dark sedan. Dressed in grimy T-shirts, jeans, and ball caps, the Titan investigative team looked like any other guys about to work on a buddy's car. Marisela dashed across the sidewalk and slid into the backseat of the sedan, waited for Frankie to climb in after her, then sucked in a calming breath when they finally tore away from the curb.

"Interesting night?" Max asked from the driver's seat, reaching over to hand Marisela a box of antiseptic wipes before handing Frankie the plug end of the universal charger he'd already connected to the sedan's conduit. Frankie immediately pulled out Parker Manning's phone.

"Seems someone doesn't like our sniffing around," Marisela replied as she wiped blood off her face, hands and neck.

Frankie leaned forward to address his question to Max. "You think Yizenia could have hired muscle to get us to back off?"

"Were they Latino?" Max asked.

"No," Marisela answered.

Frankie stared at her. "My cousin, Segundo, has red hair and green eyes," he reminded her.

"Your cousin Segundo is a freak," Marisela replied, though her opinion had nothing to do with Segundo's lack of typical Hispanic features. At three years old, he'd become famous in the neighborhood for biting the heads off of lizards. As he got older, his taste for blood only got worse.

"Not arguing with you on that, but you had no idea if those guys were Latino or not."

"Do *you* think they were?" she challenged.

Frankie smirked. "No."

"Then I doubt Yizenia was involved," Max concluded. "I've been checking up on her. She doesn't trust easily, especially not people who aren't Spanish-speaking. That's probably why she's set up shop in Jamaica Plain."

"Yizenia was there tonight," Marisela insisted. "I can feel it. She shot that guy. She saved our asses."

"Marisela, *por favor. No hables como una loca,*" Frankie insisted. "Why would she help us?"

"I don't know."

"Then drop it," Frankie ordered. "Yizenia wasn't the shooter. Not this time."

"Then who *was?*" she countered. "Some friendly neighbor who just happens to have a precision rifle propped beside their floral curtains? Just because Yizenia helping us is unlikely doesn't mean it isn't true."

Frankie didn't argue further. He couldn't. The mystery shooter had saved Frankie from a bullet. Marisela couldn't buy that this was some random act of violent kindness. The hit was too precise.

"What's *this* about?" Max asked.

Frankie cursed, but didn't respond, eyeing Marisela with a challenge. If she wanted to pursue her theory, she'd have to do the explaining. She couldn't deny that her theory was a wild one. But Marisela had seen Yizenia's work twice now, first with Craig Bennett and then with Evan Cole. She was starting to recognize Yizenia's style. The angle of shot she preferred. The sound of her weapon.

"So these guys jump us," Marisela began, leaning forward between the sedan's bucket seats. "It was a total setup—the kid messing with the car, the friends waiting in the dark alley. They take our guns right off the bat, but don't try to shoot until they're getting their asses kicked. Seems to me that they didn't plan to kill us, that they were just supposed to deliver a message. Scare us off."

"Or they could have been neighborhood thugs who didn't like us sniffing around their turf," Frankie offered.

"Or they could have been hired by someone who doesn't want us sniffing around the death of Rebecca Manning," Marisela countered.

"Or maybe Yizenia broke with tradition and paid off some local thugs to try and scare us off her tail," Frankie shot back.

Marisela shook her head. "By shooting one of her own guys? Look, we came to Jamaica Plain to find Parker Manning. Maybe he didn't appreciate my disappearing act at the bar. Maybe he figured out that I swiped his phone. He had plenty of time to call in some friends. Maybe he already had them on call and was just waiting for us to harass him again. Yizenia couldn't have set this all up. She had no way of knowing where we'd be."

Frankie's grin was infuriating. "Exactly. And if she didn't know, she wouldn't have been there to pop that jerk before he had a chance to shoot me in the back."

"Unless she caught wind of us looking for her. Maybe she was tailing us the whole time and we didn't know."

With an eye roll, Frankie shook his head indulgently, but didn't bother to respond. Marisela grunted, threw herself back against the seat, and crossed her arms over her chest. Maybe he was right. They'd been watching for tails—they always did—but that didn't mean they didn't miss her. There were a lot of people around and Yizenia was reportedly an expert at disguise. She could have been just a few steps behind them the entire time, watching them, learning about them, jumping in when it looked like Frankie and Marisela were about to bite the dust.

But why?

"Have you found Bradley Hightower yet?" she asked Max, who'd remained silent regarding Marisela's theories.

"Not exactly. We learned that he did claim his inheritance shortly after his parents' deaths. We found an old friend who claimed Brad wanted to start over with a new life. And that he missed the States."

"You think he has a new identity?" she asked.

"Very good chance," Max confirmed. "We're digging into his brother's life. Raymond Hightower also took his inheritance and tripled it. He moved to Switzerland. Before he died, he was a high-living entrepreneur and knew a lot of people all over the Continent. Chances are, if he kept in touch with his brother, one of his friends will know. Brynn ordered our Swiss office to make this investigation priority one. If Bradley Hightower is still alive, he's in great danger."

"If we can't find him, how can Yizenia?"

Max just shook his head. They had no idea what network she could tap into. For all they knew, Bradley Hightower was already dead.

"Are we going to try and save him, too?" Frankie asked, sounding annoyed.

"Craig Bennett wants us to," Max replied.

Marisela sat forward. "He's talking?"

Max maneuvered the car into one of the many tunnels running around and through Boston. Traffic slowed and the glow of the headlights reflected a glittery gold off the tiles lining the tunnel. "He's still in serious condition, but the moment he could say a few words, his wife called for Ian. Bennett was able to verify a few interesting facts. For one, he insists Evan Cole was never there that night at the campground."

Marisela's stomach clenched. If Cole had been innocent, then why was he marked for death? "What else did he say?"

"He couldn't say much, except he insisted that while Evan never showed up, Rebecca Manning certainly did. She showed up on her own, uninvited. He claims she was furious when she left, but very much alive. His main concern was about Brad Hightower. He ordered us to find him before Yizenia did. Or, we find Yizenia and stop her."

Frankie clucked his tongue. "Neither job will be easy."

Max grinned. "Nothing in this business ever is."

Except, perhaps, finding Tracy. She still might offer some insight no one else had.

"Did he say anything about Tracy?" she asked.

Max shook his head. "Ian didn't ask. Bennett barely had enough energy to tell us about Evan and Rebecca. We'll interview him again tomorrow."

The minute they emerged from the tunnel, Max took the nearest exit and stopped alongside one of the many parks dotting the Boston landscape. The phone had gotten enough juice so they could make the call, though Marisela didn't disconnect it from the charger, just in case. Before Marisela dialed, Max hooked into his team at the office with his own wireless connection. When they were set up to trace the signal, she punched in the numbers.

One ring.

"What if—"

"Sh," Frankie said.

Two rings.

Marisela closed her eyes tightly, willing Tracy to answer. She'd hate to think she'd touched Parker Manning for no good reason.

Three rin—

"Hello?"

Marisela gave Max a thumbs-up. He replied with a twirling finger, instructing her to keep the conversation going.

"Hello?" the female voice asked, this time sounding nervous.

"Hi," Marisela said.

"Who is this?" the woman replied, her voice unsteady.

"I found this phone on the sidewalk. Outside a park. In Jamaica Plain."

No response.

"Are you still there?"

A long pause. "Yes," she answered softly. "I'm here. I expected . . . it's my brother's phone. He must have dropped it or something."

"Oh! Great then. There was no name or anything, so I just hit the redial feature, thought if I found someone who knew who owned the phone, I could get it back to them. It's pretty beat-up."

Tracy's laugh was tentative but edgy. "No one in my family is that into technology. Keep the phone on and I'll have him call you. Or, wait. If he doesn't have his cell, I'm not sure how I'd find him."

Parker Manning had both a cell phone and a landline. Did Tracy only call him on the cell?

"Well, it's almost out of juice," Marisela explained, responding to Max's continued circular movements. "Maybe I could just drop it off with you?"

"Oh, no," Tracy answered. "I live too far away."

Max held his hand up flat, then after a second, gave a thumbs-up. They had the location.

Marisela could have disconnected the call, but she decided not to raise the woman's hackles. If she got spooked, she could bolt. "Why don't I give you my cell phone number? When you contact your brother, call me and we'll make arrangements."

Tracy liked that idea, so Marisela rattled off her number and then gave her best friend Lia's name, simply because, well, she'd done it before. Many times. More times than Lia had forgiven her for, actually. To guys she met in bars. To police officers letting her go with only a warning. To salespeople calling her on the phone before noon.

She disconnected the call and turned to Max.

"She said she was far away."

Max grinned. "Not that far. Natick. About fifteen miles west of the city. I've got two agents on their way right now and they'll keep her in sight until tomorrow."

Marisela frowned. "We should go tonight."

Then she yawned. Big and ugly and full of teeth that hadn't been brushed, and a body that had finally started to ache now that the adrenaline from the fight had begun to wane. Max chuckled, exchanged glances with Frankie, then started the car.

They'd wait until tomorrow.

Marisela eased back into the seat and thought about their next move.

They had Tracy's location, so she focused on that.

By tomorrow, they'd likely know if Rebecca's surviving sister had hired Yizenia, and if she had, they had a shot at finding the assassin before she killed again. But they still wouldn't know if—or why—Yizenia had come to her and Frankie's rescue.

Marisela couldn't shake the impression that there was more to this story. She couldn't dismiss the weirdness of Yizenia's making friends with Brynn and then seducing Ian when she'd come to Boston to handle a matter that had nothing to do with the Blake family or Titan International.

Or did it?

She'd expected Max to drop them off at Titan's home office for an official debrief, but instead, he pulled up in front of her and Frankie's hotel.

"Go in, take a shower," he instructed, stretching around from the front seat. "Report to the office in the morning at seven sharp."

Frankie moved toward the door, but Marisela scooted forward and laid her hand on Max's, blocking Frankie's path.

"Yizenia was there, Max. I can feel it."

Max neither agreed nor disagreed, but even in the muted light, a flash of interest played in the sparkling colorlessness of his gray eyes. "Why do you think so?"

"Who else can shoot like that?"

"Plenty of people."

"Including you?"

He didn't respond. She hadn't expected him to.

"Okay," Marisela conceded, "but when the ME

pulls the bullet, I'm betting my outrageous salary that the slug matches the one the doctors pulled out of Craig Bennett."

"You mean the slug that was supposed to kill him?" Max asked, his gray eyes intense.

She eyed him skeptically. "Yeah. Except I fired at her. Distracted her."

"Precisely," Max pointed out. "You ruined her perfect record. Maybe she *was* there tonight, Marisela. And maybe she did set you up to be in that dark alley. Maybe she wanted you there so she could kill you herself."

Marisela pursed her lips and ran that possibility through her mind. "Then why'd she hit the guy she hired?"

Max exchanged glances with Frankie, who didn't look so bored anymore with the discussion about Yizenia. "Maybe she took him out before he could identify her. Maybe you got away before she could fire again. There are a million possibilities, each more dangerous than the last. Which is why you'd better watch your back. If she's gunning for you, I don't think she'll screw up again."

On that happy note, Marisela slid out of the car. She crossed the lobby quickly, catching up to Frankie, who held the elevator open for her. As soon as the doors shut, she pushed herself high on the balls of her feet. Up and down. Up and down.

She'd been exhausted in the car, but once she'd hit the crisp night air, she'd felt instantly re-energized. The blood cells pumping through her veins seemed to have little ticklers on the edges, chafing her from the inside, forcing her to move or face madness.

"Can't stand it, can you?"

Leaning against the back wall of the elevator, Frankie had his arms crossed over his chest and a gleam in his hazel eyes that made the green flecks glimmer like shards of colored glass.

She braced herself, even as the hair on her arms reacted to a chill that didn't exist. "Can't stand what?"

His smile was crooked, the smirk accentuated by the slim lines of his moustache. "The rush."

She tried shoving her hands in her pockets, but the denim was too tight, so she opted to cram her fingers into her back pockets instead, forcing her breasts to jut forward. The minute his heated gaze struck her flesh, her nipples hardened, tweaking the nerve endings so that jolts of pure fire flashed toward every pulse point in her body. Frankie's generous lips curved into that tiny smile. Just in time, the elevator doors slid open and she beat a hasty path to her door. She slid the card key. When the tiny light turned green, Frankie slid one hand around her waist and the other up the side of her thigh.

"What do you think you're doing?" she said, her voice a raspy whisper.

With a flick, he unbuttoned the waist of her jeans. He leaned in to her neck and inhaled. "I'm touching you. I've wanted to all day. You're torturing me, you know that, ¿si?"

"Your own damned fault," she replied, her eyes drifting closed as his fingers danced along the lower edge of her belly. "You can't beat your chest around me, Frankie. Get all jealous and macho. That doesn't turn me on."

He stroked a finger across the top of her panties. "Maybe not, but I know other ways to make you wet, *vidita*. I know you, Marisela. I know your body. I know how you think. No other man will ever give you what you need the way I can."

He wasn't talking about a vague, unnamed "other man." He was talking about Ian Blake.

She arched a brow, holding back a pleasured gasp as his fingertip dove deeper. "You think so?"

"I can prove it."

Too exhausted and too turned on to argue, she entered her room. Behind her, he shut the door. Clicked the lock. She'd already fought so hard tonight. Did she really have the power to struggle further against what was so instinctual, so natural?

But she was hot, dirty, and sore. She went into the bathroom, and peeled off her bloody, sweaty clothes. She needed a few minutes to herself. To prepare. To rein her raging hormones under control so the loving could be slow and sensual instead of hard and fast like the night before.

Unfortunately, the scalding water did nothing to lessen her overloaded senses. Every shard of water that burst against her skin enflamed her. The smell of the soap and shampoo lured her with the headiness of mint and cucumber, heightening her hunger—a hunger no simple food would sate. Then she heard him.

With steam clouding the shower, Frankie was a shadow on the other side of the glass. She flattened her palm on the door, but didn't dare wipe a clear view. She didn't want to see him approach, didn't want to confront the torture she knew he planned for her. And damn it, she had no desire to resist. And he knew it. She hated the surge of confidence that knowledge gave him, but she hated missing an opportunity to make love to him even more.

Like an addict, she'd imbibed the forbidden and wanted more. She watched him shrug out of his jacket. He stretched his shirt over his head, revealing the dark, bronzed expanse of his chest, muted by the fog and glass, but perfect nonetheless. He must have ditched his shoes before he came into the bathroom, because once he shed his jeans and briefs, he was nude.

When he neared, the distinct outline of his aroused sex held her in thrall. And yet, she still held the handle to the door tightly so that he couldn't come inside.

"Marisela, stop playing games," he said, gently rattling the handle.

"Are you done being jealous of Ian?"

His mouth tightened. "I'm not jealous."

"Eh," she said, mimicking the sound of a buzzer. "Wrong answer. Try again."

"Why should I be *celoso* when I'm the one in your bathroom naked, huh?"

"But if I chose, he could have me," she said. She cared about her ex, but she wasn't ready for anything more than sex between them. She'd been there, done that. Her options had to remain open.

He leaned forward so she could catch the white gleam of his toothy smile. "Then know this. If you ever fuck him, I'll be done with you."

She stepped back, but tightened her hand on the door handle. "Is that a threat?"

"No, *vidita,* just the way it is."

"So no man can have me but you?" She yanked the door open. "I hate to break this to you, *cabrón,* but you're not that important to my decision-making process. I can fuck whoever I want, whenever I want."

He pushed his way into the shower stall. "Then fuck me now."

"No," she said, wrapping her arms around his neck. "*Dios, ayuda me.* Never you."

In an instant, his lips crashed over hers. His hands slid over the silky wetness drenching her skin from the inside out. His palms, dry and rough, instantly sought her breasts and buttocks. She gasped. He felt so good. So solid. So hard.

So hot.

She pushed away. This was too fast. She landed right under the spray from the shower. Cursing, she pushed her damp hair and the veil of water out of her eyes.

"Stop!" she commanded, palm out.

And oddly, he listened.

She sputtered. "What? What was that?"

"You asked me to stop."

"So? Since when do you listen to me?"

"Since I saw how hot you get when you think you're in charge."

She couldn't deny that Ian's trust in her earlier had pumped her up. And clearly, that had given Frankie inspiration for this seduction. He'd turned his jealousy into some sort of competition with their boss. But what did she care? If he won, so did she.

He took her hand and, with a gentle tug, swapped places with her in the shower. He leaned his head back under the water, then as an afterthought, unbound his hair. As long and silky as the style was, Marisela had never seen anything more masculine, particularly when those dark strands were stretching over his perfectly muscled shoulders.

He turned and grabbed the soap. She could hardly concentrate as he rubbed the soap sensually over his body, building the lather into a silky foam amid his dark chest hair and square-cut pecs. When he dropped his hand lower and created a collection of suds over his cock, Marisela had to lean against the tile to keep from slipping to the bottom of the tub on rubbery knees.

"Stop doing that."

He yanked his hand away, stepped out of the water stream, and offered her the soap. "I need to get clean, babe, but if you want, take over."

Was he serious?

She took the soap. Licking her lips, she rubbed the slick bar between her hands, creating satiny bubbles she couldn't wait to spread over his hot skin.

"You're really letting me call the shots?" she asked.

The corner of his mouth quirked in a grin. "*Tu deseo es mi orden.*"

Your wish is my command.

She closed the distance between them. "You may regret this."

But she certainly wouldn't.

Their relationship, such as it was, had evolved over the years. At first, they were teenagers stumbling and groping their way to orgasm. Then they'd parted for a decade, and when they'd crashed together yet again, they'd fallen back into the pattern they'd developed in the backseat of Frankie's car.

She wants him, but she fights it.

He wants her, so he fights harder.

She teases and taunts. He trumps. The sex is hot, hard, and fabulous—but now that Marisela thought about it, Frankie had always set the pace.

How the hell had she let that happen?

The only thing that had changed was that they both had more experience—and thankfully, more finesse.

She handed him the soap. "Lather up your hands."

He obeyed, his eyes locked with hers, the jade-green jags of color bright with arrogance. Even when taking orders, the man held tight to his confidence.

Tossing the soap onto the ceramic tray built into the shower wall, he held up his bubbly hands.

"Wash me," she directed.

He chuckled. "And here I thought you'd ask me to do something I wouldn't enjoy."

Frankie didn't miss an inch. Starting with her neck, he smoothed his hands over her skin, painting her flesh silky white. He left her breasts bare while he washed her back and stomach, then dipped to her hips and thighs, again leaving her most sensitive areas free from the scented lather. He dropped to his knees to attend to her calves, and when she lifted her foot onto his shoulder, he moved forward to take her *concha* into his mouth.

"Not yet," she said softly, even though she throbbed for the sensation of his lips on her. Denying him, even for a few moments, heightened her sense of power.

Again he obeyed, retrieving the soap and replenishing the froth on his fingers and palms. The moment he slid his slippery hands into her wet curls, she grabbed the towel rack above her for support. As he coated every nook and cranny with the cool soap bubbles, he explored her, pleasured her, destroyed her ability to think beyond the sensations.

Reaching up with his other hand, he finally attended to her breasts. The combination of the hot steam, the sleek foam, and his silken touch spawned an electric current that rode over her skin.

"Ready for the rinse?"

Marisela opened her eyes. He waited expectantly, and with her tiniest nod, he removed the handheld showerhead. *Dios mio.* And from the wicked gleam in his eye, she knew he wouldn't allow the shower feature to go to waste.

Adjusting the head so the water came out in a strong pulse, he doused her, running the stream close to her skin, pounding into her muscles. He took his time on her breasts, letting the water work its magic long after all the soap had dribbled away. Sensations rippled through her in a staccato rhythm sexier than any Latin beat. By the time he turned the concentrated stream of water onto her sex, she climaxed instantly. Flashes of color. Light. Dark. Orange. Red. Her body quaked, and from deep in her throat, she cried out his name.

He grabbed her bottom and held her while she rode the wave of pleasure. Just when she thought she'd had enough and he'd moved the water away, he started again until she cried out for mercy.

She pointed to the faucet, and he put his instrument of delicious torture away and turned off the water. He retrieved a towel, wrapped her first, then tossed a white rectangle around his waist before sliding open the door and carrying her out onto the bed.

"Now, what, *vidita*?"

The air conditioner had kicked on, coating their bodies with an icy shiver. "Blanket."

He complied, retrieving a blanket from a shelf in the closet. He dropped his towel before climbing beneath the covers with her.

The lingering heat from the water clung to their bodies, even as their skin dried. Frankie curled around her, his hard sex pressed against the small of her back, reminding her of what he ultimately wanted, of what she had the power to give.

She twisted around beneath the blanket.

"Something else you need?" he asked.

"You. Inside me."

The water had actually parched her skin, but Frankie wasted no time replenishing the moisture with his skillful mouth and deft fingers. Soon, he was poised over her, but even as the tip of his cock pressed against her, he stopped. "Are you sure?"

Cabrón. He wanted her to beg?

"You want something different?" she asked.

His chuckle was deep and filled with sin as he entered her and his long, luxurious strokes milked the last drops of pleasure from her body even as he filled her with his. She called out his name again as she came, the sound threaded with his own gratified groan. By the time they both dropped to the bed, Marisela wondered if she'd really been in charge at all, or if she'd just fallen for the most delicious, devious scam her ex had ever devised.

Twelve

"DID YOU DOUBLE-CHECK the GPS system?" Frankie asked as Marisela attempted, for the fifth time, to close the hidden compartment behind the passenger seat of the sleek, black Corvette he'd requisitioned for the trip to interview Tracy Manning. The garage beneath the Titan home office was temperature controlled, but the exertion was making her sweat.

Winded with frustration, she spun around and knocked her head on the car's low roof. "Does it look like I've had time? Why do we have to pack all this firepower, anyway? We're just meeting Tracy Manning, right?"

Frankie clucked his tongue at her in a way that made her shove her hands under her knees so she didn't slug him.

"Can't be too prepared," he said, strapping his 9 mm into his shoulder holster. "We still don't know who tried to kill us last night."

"Or scare us," she mused.

"You scared?"

"Hell, no. I'm just pissed."

"Good, then fold that vest the right way, get it under the seat so I can't see it, and make sure the coordinates to this farm in . . . Natick . . . are programmed in so we don't waste time once we're on the road."

She arched a brow at him. "Bossy much?"

He winked at her. "After last night, I earned it."

Marisela rolled her eyes. She knew she'd pay for her domination in the bedroom—more specifically, the shower—one way or another.

She'd finally gotten the lid of the storage compartment to click shut when a touch on her shoulder nearly sent her out of her skin.

"Ian."

Her employer slipped his hands into the pockets of his perfectly tailored slacks. "Jumpy?"

"I almost got sliced open last night," she said bitterly. "Tends to make me a little nervous."

Ian tilted an eyebrow. "Clearly too much leftover adrenaline. The Marisela I knew a few months ago would have . . . worked off the excess hormones." He streaked his gaze down her body. Even though she'd dressed in snug, boot-cut jeans, a two-layered cotton T-shirt, and her favorite thick leather belt with the flashy silver buckle in the shape of handcuffs that she'd found at a shop catering to the biker-chick, S–M crowd, his glance undressed her in a flash.

She unfolded herself from the car. "And how exactly should I do that?" she challenged.

He licked his bottom lip, and then cleared his throat and straightened his jacket. "Solving this case in short order would be a good start."

She smirked. Big boss man couldn't say what he really wanted to. Well, *wouldn't* was more like it. She supposed she couldn't blame him. His place in the company had become precarious since Brynn had breezed back into town. He couldn't go around messing with the help. Besides, if their truce yesterday had unnerved him half as much as it had her, she could understand his reluctance to fuel the fire.

But just for fun, she sidled up closer to him until she could smell the distinctive leather and spice scent of his heady cologne.

"According to Max, you sent Frankie and me home last night. Ordered us to take it easy. You don't think we found a way to work off the rush?"

His jaw clenched. Not a lot, just enough to display a tiny tic she only noticed because she was standing so close.

"What you do with Frankie is none of my concern," he explained icily.

"You sure?" she teased. "Maybe we could use a third—"

The slam of a door behind them quashed any additional flirtations, such as they were.

"Any last-minute instructions, Blake?" Frankie asked, keeping a tight, probably tentative hold on his cool.

Ian swept Marisela with an unruffled gaze. "We've electronically blocked Tracy's phone, so if her brother tries to warn her against talking to you, he'll get a message that the network is temporarily down."

"What's to keep Manning from going to his sister directly?"

Ian grinned. "We have Mr. Manning under surveillance and we're making no secret of the fact. He'll stay away or risk leading us straight to her. We'll cut him loose one you have what you need. You'll relieve the team currently watching Tracy. Do you need additional backup?"

Marisela smoothed her jeans and wiggled until the gun she'd tucked into the back of her waistband wasn't jabbing her. "I think we can handle it."

"Unless she's the wallet behind the muscle from last night," Ian reminded her.

Frankie slid into the driver's seat. "We can handle that, too."

Seconds after the engine purred to life and they'd left the Titan garage, Ian's voice echoed over the sound system. "Watch for a tail more carefully this time."

Frankie cursed and Marisela couldn't blame him. During their briefing this morning, Ian had been ruthless. He'd criticized their every action the night before and he hadn't been completely out of line.

The tampering of the truck had been bait and they'd fallen for the ruse hook, line, and sinker. And they were no closer to figuring out who had sicced the attackers on them. Parker Manning? Yizenia Santiago? Some as yet unnamed player in this game of cat and mouse?

Marisela twisted the rearview mirror so she had a view behind the car, but Frankie instantly moved the device back into place.

"Any other suggestions?" Marisela asked Ian, annoyed.

"Just to reiterate that Tracy Manning should be handled with kid gloves, in case she is as fragile as her brother and her file seem to indicate. Focus on figuring out if she had the cash to pay our shooter or if she has any knowledge of her brother's involvement. And of course, see what she knows about the night her sister died. Tracy might be our last chance at finding out what really happened."

"Affirmative," Frankie replied, then turned the radio off, shifted into drive, and eased the ground-hugging machine onto the uneven cobblestone road outside the Titan International office.

"Shouldn't we maintain radio contact?" Marisela said, somewhat surprised that Frankie had cut Ian off so absolutely.

"He can call our cells."

Marisela snapped her seat belt secure. "Now you're getting all bossy with the boss. Is that what playing love slave does to you?"

If looks could kill, someone should have been dialing Marisela's next of kin right about now.

With a grin, Marisela eased back into the seat while Frankie maneuvered the car toward the highway, punching up the directions on the GPS. Marisela turned the radio back on, finding a Cuban station playing a great mix of Timba music. As they slipped onto Highway 93, Marisela leaned back, closed her eyes, and tried to forget that Frankie was sitting so close to her that his body heat affected the temperature in the car. She opened one eye long enough to consider adjusting the air conditioner, but opted instead to dig into the files Max had provided during their debriefing. She should have read them before she left, but she'd chosen a second cup of coffee and a quick phone call to Lia in Tampa instead.

Nothing interesting was happening at home, other than Lia's disenchantment with the political process. Her boss, the mayor, was looking at serious opposition and might not be reelected, leaving Lia without an upstanding, well-paying job for the first time since age sixteen. Well, until Lia lined something else up, of course. Which she would. Probably by tomorrow.

Marisela, on the other hand, was keenly aware of her limited choices. She glanced at Frankie. He was so keen to leave all this behind. The money. The excitement. The challenge. All to be his own boss. She understood the draw, but for once in her life, Marisela needed to act on reason and smarts, not emotion and pride.

"What's that?" Frankie asked, tapping the folder on her lap.

Marisela glanced down. "Intel on Tracy Manning."

"Weren't you supposed to read that during the morning debrief?"

Marisela cocked an eyebrow. If he kept pushing that tone on her, she was going to invest in some whips and chains. Then next time he wanted to get naked, she'd really show him who was boss.

"That was the plan," she admitted.

"But you don't follow the plan," Frankie guessed.

"Not usually."

He shifted the car and flashed a look behind them. "What does the file say?"

The car had an incredibly smooth ride, so Marisela had no trouble reading as they sped along the sixteen miles between the city of Boston and the smaller city of Natick, exiting the highway onto Route 9. Southwest of the small city's hub, they'd find Bliss Haven Orchards. And amid the apple trees and, Marisela guessed, farm equipment and various clucking and neighing animals, they'd find Tracy Manning.

"According to this report, Tracy's parents sent her away shortly after her sister's funeral."

"Where'd they send her?"

Marisela skimmed the brief, frowning more deeply as she read. "*Pobrecita*. They sent the poor kid all over. To grandparents in Virginia first, then to an aunt in Chicago, and finally a distant cousin who lived in San Francisco. She stayed there, finished school, and enrolled in college to study psychology, which . . ." she said, turning through the pages, "makes perfect sense since she was under the care of no less than three shrinks at the time."

"Three? Wouldn't one do the trick?"

"*Yo no sé,*" she replied with a shrug. "Therapy for me is a hard workout with a very sturdy punching bag."

Frankie adjusted the rearview mirror again and then smoothly changed lanes. "Is she still having her head shrunk?"

Marisela chewed on her lip as she scanned through the report, which included a badly photocopied psychiatric evaluation from a place called Windchaser Farm. Farm? Ha! From what Marisela read on the reports, the only thing the place seemed to breed was paranoia and addictions to antidepressants.

"Her last stay was only a year ago, but for outpatient care. Maybe that means she's getting better."

She continued to review Tracy's file, but there wasn't much more to share except that no bank accounts or credit cards or property titles were listed in Tracy's name. According to her suppliers, for the farm she paid cash for everything.

At a light just before they crossed outside of the city of Natick and into the countryside, Frankie pulled over into the parking lot of a convenience store and pretended to consult a map, which, thanks to the GPS, they didn't need.

"What else have you got?" he asked, looking behind them.

"Is someone following us?"

He arched a brow. "Not anymore."

Instinctively, Marisela looked behind them. She'd been engrossed in Tracy's file and hadn't noticed Frankie executing any maneuvers meant to elude a tail. He always was smooth.

"Who was it?"

Frankie flipped the map over. "Don't know. Blue van. Probably nothing. I got off one exit early to see if they'd come by. They haven't."

"Maybe they know where we're going," she suggested.

"Maybe they'll double back just to make sure. Tell me what else we know about Tracy."

"The orchard where she lives is owned by a trust." She flipped the page. "A trust whose executor is none other than her dear brother. That explains where her money is coming from."

"Is it a big trust?"

Marisela scanned the financials, then frowned. "Not really."

"Enough to pay Yizenia?"

She flipped back a few years. The amount in the trust steadily declined with expenses and rose with interest. No huge withdrawals that she could see.

She frowned. "Not sure."

"Then we'd better watch our backs. What kind of stuff does she buy?"

"Equipment, seeds, veterinary care. Oh, there's an investment in a co-op. This brochure for Bliss Haven

Orchards says that for a fee, she'll let you pick apples when the harvest comes around. Looks to me like she pretty much lives off that money, so she's not exactly floating in cold hard cash."

"Not that we've found yet," Frankie said. "People can be very sly about hiding their money. Of all the people who would hate those rich boys, this chick's gotta be the angriest. Brad Hightower used her. Used her sister. I'm betting that even if she didn't hire Yizenia, she might be very grateful to anyone who did."

They parked the car and went inside the convenience store for sodas and a bathroom break, then shared a Snickers bar while leaning against the rear spoiler, weapons close by. Once Frankie was certain the blue van hadn't returned, they continued on. After a mile or two on the back roads, they spotted the open gates of Bliss Haven Orchards—and the dark Titan sedan sent to watch Tracy Manning.

They stopped and chatted with the agents, who reported seeing no one anywhere near the farm all night. After calling in to Titan to verify the change of shift, Frankie maneuvered the Corvette through the gates, directed by a small, hand-painted sign that announced the presence of the farm with a crooked arrow and an invitation to taste the brand-new crop of strawberries.

"You like strawberries?" Frankie asked.

"I always wanted to try them dipped in chocolate," Marisela answered seriously. "But I thought strawberry season was like February."

Not that she was a particularly agricultural-minded person, but Tampa wasn't far from Plant City, Florida, where the locals kicked off strawberry season with a festival that she and Lia had attended yearly, if only for the *delicioso* strawberry shortcake and *decadente* elephant ears. The event was pig-out heaven.

"Apparently not in New England. Looks like we're in luck."

Frankie pulled up the drive, which was nothing more than a dirt and gravel road leading through ramshackle fences that likely couldn't keep the most contented animal penned in. He drove the length of the road, past the house and barn, deep into the orchard, looking for signs of the blue van—or any other vehicle that might be where they shouldn't. The Corvette reacted to every pothole and divot, causing Marisela to wince more than once as the fiberglass chassis scraped the gravel.

"Next time we're heading out to a farm, maybe we should requisition another truck?" she offered.

Frankie grinned. "And miss this primo ride? Ian can afford body work."

Once he was certain no one else was on the property, Frankie turned around and returned to the house near the entrance, pulling up beside a rusted white pickup. Colorful curtains flapped from the windows of a small cottage, painted in what at one time was probably a bright blue but had faded to nearly gray. The lawn, what there was of it, was overgrown, as if the goat penned near the barn, which overshadowed the house like an architectural David and Goliath, hadn't been let near the house in way too long. Marisela waited for the dust kicked up by the Corvette's tires to die down before she opened the door and slid out.

When a cool breeze and barely seventy-degree temperatures greeted her, Marisela decided she could get used to summer in New England. The apple trees, lined in neat rows on either side of natural wood fences, had bright green leaves. Clusters of white, star-shaped flowers, some still clinging to the trees, some on the ground, emitted a fresh, sweet smell. On the backside of the barn, Marisela recognized the raised rows of strawberry plants. Intermixed with the scents of fertilizer, apple blossoms, and country fresh air, Marisela caught a whiff of the ripe berries and her stomach gave a little rumble.

Unfortunately, Frankie was close enough to hear the sound. "The candy bar didn't do the trick? Should have had a real breakfast before you left the hotel."

"I was too busy with some *varón* I found in my bed this morning."

He clucked his tongue. "You didn't look too disappointed when I woke you up by sucking those sweet—"

The screech of an unoiled screen door cut off the rest of Frankie's dirty talk—dirty talk that, Marisela had to admit, inspired a steady pulse between her thighs.

"Here for the berries?"

The woman in question was clearly Tracy Manning, judging by the resemblance to a yearbook picture Max had tucked in the briefing file. Her hair, once a large pouf, leftover-from-the-big-hair-eighties style, was now darker, thinner, and longer. Her eyes greeted them warily.

Frankie waved. Tracy's smile was tentative as she donned a large-brimmed hat. When Marisela held out her hand, Tracy hesitated before accepting it. When she did, Marisela felt a delicacy in the bones that seemed out of place with running a farm.

"I'm Tracy," she said by way of hello.

"I'm Marisela. This is my—" Wow. They hadn't practiced this part. It wasn't as if they were deep undercover or anything, so they'd at least decided to use their own names. But they'd planned to wing the rest.

"*Novio,*" Frankie provided.

Boyfriend? Ha! What was he smoking? Lover, maybe. Ex, definitely. Friend with benefits? She thought that one had potential, if not for the fact that they were constantly at each other's throats when they weren't pleasuring other parts of their bodies.

He took Tracy's hand in his. "Name's Frank. Beautiful farm you have here, not that I'd know a beautiful farm from an ugly one."

Tracy gave him a short grin. "Oh, I think you'd know."

Flirt.

"Are you visiting the area?" she asked them.

"On our way to Boston to see the Red Sox. Frank here used to play," Marisela said.

"Professionally?"

No, in the sandlot two blocks away from where

they'd grown up, but Tracy didn't need to know that.

"It was a long time ago," Frankie said. "But I'm a baseball freak as much as my woman here loves fresh fruit. Thought we'd stop by and pick a quick snack for the rest of the trip to Fenway."

"I'll grab you some baskets," Tracy answered briefly, her eyes lingering with a tinge of suspicion on Frankie.

Marisela figured she'd need to be chatty with this one.

"This place is so adorable. Is it a family farm?"

"Sort of."

Tracy waved at them to follow her through the barn to the strawberry field on the other side. Just steps from crossing into the two-story opened door, Marisela stopped up short when a strong odor shoved its way up her nose.

"What's that smell?"

Tracy lifted her hand to her mouth, trying unsuccessfully to stifle a giggle. "Horse manure, likely. I haven't made it out to muck the stall yet today."

"You do that yourself?"

The shocked expression on Marisela's face finally broke the ice and Tracy allowed herself to laugh. "Does it look like I can afford a lot of help? Some kids from the high school come over nearly every day and do some chores in exchange for credits for their agriculture class, but that's later in the afternoon. I'm not as weak as some people might think."

Marisela stepped into the cool, shadowy barn, ignoring the overwhelming stench. "No, no. *Perdone.* I'm just a spoiled city girl. You don't look weak to me. Not at all! Look at the size of this place. And you take care of it all on your own?"

Tracy gave a humble shrug, like a child who didn't know how to take a compliment.

"I'm very impressed. Aren't you, Frank?"

Frankie, engaged in a staring contest with the horse, a huge dun-colored animal with large black eyes who didn't seem to like the strangers in his domain, didn't respond right away.

"Is that one of those beer horses?" he asked.

Tracy laughed again, every giggle a step closer to trust. "Pack likes to think he's a Clydesdale, but he's not even close. Just your average farm horse. He's harmless, mostly. Just doesn't like men much. I think his last owner was a son of a bitch, if you know what I mean."

As they walked through the barn, Tracy pointed out the various animals penned there, including a smaller pony named Freddy, an assortment of goats, hens, and a collection of lazy cats who seemed more interested in finding the right strand of sunshine to bask in than they were in the strangers who'd invaded their home. By the back door, Tracy retrieved two straw baskets and handed one each to Marisela and Frankie.

"So is there a trick to this?" Marisela asked, only half kidding when she looked at the plants as if they were tarantulas rather than bearers of sweet, juicy fruit.

With a shy grin, Tracy walked with them into the field and instructed them on which berries were ready for picking and which ones should remain a few days longer. After making a selection, Marisela brushed a choice, red fruit on her sleeve and relished the sweet succulent taste. Frankie eased into her personal space just as she was about to plop a second treat in her mouth, his eyes glittering with hunger that couldn't possibly be sated with a fruit that size, but since Tracy's eyes were trained tightly on them, she fed him with all the adoring indulgence she could muster.

He'd pay for that. Later.

When the private moment nearly sent Tracy away, Marisela piped up. "You know, my grandmother grew figs in her backyard when I was a kid. I used to bribe my little sister to do the picking and washing. I preferred the eating part."

Tracy's smile was soft and melancholy. "My sister probably would have worked the same sort of deal, if she'd ever gotten within five hundred feet of a fruit tree, which she never did. Except maybe to carve her and a boyfriend's initials in the trunk."

Marisela chuckled and exchanged a glance with Frankie. She spoke pretty easily about her murdered sister for someone who was supposed to be so screwed up. But her eyes darted away quickly and she shifted uncomfortably from foot to foot—as if she hadn't expected to share that memory out loud.

Marisela decided not to push. Too much, too soon, and the chick could clam up for good.

"Oh, I remember doing that," Marisela shared, "on the only pecan tree in our neighborhood. We're from

Florida, so when we hit the backyard, we had our pick of produce," she explained, chattering about the sour oranges her mother used to make her garlicky *mojo* until Tracy relaxed. She listened raptly, asked questions, always watching Frankie warily, but after a little less than half an hour, she was grinning broadly at the two overfilled baskets of berries and yakking as if they were old friends.

"Why don't you wash these up in the barn before you get back on the road?" Tracy asked.

"That would be great," Marisela said warmly. "Is there somewhere I can wash up, too? This is hard work, farming."

Tracy hesitated for a moment, then, tentatively, nodded toward the house. She walked ahead of them hurriedly.

"Just let me clean up a bit," she said, her voice shaky. "I live alone. I'm not used to company."

Marisela and Frankie stopped on the porch and allowed Tracy to slip inside. Marisela leaned in close to Frankie, looking like any adoring girlfriend when all she really wanted to do was talk to him without being overheard.

"Think she's really cleaning up?"

"Either that," he said, eyeing the house over her shoulder, "or hiding something she doesn't want us to see."

Thirteen

AT THE DOOR, FRANKIE HESITATED. "You should go in with her alone. She's warming up, but I think I still make her nervous."

Marisela skimmed her fingertip down the slim line of facial hair on Frankie's face, loving the sharp feel beneath her skin, though she wouldn't admit her weakness, even under torture. "Can you blame her? With that beard and moustache, you look like *el diablo*."

"Last night, you thought it was sexy enough."

"Yeah, well, I've got a thing for fallen angels. Not all women need a danger fix the way I do."

For an instant, Marisela felt herself rising on the balls of her feet, her mouth inches from his, her gaze riveted on the lips that had brought her such decadent pleasure the night before. Frankie could be macho and rude and intimidating, but she couldn't manage to kick him out of bed for his faults, not when he was so damned skillful underneath the covers. And on top of the covers, for that matter.

"I'll call in to Titan," Frankie said, watching over Marisela's head as Tracy scurried through her house, cabinet and drawer doors slamming shut as she moved. "See if you can get her to open up."

Tracy appeared at the screen door, slightly breathless and red-faced. "Come on in!" she said with an animated friendliness that completely contrasted with the shy woman who'd first greeted them. "I've got some iced tea, if you're interested."

"That would be wonderful," Marisela replied, swinging around Frankie. "Honey, why don't you make that call and meet us inside?"

He handed over the berries and headed toward the Corvette.

With a basket hooked on each arm, Marisela smiled as Tracy pushed open the door. Once inside, the clutter silenced her. The couches, two of them, overflowed with a dozen pillows in various colors, textures, and types. Shelves upon shelves, those on the walls or inside curios, were crammed with collections of all shapes and sizes—candles and candlesticks, snow globes and music boxes, statuettes of everything from birds to bun-

nies to bears. And where there wasn't bric-a-brac, there
were books. The woman could open a library. Stacks
of tomes from worn leather hardbacks to the latest paperback bestsellers were stacked two and three deep.
The ceiling glistened with what Marisela guessed were
tacks and fishing wire, supporting a wild array of wind
chimes, dreamcatchers, cut pieces of crystal, or discs
of artsy stained glass. Surprisingly, the floor was clear
except for rugs, yet every other space swam with something to grab the attention.

And perhaps distract from the sadness in the soul.

"I have a lot of collections," Tracy explained flip-
pantly, watching as Marisela's gaze swept through the
living room, dining room, and front hall.

Marisela pressed her lips tightly as she formulated
an answer that wouldn't be rude. "That's one way to put
it." She smiled and winked.

"I guess you could say I've got issues," Tracy replied
with a nervous twitter of a laugh.

"Who doesn't?" Marisela shrugged, which sent a
few berries skittering to the floor. She put down the
baskets and retrieved the escapees. "You should see my
shoe room."

Tracy's eyes widened to the size of the dozen or
so saucers she had lined up on the mantel. "A whole
room?"

It was a lie, of course. Despite her admiration and
recognition of a good Jimmy Choo, Marisela was the
sort of woman who could make do with flip-flops
from Wal-Mart, decent leather boots like those she

wore today, a couple pairs of sexy high-heeled sandals for special occasions, and running shoes in three states of existence—old and grungy, broken in, and brand, spanking new. However, she knew women well enough. Shoe-bonding was genetically ingrained.

"I converted a guest room," she replied.

Tracy's smile warmed. "I used to love shoe shopping," she said wistfully, and for the first time, Marisela heard a child-like quality in her voice that she'd attributed to simple shyness before. Now she realized that while Tracy might have aged physically since her sister's murder, her mental state was trapped in teenage angst.

No wonder her brother freaked when they threatened to speak to her about Rebecca's death. She was practically a poster-child for innocence, all laced up in gut-wrenching tragedy.

"I hear there are great boutiques in Boston," Marisela said. "At least, there had better be or Mr. Baseball out there isn't going to be making it to any bases tonight."

Tracy blushed and timidly gestured toward the kitchen. "I don't need fancy shoes out here. Just a good pair of work boots and fur-lined slippers when the nights get cold."

Marisela followed, placing the baskets of berries beside the sink and accepting the glass of iced tea Tracy offered. She took a sip and the sweet, tangy flavor soothed the throat she hadn't realized was parched. Man, picking fruit was no picnic.

"You stay out here on the farm all the time?" she asked.

"Mostly," Tracy said, reaching into a carved cabinet to retrieve a battered aluminum colander. "I'm not very social . . . anymore."

There it was. Her in. Marisela glanced out through the window and saw Frankie leaning on the back of the Corvette, phone in hand.

"Did something happen?"

Tracy turned away, pretending to look for something when Marisela couldn't imagine what else she'd need to rinse off the berries other than the colander she had in her hand, the berries, and some tap water.

"I'm sorry," Marisela said, reaching out and touching Tracy softly on the shoulder. "That was rude. I shouldn't be nosy. It's just that, I don't know, you seem like a really nice person. I'd hate to think of you all cooped up."

Tracy turned around slowly, her eyes a little glossy. "I like living like this. Beats the alternative."

"Which is?"

Tracy turned on the water, sliding her fingers underneath the stream to test the temperature. "Well, my choices have always seemed to be either hanging out with the wrong crowd and making stupid choices or in-patient therapy. I prefer this farm to Windchaser Farm."

Marisela pressed her lips together tightly. Tracy wasn't exactly mincing words. "Sounds like a tough life."

"I'm sorry," Tracy said, her voice more forceful. "That's an awfully personal thing for me to share."

Marisela waved her hand as if Tracy's confession hadn't struck her hard. "Hey, we all screw up sometimes."

"Some more than others. I've been a serial screwup for fifteen years. But out here, in the isolated farm country, I tend to do better. Least I have for nearly a year now. One day at a time."

"You know that's right," Marisela insisted, attitude lacing every word. The girl-talk angle was working. Now she just had to ramp up the stakes. "I got in with the wrong crowd when I was in school. Wasn't pretty for me, either."

Tracy turned the berries into the colander. "Drugs?"

Marisela winced uncomfortably. "Selling, not taking. Mostly, I was a petty thief and a major thug. Some bad shit went down. I learned my lessons the hard way."

"What happened?"

Tracy's stare was intense, intimate. She wasn't asking because of Marisela, necessarily, but for herself. She was seeking the secret. The magic bullet. The trick to escaping the downward spiral.

"I was attacked," Marisela said, twisting the truth a bit to gain Tracy's trust. "I nearly died. I literally had the sense beat into me, as my papi likes to say."

The colander dropped noisily into the sink, but Tracy didn't seem to care.

"Beat into you? By whom?"

Marisela reached out for the colander, took it and busied herself by shaking the water around the metal sieve. "Bunch of girls jumped me."

"A bunch?"

Marisela nodded. "After a basketball game in the gym parking lot. Nearly killed me. Trust me, they wanted to. They tried. I was in the hospital for two weeks."

None of which was a lie. She'd just described, in scant detail, her bleed-out from *las Reinas*. The only part of the story she'd failed to mention was that she'd asked for the beating as a way to permanently exit the gang. That detail might not help her stir Tracy's sympathy.

"How'd you get away?" Tracy's voice vibrated with breathless desperation. She slid out a metal kitchen chair and dropped into the floral-patterned seat.

Marisela twisted the faucet and pumped some liquid soap into her hands.

"I fought back," she said with a shrug. "I was a tough kid."

"I hate violence," Tracy said, her voice faint and faraway. From her seat at the table, she was staring out the window, but not at Frank. He wasn't standing by the car anymore. Tracy's gaze was now lost in the turquoise-blue sky where not even one fluffy cloud dared dispel the perfect morning scene.

Marisela grabbed a dishtowel and approached Tracy slowly.

"Most people hate violence," she concluded. "Doesn't

mean we all aren't capable of kicking a little ass when it's necessary."

A sob caught in Tracy's throat and her eyes instantly filled with large, gelatinous tears. Marisela could now see that Tracy wasn't staring out the window at all. On a small shelf beside the fluttering curtains was a small picture frame. In the center, two girls in black-and-white, like one of those photographs taken at a booth in the mall, smiled as if they owned the entire world. Looking more like twins than sisters, Tracy and Rebecca Manning's grins were toothy and genuine, with that special teenage goofiness that only emerged in the company of close friends. Marisela and Lia had a whole collection of pictures just like this one.

She took the picture down and noticed there wasn't a speck of dust on the polished metal frame.

"Is this you?" she asked.

Tracy cupped the photograph lovingly in her palms as tears slid with painful slowness down her cheeks. "Me and Becca."

"You look so much alike."

"She was my sister."

"Was?"

"She died," Tracy said.

Not she was *murdered*? Not she was *killed*? Just *she died*?

"I'm so sorry," she replied.

She put her hand softly on Tracy's shoulder, and was surprised when the woman didn't flinch. Instead she traced the tiny, smiling face in the photograph with her quaking touch.

"We were born only thirteen months apart. Irish twins, right? "

Two fat drops fell from her eyes, splashing on the glass.

"*Pobrecita*," Marisela said softly. "You don't have to talk about it. I'm so sorry. I shouldn't have asked."

That wasn't honest, but Marisela had to play this out. She was in too deep to turn back now. And she was making progress.

Tracy shook her head. "No, no. It's okay," she said with a sniffle and a deep, fortifying breath. She swiped the tears off her face brutally. "No one ever wants me to talk about it. Well, my brother never wants me to. He says it's too painful. That I shouldn't torture myself anymore." Tracy glared up at Marisela, her light brown eyes intense with more than just fifteen-year-old grief. "He doesn't know the half of it!"

Near-hysteria pitched Tracy's voice higher, so that she startled herself with the sound. She clamped her hand over her mouth and shot out of her chair. With jerky hands, she shoved the picture frame back on the shelf, knocking down the tiny kitty-shaped salt and pepper shakers perched beside it. Tracy screamed.

One bounced. The other dropped onto the linoleum and rolled under the table. Tracy immediately dropped to the ground on all fours, scrambling for the runaway knickknack and crying openly now with no immediate sign of stopping.

Marisela dropped to the ground beside her. "*Mijita*, what's wrong?"

"These were Becca's! They can't break. They—"

The rest of her sentence was captured by a panic-stricken sob and even as Tracy recovered the runaway kitty, her shaking hands sent it clattering to the ground once again. Marisela slid under the table with Tracy, and taking a cue from her mother, who was a hell of a lot better at this shit than Marisela was, wrapped Tracy in her arms. Instantly, Tracy pressed her face tight to Marisela's shoulder, the moisture of her misery almost instantly sinking through.

Please let this pay off. Please let this pan out.

Not that Marisela was coldhearted, but damn. It had been fifteen years.

For a few moments, Marisela crooned to Tracy in Spanish, telling her not to worry, encouraging her to let out her emotions. She was certain the woman had no idea what she was talking about, but somehow, speaking in the native tongue of her parents had a musical effect that went a long way toward communicating, even if the words were unintelligible.

Soon after, Tracy seemed to calm. The rivers of tears drenching Marisela's jacket trickled down to a steady but lessening stream. Without words, she helped Tracy to her feet, then slid her back into her chair at the kitchen table. She grabbed the iced tea Tracy had poured for herself, but hadn't touched. "Here, *mija*, take a drink."

Tracy obeyed. "I was only fifteen."

"You were a baby."

"I was so angry with her! She was ruining every-thing."

Marisela slid into the chair next to Tracy's then scooted closer. "Big sisters do that," she commented, thinking that her own sister, Belinda, likely had a damned long list of all the ways Marisela had effectively screwed up her childhood.

Tracy used the dishtowel as a handkerchief, wiping her face and blowing her nose. "You don't understand. She wanted to destroy him, but she ended up destroy-ing me."

Marisela's heart clenched. This was the information she needed. Right here. Right now. "Who? Who did she want to destroy?"

Tracy shook her head. "You're not from around here. You don't know the story."

Marisela reached out and cupped Tracy's quivering hand. "No, I don't know the story. But if you want to tell me, if it'll make you feel better, I'll listen."

Tracy shot out of her chair. "I can't! I appreciate—"

"I'm not just a stranger, Tracy."

The words tumbled out of Marisela's mouth in a rush, but she had to trust her gut.

Tracy's head tilted in confusion. "What do you mean?"

"Your sister died. She was probably killed. That's torn you apart over all these years, hasn't it?"

"Who are you?"

Marisela stood. "My name is Marisela Morales and

I work for an organization called Titan International. Two days ago, someone tried to kill Craig Bennett, the congressman. A few weeks ago, Raymond Hightower was murdered on a mountaintop in Switzerland."

With each tidbit of information, Tracy's face lost a shade of color. She went from red to pink and splotchy to blushing pale.

"And yesterday, Evan Cole was shot on his way to visit your sister's grave."

What was left of Tracy's color instantly drained from her face. She brought her shaking hand to her mouth, whispered what Marisela thought was Evan's name, and then fainted dead away on the floor.

Marisela shouted for Frankie, but hearing no response, she grabbed the dishtowel, doused it with water from the sink, wrung it out as quickly as she could, and then slid next to Tracy on the floor. She cursed as she moved Tracy's head, checking for bumps, but she couldn't feel any. Marisela ran the wet towel over Tracy's face, and almost instantly, the woman's eyes fluttered open.

"What happened?"

Marisela helped Tracy sit up. In the silent seconds that followed, Tracy's memory slammed back into operation.

"Did you say Evan . . . was killed . . . at Rebecca's grave?"

"Didn't you know he was dead? It was all over the news."

Tracy shook her head, groaning and clutching at her temple. "I don't watch the news or read newspapers. Too depressing. Oh, my God. Evan?"

To her credit, Tracy didn't dissolve into tears again. Marisela retrieved the iced tea and held the glass to Tracy's mouth, so she could take a few sips.

"Who was Evan Cole to you?"

Tracy's eyes widened with fear. "What is this Titan group you work for?" she asked, after pushing the glass away.

Marisela focused. Okay, she had to drop the Evan Cole questions. For now. Concentrate. Employ a dash of honesty. Judging by the bits and pieces Marisela had heard so far, Tracy obviously knew more about the night her sister died than she had told the police all those years ago. And her knowledge could be the key to finding out who had hired Yizenia Santiago to exact revenge for a fifteen-year-old crime. So far, she saw no evidence to indicate that Tracy was behind the killings. The woman appeared haunted, not bitter. And her shock at hearing about the fates of the men she'd once hung around with had been too genuine to be faked by a woman so emotionally fragile.

"We're a private investigation firm. When Craig Bennett was shot, his wife hired us to protect him and find out who was trying to kill him. Certain evidence leads us to believe that his attempted murder was retribution for what happened to your sister on that island fifteen years ago."

Tracy braced her hands on either side of her in an attempt to stand, but she seemed to have no strength in her arms.

"Oh, God. You said someone tried to kill Craig. Is he—?"

"No, he's recovering. Slowly."

Tracy's lips pressed into a tight line. Not good.

"You were dating Bradley Hightower," she said, her tone matter-of-fact. Nonthreatening. "After he dumped your sister."

She gave a little nod.

"She was supposedly furious about that. Did she go to the island that night to confront the two of you?"

Tracy shook her head.

Marisela grabbed her arm at the elbow, firmly but gently. "Raymond Hightower is dead, Tracy. Evan Cole, who wasn't even there that night, was ruthlessly murdered yesterday right in front of me."

The waterworks renewed, though the tears flowed silently.

"Craig Bennett is clinging to life in a hospital and could spend the rest of his days living in fear if we don't find out who is trying to kill him. And Brad Hightower! We can't find him yet, but he's in danger and could be next on the killer's list. If there was anyone else there that night, anyone else who might become a target of this killer, we need to know so we can protect them. Do you understand?"

Tracy managed a nod.

"Was anyone else there that night?"

"No," she said weakly. "Craig and Bradley had gone camping."

"Just the two of them?" Marisela asked.

Tracy nodded. "Evan had a party for his parents. I don't know why Raymond didn't go. He usually did. I was in bed that night"—her voice grew stronger—"sleeping. But Becca came in, all psyched up about something she just had to show me. Had to! We snuck out our bedroom window. I don't know how, but she'd gotten Raymond to drive us over to the marina where she stole a boat and made us go with her to the island."

Marisela helped Tracy stand. They slipped back into the kitchen chairs, but not before Marisela glanced out the window. Still no sign of Frankie. She was starting to wonder where the hell he'd run off to, especially since she'd called out for him minutes ago and he'd yet to respond.

That wasn't like him. Wasn't like him at all.

But before Marisela could suggest she go find him, Tracy continued to talk. "Becca had this crazy look in her eye the whole time. Like she knew something we didn't know. Like she was finally going to get everything she ever wanted. Halfway there, Raymond wanted to turn back, but Becca wouldn't let him. She said we had to see what was really going on."

"If Evan wasn't there that night, why did someone kill him?" Marisela asked, trying to move Tracy along. An icy hand clawed at Marisela's spine the longer Frankie remained out of contact. She needed Tracy to spill. Now.

Tracy shook her head, slowly at first, then with growing speed. "No one knew. No one but me."

"No one knew *what*? What happened that night, Tracy? What you tell me could save Bradley Hightower's life. And maybe yours. You were there, weren't you? Rebecca made you go. What if this killer is simply targeting everyone who was there that night, including you? You need to tell me everything so we can protect you. How did your sister go from leading you on some expedition to being murdered? Why didn't you tell all this to the police? What have you been covering up all these years, so much that it's been eating you alive?"

Tracy took a deep, vibrating breath. She opened her mouth to speak, but Marisela silenced her when, out of the corner of her eye, she caught sight of someone sneaking past the kitchen doorway.

Marisela reached for her LadySmith. The weapon, smaller than her Taurus 9 mm, was easier to hide, but she didn't want to pull it in case Frankie was the one who'd invaded the house. But why would he sneak around? To search Tracy's stuff? Possibly . . . but that hadn't been the plan.

She glanced out the window yet again and saw nothing, including no new cars in the drive. Just Tracy's white truck and the Corvette, still and untouched. But with all the boo-hooing going on in the kitchen, she supposed someone could have come up the gravel drive without her or Tracy noticing. And the vibe didn't feel right. She'd bet her newly stuffed bank account that Frankie wasn't the one in the house.

"What's wrong?" Tracy whimpered.

A noise from the back of the house forced Marisela to spring to action. Spotting Tracy's keys on the counter, she grabbed them and tucked them tightly in Tracy's hand. "You need to get out of here."

The sound had startled Tracy, but she hadn't processed that her home had been invaded. "What's happening?"

Marisela shushed her and spoke directly into her ear. "I'm not sure, but you need to get to your brother. Can you do that?"

Tracy's eyes widened with fear. "Why? What's wrong?"

Marisela pulled her gun, but pointed it away from Tracy. "I think someone just broke into the house."

Tracy stood, her arms and legs unsteady, her eyes darting around as if the collections she'd amassed were her primary concern, ahead of her life. "Who?"

"I don't know," Marisela whispered, taking Tracy by the arm and leading her toward the archway that separated the kitchen from the hall. "But I'm going to find out."

"Where's Frank? Your boyfriend. Is he really your boyfriend?"

"Good question," Marisela replied, answering the location question, not the boyfriend one. "I'll find him, too. Trust me."

Marisela would have loved to believe that Frankie

had been distracted by the animals in the barn or something equally unbelievable, but she knew he wouldn't take off on her. Not by choice.

After glancing up and down the hall, Marisela tugged Tracy into the front room, her gun at the lead. She considered calling out to Frankie again, but decided not to reveal their location. For all the intruder knew, she and Tracy were still weeping in the kitchen. She stopped at the front door. Once they opened that squeaky screen, their position would be revealed.

"Is there any other way out of the house?"

"Back door," Tracy answered.

Marisela spun around, shaking her head, knowing the figure she'd seen—the one she was nearly certain wasn't Frankie—could be waiting for them there. "Any other?"

"Windows. The one in the bathroom has a broken screen."

"Can you climb through?"

Marisela only allowed Tracy half a shrug before pushing her gently into the bathroom. Once Marisela was sure Tracy could make it outside, she moved to the door. "Lock this door behind me. Stay in here until I tell you it's safe to move, then make a run for your truck. Don't look back. Go to your brother."

"Shouldn't I call the police?"

Oh, yeah, that would be fun.

"Let me worry about the police. You just get out of here. Don't let Parker talk you into going anywhere. You stay put until other Titan operatives arrive. Tracy,

look, I came here thinking that you hired the assassin
to kill the—"

"I didn't!"

Marisela nodded. "I believe you, but you could be
in danger. Do you understand?"

"This is my home, Marisela. I can't . . . "

Figuring Tracy had simply depleted her tear stock-
pile, Marisela watched the woman's features melt into
utter despair. "You can, Tracy. Don't be a victim to some
two-bit punk who probably followed us here to jack our
car."

Tracy took a deep breath, nodded decisively, and
then closed the door.

Marisela waited to hear a click before she made her
way toward the back of the house with the most silent
steps she could manage. She made it all the way to the
back door before a hand shot out from around the corner and dragged her into the darkness.

Fourteen

MARISELA THREW HER ELBOW BACK hard, satisfied when she heard a breathless grunt. Spinning in the opposite direction, she built momentum so that when her fist, clutching the gun, connected with the nose of her attacker, blood spurted and the assailant dropped to the ground. She stepped back into the light as his body fell.

Good, it wasn't Frankie.

Not that she'd feel bad if she knocked him out. He knew better than to grab her like that—which is why she hadn't hesitated.

She quickly checked to see that the guy moaning on the ground wasn't armed, then she pistol-whipped him to silence, dragging him back into the closet from where he'd emerged. The hallway was narrow, so a chair from the kitchen jammed between the door and wall would keep it closed even after the guy woke up. Where was Frankie? Had he been attacked while she was in the house? She and Tracy had been talking for a while. Was this another warning, another attack to convince them to back off?

Marisela crouched down and scrambled back to the bathroom. She knocked lightly on the door.

"Don't open it, Tracy. It's me. Are you still in there?"

She heard a whimper.

"Are you okay?"

A long pause. "I'm . . . okay."

"Get ready to bolt. I just found the guy in your house."

"Where?"

"Don't worry. I took care of him, but I don't think he was alone and I think his friends may have jumped Frankie. I'm going to cause a diversion out front. When I do, I want you to scramble to the truck, got it? Don't look back. Just get out. Drive like a bat out of hell. Don't stop for red lights. In fact, don't stop until you're with Parker. Can you do that?"

The whimpers increased, followed by a series of deep, nearly hyperventilating breaths.

"Tracy?"

"I don't know where he lives," she confessed. "He always visits me!"

Damn. Damn, damn, damn.

"Okay, where can you go?"

"I have a neighbor, a few farms down. Her husband used to be a marine. I'll be safe there."

Marisela blew out a relieved breath. "Good thinking. You bust your ass getting there and then stay inside until I personally come get you, got it?"

"Yes," Tracy said.

Satisfied that Tracy would follow her directions, Marisela made her way to the back door, crouched down so no one peeking through windows would see her. Not only did she want Tracy safe, she wanted to hear the rest of the story. So much didn't make sense. There was a good chance that somewhere in the blanks Tracy had yet to fill was the answer to who had hired Yizenia Santiago. Marisela couldn't imagine that Tracy had had anything to do with the assassin. She wasn't yet a hundred percent sure about Parker, but she doubted he'd knowingly put his remaining sister in harm's way. That left the identity of the person who hired Yizenia wide open—which put them all in danger.

The guy who'd attacked her in the hall wasn't the same sort of punk who'd ambushed them last night, but he was only a slight upgrade. She could smell hired muscle, and this jerk stank. But who had hired him? Did he work for Yizenia? Parker? Some third unknown party they still knew nothing about?

She hurried to the back door and caught sight of movement inside the barn. Her main firepower was in the car, so Marisela cut around to the front of the house. She sprinted across the yard only to find the Corvette door locked, and Frankie, wherever the hell he was, had the only key.

If she'd had her tools, she'd be inside by now. She could break in, but in the time it took for her to crack through the glass and retrieve her big guns, she could be ambushed. She'd have to improvise.

She promised Tracy a diversion, but thought better of it with no one visible in the front yard. The animals weren't happy in the barn, however, giving Marisela a clue to where the real action was going down. She dashed around the house to the bathroom window, knocked vigorously so Tracy would leave, then cut across the yard until her back was pressed flat against the outside of the barn.

She anticipated that the sound of Tracy's engine revving might bring the attackers out of hiding, so she waited while Tracy hopped into the cab, turned the ignition, and sent the truck flying backward in a cloud of gravel and dust. Just as she ground the pickup into drive, someone flew out of the barn. Marisela waited the split second to make sure it wasn't Frankie, then she kicked the guy in the small of the back, sending him sprawling onto the dirt and gravel road.

"Move and I'll blast your fucking head off," she screamed, gun aimed and ready, though she had no intention of killing the man. This day wouldn't end in more questions. She wanted answers.

He looked about ready to jump to his feet when the sun glinted off her weapon. He held up his hands. "Don't shoot!"

"What? And ruin my fun?"

She cocked the hammer.

He froze like a popsicle.

"That's more like it," she said, her tone even. "Toss down your weapon."

"I'm clean," he insisted, hands high. "I swear!"

She arched a brow, but wasn't going to chance patting the guy down. "You came here unarmed? That's not too bright. Who are you?"

"Look, lady. We're just here to make you stop."

"Stop what? Picking berries? Where's my partner?"

The man's eyes widened. His lips twitched. "What partner?"

His gaze shifted suddenly and Marisela dove over him, certain she felt a presence behind her. By the time she rolled back to her feet, she saw her instincts were right. She fired, but the guy she'd vaulted over kicked the weapon out of her hand before she could make her mark, sending the LadySmith flying into the nearby grass.

Marisela's mouth dried. Her fingers throbbed just enough to fill her with the rage she needed to take on these two *pendejos* and anyone else they might have lurking in the shadows.

She raised her hands, balanced her stance, ready

to strike. When the guy on the ground started to stand, she kicked out, sending gravel and dirt into his eyes. He screamed, giving her a split second to charge his cohort, grab his shoulders, and in his surprise, yank his torso down as she kicked up with her knee. Bone connected with his chin and he stumbled back, dazed.

Marisela spun, hammer-fisted the jerk in the back of the neck, and sent him to the ground. She kicked him twice in the gut, retrieved her gun, and then ran into the barn.

As she dashed through the structure, she came up short when she heard a very human groan coming from the largest stall. She doubled back and caught Frankie half buried in the hay, only moments from being stomped by a very large, very angry horse.

Marisela yanked on the latch.

"It's okay, um, horsie." What was that animal's name? "Shhh . . . Trust me, he doesn't want to be in your space any more than you want him there."

The beast snorted and stamped at the straw with his front hooves. Frankie was dazed, but coming to. Marisela fought with the latch until she won, threw open the door and with her hands stretched out in surrender, tried to soothe the animal with soft knickers and nonsense words.

She even tried Spanish. What the hell? Worked on Tracy.

The horse backed up.

"You okay?" she asked Frankie.

"Three . . . bastards . . . jumped me."

But they hadn't shot him, which had to mean something.

"Only three? You're losing your touch."

He rubbed the back of his neck. "Just give me a minute."

"Mr. Ed doesn't like you hanging in his crib."

Frankie managed to lift himself as far as his knees. "Remind me to hurry your ass after you've been bashed on the head with a tire iron."

Marisela watched behind her. The two guys hadn't yet come back into the barn. Had they left? And what about the third guy she'd locked in the closet? Had he worked himself free yet?

"What do they want?" she asked.

"They didn't stop to chat."

"What, no threats? No deep-throated laughter as they explained their evil plot?"

"You and your *telenovelas*. I was talking to Brynn on the cell. Two came at me from the barn, one behind me with the iron. They knocked the crap out of me and tossed me in here. With the horse shit."

Marisela took a sniff. "Not only am I driving the Vette on the way out of here, you're riding on the roof."

The horse's anxiety spiked again. He charged forward, but Frankie was finally able to find his legs.

"Where's Tracy?" he asked.

"I got her out. Maybe we've missed something. What if Yizenia is out to hit everyone who was on that island that night? That puts Tracy in danger, too."

Frankie shook his head, but Marisela couldn't tell if it was from disagreement or from his futile attempts to regain his equilibrium. "So Tracy was there?"

Marisela didn't have time to reply. Two men approached them from the tall, wide front entrance to the barn and the third man, likely released by his pals, came from the back, a crowbar clutched in his hands. The other two preferred rage as their weapons—and they looked like they knew how to use it.

Marisela had her gun, but Frankie forced his hand over hers, silently insisting she put away the weapon. Killing was a Titan option, but shooting was never the first choice—particularly since she and Frankie both had criminal records. They had to keep this clean if they could—and they needed information, not more dead bodies. Marisela shoved the LadySmith in the back of her jeans. These guys clearly didn't want to kill them or they would have by now.

Frankie glanced upward and then turned toward the guys in the front. Marisela followed his quick gaze and caught sight of a collection of ropes, chains, and pulleys dangling above their heads. She could never jump that high. Not without help.

The men rushed forward. Frankie yelled, lunged to the side, and caught Marisela's foot as she shoved it toward his hands. Frankie flung her high and she grabbed the looped chain and hoped to hell she didn't crash to the ground for her trouble.

The chain held. Frankie latched onto her legs and gave her a swing so that by the time the big guy with the crowbar was inches away, her foot connected with his chin. Marisela twisted in the air, then gave him a swift kick on the way back. He crashed down, passed out cold.

That left two.

With a grunt, Marisela swung herself up onto the half-wall of the pig's stall, reached down and grabbed the closest farm tool with the longest handle, which ended up being a four-pronged pitchfork. She shouted in triumph, which caught Frankie's attention, giving her the chance to toss him the tool just as the guy with the gravel-cut face charged. The men struggled over the handle, and when his friend attempted to join in, Marisela dropped on top of him.

The man cursed as they struggled, but Marisela pressed hard against his throat before he flipped her off him.

"You fight like a girl," she taunted, scrambling to her feet.

"I'm just getting warmed up," he spat.

She shifted her weight, hands loose, eyes alert, feet balanced.

She didn't have to wait long. The guy rushed her, but Marisela shifted and avoided his tackle. She struck out with the side of her fist and connected with his ear as he rushed by.

She turned to see Frankie pin his assailant to the barn wall with the handle of the pitchfork stretched tight across his neck. The choking sounds intermingled with the clucks, neighs, and bleats from the farm animals. Before she could intervene, she was attacked with a head-butt to her midsection. She curved her body as she fell, allowing the momentum of the blow to facilitate her kick into his stomach.

The air squeezed out of him, Frankie's attacker fell to the ground, unconscious. Frankie tossed her the tool, and before Marisela's assailant could get to his feet, she had the sharp prongs leveled across his chest.

"Stop! Wait!"

"For what?" She raised the fork an inch, clearly needing a little more space to make a clean slice through his skin, muscle, and bone.

"Boss told us to scare you off, not kill you."

Frankie walked up behind her. "Could have fooled us, *muchacho*," he groused. "Who sent you?"

"I don't know!"

Frankie cursed. "Don't you guys ever know who hired you?"

"He was just some guy. Paid us cash. We do jobs for him sometimes . . . on the side."

"You work for him regular and he has no name?"

The man's eyes darted from side to side.

She stabbed the pitchfork downward, pinching through his shirt.

"Wait! Please! I swear. The guy knows my boss, okay. He ordered us to follow you. Told us to keep you away from the girl, but we lost you on the highway."

Marisela clucked her tongue. "I told you, Frankie, you drive like a maniac."

"You knew where we were going," Frankie said, ignoring her crack. "Why wait so long to grab us?"

"The girl was with you. The boss said to make sure you didn't touch her. Told us to warn you to back off. To tell you to leave the past alone."

Incensed, Marisela leaned forward just enough so that the guy was going to have four bloody indentations across his chest when he took off his oversized Tommy Hilfiger T-shirt. "You sure it wasn't a woman who hired you?"

The man looked at her, confused. "A woman? No."

"Then tell your boss that we don't take orders from nameless, faceless creeps who can't do their own dirty work. Now, get up! ¡Rápido!"

Marisela backed off just enough to give him room to move, and he winced, clutching his chest as he half crawled, half dragged himself in the direction Marisela indicated with the pitchfork. Frankie snagged the other guy, still unconscious, by the collar and lugged him toward an empty horse stall with walls straight to the ceiling. He tossed the guy inside and Marisela forced his friend to follow. Together, they pitched in the third man, still dazed and confused. Once they had them caged, Frankie clicked on a large padlock he'd found hanging on the wall.

They walked out into the sunshine. Marisela leaned against the barn and tried not to think about the aches and pains she was going to feel in the morning, while Frankie found the keys to the Vette and retrieved his cell phone, which had been buzzing incessantly. He answered, talked quickly, then returned to Marisela.

"Backup is on the way," he informed her. "They left as soon as I lost my connection with Brynn."

"Think those creeps are good for any more information?"

"Give me a minute," he said, rubbing the tangerine-sized lump on the back of his head. "To catch my breath. We'll find out what they know."

"I've got to go get Tracy. She was terrified."

Frankie pulled out a 9 mm from the storage compartment and tossed her the keys. "I've got these guys covered. Tracy tell you anything interesting before these *pendejos* crashed our party?"

"Oh, yeah," she said, heading toward the car. "But she only just got started. She knows what happened to her sister. The trick now is to get her to tell me."

Marisela was greeted by a three-hundred-pound, flannel-clad, former marine farmer with a twelve-gauge shotgun. After cruising up and down the dirt road that connected the farms in Natick, searching for Tracy, she'd finally spotted the tail end of Tracy's truck tucked behind a rusted green tractor at the farm west of Tracy's orchard. She'd pulled the Vette up to the main house and quickly exited, anxious for Tracy to provide the rest of the story about the night of Rebecca's death. If Evan Cole hadn't been there that night, why had he been killed? Why had Rebecca dragged her little sister and Bradley's brother to that island in the middle of the night, and what exactly had Tracy seen there that had haunted her all these years? Had she seen her sister murdered?

So many questions swam through her brain that she decided not to challenge the big guy with the gun. She even complied with his order to raise her hands high over her head without flinching.

Tracy ran out of the screen door. "It's okay, Bobby. That's the woman who saved me."

Bobby didn't look too convinced, but he lowered his gun.

"Marisela, this is Bobby Dawson," Tracy introduced.

"Call the cops?" she asked Tracy's protector.

"Should have," Bobby said gruffly, his eyes darting to Tracy, who shook her head.

"*Gracias,*" Marisela said, the Spanish evoking an even more confused look from Tracy's neighbor.

"Tracy says you're some sort of cop?" he questioned, the shotgun still gripped tightly in his beefy hands.

Marisela gingerly lowered her arms, then reached into her back pocket for her business card. "I'm a private investigator."

Bobby took the card and read every word. Twice.

"What do you want with Tracy? She's a nice woman. Don't do no harm to no one. She don't need trouble."

Tracy laid her hand softly on Bobby's massive shoulder. "I've already got trouble, Bobby. But I think I can get out of it, finally, with a little help from Marisela, okay?"

Marisela smiled. She liked Tracy. For all this woman's troubles, she wasn't stupid.

After a few quiet words exchanged with Bobby, he went back inside the farmhouse. Tracy lingered on the porch, grinding her teeth and trying to find something to do with her hands. Marisela stayed on the lush green lawn and waited for Tracy to make the right decision. After a few minutes, Tracy took a deep breath and swept her hand across her sandy hair, then marched down the steps. Her eyes were clear now. No more tears. And she spoke with a steady voice.

"What happened at the orchard?"

"Three guys jumped my partner," Marisela explained, "threw him in a horse stall and were waiting to come after me. I messed up their plan by spotting the guy in the house."

Tracy's brow scrunched with worry. "They weren't after me?"

Marisela shook her head. "I don't think so. I think the guy in the house might actually have been there to protect you. From me."

Fear skittered across Tracy's face.

Marisela reached out and placed her hand softly on the woman's arm. "Tracy, I know you don't know me. You have no reason to trust me. But I'm telling you here and now that you might be in danger. Other people, too. And maybe, with your help, we can stop this craziness before someone else gets killed."

"You mean Brad Hightower."

Marisela nodded. "And Craig Bennett. He's lucky to be alive and it's our job—Titan's job—to keep him that way."

Tracy rubbed her arms as if suddenly very cold. "I tried to call Parker, you know. The recording said the network was down."

"That was us, making sure your brother didn't try to stop you from telling the truth," Marisela replied.

"That's real clever," Tracy said. "He would have told me to leave. Or to keep my mouth shut. What I don't understand is why Parker didn't come out here himself."

Marisela patted Tracy's shoulder gently. "I can't say what's keeping him, but I'll find your brother for you myself once I know the whole story and I know you're safe. Why don't we start with my biggest question— would your brother hire someone to kill Craig Bennett and his friends?"

"Parker? No way! He'd never dig all this up again. Never."

"Why not? He hated those men. He blamed them for your sister's death."

"At first, yeah," Tracy said desperately, "We all did." She stepped away and her voice became so tiny, Marisela nearly didn't hear her when she said, "We were wrong."

Marisela didn't try to hide her confusion. "Tracy, you need to tell me everything you remember from that night—everything you know to be true. If you were there, you could be in danger, too, maybe not from those guys back at the barn, but from the assassin herself."

"It's a woman?" she asked, shocked.

Marisela arched a brow. "You don't think a woman can kill?"

Tracy's face went white and the shaking she'd had a handle on moments before returned in full force. "No . . . I know we can."

We?

Marisela decided to take the tension down a notch. "Why don't we go for a drive?"

Tracy eyed her warily. "I want to go back to the orchard."

Marisela shook her head. "Frankie's a little busy right now. He's probably, very politely, finding out what else those goons know. And in a few minutes, the place will be swarming with Titan operatives. Wouldn't you rather go somewhere private?"

Tracy hesitated, her eyes hooded. When she finally looked up, Marisela saw a flash of determination. "Maybe it's time."

With that cryptic statement hanging in the air, Tracy started toward the Corvette. Not one to let an opportunity slide, Marisela clicked the alarm off and jogged to the car. The minute she turned the ignition, Ian's voice crackled over the radio communicator.

Tracy nearly bolted out of the passenger seat. Marisela calmed her with a hand to her thigh.

"Marisela here, Ian. Tracy's with me."

Ian's voice instantly softened. "I hope you're all right, Ms. Manning."

Tracy looked around, unsure of where—and to whom—to respond. "I'm . . . fine."

"Agents are on the scene with Frank," Ian announced. "He was able to convince the attackers to give up the name of who hired them."

Marisela grimaced. She hadn't doubted Frankie's skills at coercion, but she had a feeling the information wasn't something Tracy would want to hear.

"Let me guess. Parker Manning?"

"No big surprise, I suppose," Ian confirmed.

Tracy's eyes widened. "My brother sent men to hurt you?"

Marisela turned to Tracy. "Your brother didn't want us to talk to you. Maybe because you know that he hired the assassin and he didn't trust you to keep quiet?"

Tracy laughed, but the tone was completely absent of humor. "Parker knows I can keep a secret better than anyone. And he didn't hire any assassin. First, he doesn't have the money. Those thugs at my place are probably guys who owed him favors or guys he drinks with in bars."

"They said this was a side job," Marisela confirmed.

"See? He's only protecting me. Like always. Since Becca died, I'm his only family. Our parents totally checked out. Parker and I . . . we only had each other. I can totally see him trying to get you to back off, but he'd never have anyone killed, especially not Evan Cole. Or the others. He wouldn't."

"Why not?"

Tracy's gaze skittered around the car. She knew Ian was listening. She hesitated, but finally took a deep breath and then spoke. "Because they didn't kill Becca. I did."

Fifteen

ON IAN'S ORDERS, Marisela used the GPS system in the Corvette to maneuver the car back to Boston immediately. If Tracy really had killed her sister, then she could be in very real danger from Yizenia's determined bullets. For all they knew, Yizenia had been looking for Tracy, too, and Titan had led the killer right to her next target.

"Murder has no statute of limitations," Tracy said softly, as Marisela shifted the car into fifth gear.

Marisela focused on the road, sparing Tracy only a quick glance and a soft pat on her thigh. "You didn't murder your sister."

"Yes I did." Tracy sniffled, but contained her tears. Marisela expected Tracy to continue, but she was looking around the car, as if expecting Ian's voice to break in again.

With a sigh, Marisela spoke aloud. "Ian, I'm disengaging the communication device for a few miles."

"Understood," he said. "We have a car on the way to intercept you, to watch your back until you get Tracy safely to the office."

"Thanks." She flipped off the radio, then glanced at Tracy with a smile. "There. No one's listening. No one but me."

"You could testify against me," she said. "I could go to prison. Maybe I deserve to."

Marisela bristled. She didn't need Tracy indulging in her emotions. Painful as they were, Marisela needed the facts.

"Give me a dollar," Marisela suggested. "A dime. Whatever you got." She'd seen this on television. On the lawyer shows. She figured the same privilege applied to private investigators, because Ian had reassured Denise Bennett in the hospital that since she was his client, he could not be compelled to testify against her.

"I don't have any money on me," Tracy said.

Marisela frowned. She didn't have any cash on her, either. "Okay, give me the keys to your truck," she suggested. It was a stretch, but all laws were elastic in her way of thinking.

Tracy complied.

She tossed the keys in the console. "Okay, you gave me your truck as collateral. You're now my client. Anything you say to me is protected. Besides, in a court of law, it'd be your word against mine, and no judge or jury is going to consider me a credible witness."

"You don't have multiple stays in drug rehab on your record," Tracy pointed out.

"No, but the record I do have includes a laundry list of misdemeanors and one particularly ugly felony."

The GPS on the car instructed Marisela to get onto the highway, so she slowed long enough to make a quick lane switch. She checked the rearview mirror and noticed a car following closely behind them.

She held up her hand to Tracy, who'd opened her mouth to speak.

She flipped on the radio-based communicator.

"Ian? Tell me those are the Titan agents behind me."

"Not in the mood for evasive maneuvers?" he asked.

"Tracy's been through enough terror for today," she quipped.

"Look behind you."

The headlights on the car blinked twice.

"You're so sweet," Marisela crooned.

"Don't tell anyone," Ian said. "Headquarters out."

Marisela once again turned off the communication system. "Now we can both feel safe and you can tell me the whole truth."

Marisela wished she didn't have to keep her eyes on the road. She often relied on observation to decide whether or not someone was telling the truth. But then, why would Tracy lie? She was, after all, admitting to murder.

"Becca was furious when Brad broke up with her," Tracy began, her voice crisp and clear and, Marisela guessed, just a bit angry. "He was so perfect, you know? Tall, muscular, handsome. Rich. I think rich was what turned Becca on most of all. But after a few months, she started getting annoyed with him. She said he was too much of a gentleman. He like, hardly ever wanted to make out with her and when she'd get all hot and heavy on him, he'd pull back. Say stuff about respecting her."

"What a load of bull," Marisela commented. The guy was using her for something—just not for sex.

Tracy laughed nervously. "Yeah, I guess it was. Anyway, he got tired of her complaining and he dumped her."

"And he was immediately interested in you?"

Marisela caught Tracy's frown out of the corner of her eye.

"I was always hanging around. I guess I was an easy target."

"You don't seem flattered."

A sob caught in Tracy's throat. "It wasn't Bradley I was in love with."

Though she couldn't see a player going for a girl like Tracy—quiet, a little shy, not rich like him—the signs were all there. "You loved Evan Cole," she concluded.

Tracy nodded silently, a tiny whimper spilling from her lips.

"Not to speak ill of the dead or anything," Marisela ventured, "but weren't the two of you . . . different?"

"Oh, God, yes. I didn't even think he knew I was alive! But when I needed him, he was so good to me. He . . . "

"He what?" Marisela prodded.

"He protected me," Tracy admitted in a rush. "No one knew. No one knew he was there that night. Not until after the funeral. He came to see me. Snuck over to my house in the middle of the night. Threw pebbles at my window! God, I'd dreamed of him doing that so many times, but not like that. Not to tell me what he told me."

Marisela remained silent, waiting for Tracy to finish the tale. When Tracy didn't continue on her own, Marisela cut to the chase. "What happened that night? Why did Rebecca take you and Raymond Hightower to that island?"

"She said she had something to show us," Tracy said, her voice laced with disgust. "She wanted to ruin everything. She wanted to prove that Bradley didn't dump her because of her, you know? That it wasn't *her* fault. She suspected that Brad and Craig were doing something in that tent that night. Something they shouldn't."

Marisela nearly slammed on the brake, but managed to maintain a steady speed. "Craig Bennett is gay?"

Tracy shook her head. "I don't know! Becca said he was. She said so once we were on the island and were just feet away from the tent. She burst in and started screaming and Bradley came out and he wasn't wearing anything and Craig was huddled in the corner. I didn't stay. I ran. How could she? She'd been so cruel and mean. To expose Bradley that way, in front of his brother? God, what had she been thinking?"

Marisela blew out a whistle of a breath. "Your sister didn't fuck around. She wanted revenge. She went for the jugular."

Tracy gasped.

"Sorry," Marisela said quickly.

Tracy's hair flew around her face as she shook her head violently. "No, no! You're right. She was horrible, and every step I took away from that tent, every twig I crunched under my shoes, every bramble I yanked out of my hair, made me angrier and angrier at her. She'd ruined everything! Brad was my way to stay close to Evan, who I thought didn't even know I was alive. And Brad was nice to me. Treated me like a lady. With respect. I didn't care what his reasons were. After what she did, I knew . . . everything . . . about him and Craig was going to get out. My life would be torn apart and I would never see Evan again. Bradley would be destroyed, probably sent away by his family. I was so furious! Maybe I meant to kill her. Maybe it wasn't an accident."

At this, Marisela pulled over. When the tail caught up behind them and the agents rushed out, she rolled down the window and waved them back.

Tracy was crying again and Marisela turned to her, taking hold of the woman's quaking hands.

"Tell me what happened," Marisela insisted.

Tears streaked down Tracy's cheeks. Her words came out in a rush. "When I ran away, Becca followed. She was screaming about how right she was, how no one would laugh at her again for getting dumped by the big jock who was a queer. She was practically cackling with glee, not for one minute realizing how humiliated Brad was, how humiliated I was. How none of us deserved this. She couldn't just tell me? She had to drag me out and show me? I could hear the boys yelling at each other. Brad and Raymond. Brothers who were always best friends. She'd ruined that, too. She was so selfish!"

Marisela nodded. While she admired a good scorned-woman tale and had a few of her own to tell, she winced inwardly at the damage Rebecca's tantrum had caused.

"What happened next," Marisela encouraged.

Tracy took another deep breath. "I just wanted to get away. I was going to take the boat and leave Becca and go home. I didn't want to see her or talk to her. But I got confused in the woods and I got lost. Becca caught up to me. She was still laughing. She grabbed my arm. I pulled away. I told her not to touch me. Ever! That I hated her. But she wouldn't stop. She kept grabbing me. I pushed her. She fell. I ran. I got lost again, but Evan found me."

"So he was there," Marisela said.

Tracy nodded. "He'd snuck away from his parents' party to hang out with the guys. I guess he had no idea what was really going on. Anyway, I practically ran into him. I was hysterical. I tried to tell him what happened, but I couldn't get it all out. I told him I pushed Becca, that she fell, that I had to get away. I started running and he stopped me, said I was going to end up in the marsh if I kept going in that direction. I didn't know. He brought me back to the boat Becca had stolen, and I took it to shore. I went home. I showered and went to bed. I kept expecting Becca to come home and yell at me or laugh at me, but she didn't. Then I figured she was staying away to punish me."

"But she never came home."

Tracy shook her head violently. "No, but Bradley was so furious! And Raymond, too! I thought maybe she'd gone back to goad them some more and that they were so furious, they killed her. It wasn't so hard to imagine. I hated her so much for what she did."

Marisela bit her bottom lip. No wonder the woman had tripped on the drugs. She'd been dealing with several layers of serious guilt.

"When did you figure out what really happened?" Marisela asked.

"On the night after the funeral, when Evan came to my room. He didn't realize that I didn't know. He didn't realize how out of it I'd been. I swear, I hardly remembered anything, it was all like a nightmare. He started talking about how he'd never tell, about how he hid her so that no one would find her. I didn't know what he was talking about at first, but then I realized. When I pushed her, she hit her head on a rock or something and died. She was dead when he found her."

Marisela sat back in her seat, absorbing all that she'd been told. Tracy covered her face with her hands and cried and damn it if Marisela could blame her. She wasn't close to her own sister and she'd pretty much made Belinda's childhood a living hell most of the time, but if anything had ever happened to her sister because of Marisela, she wasn't sure what she'd do.

She banged the steering wheel with the heels of her hand. Craig Bennett hadn't been lying when he said that Rebecca Manning had been alive when she left their campsite, and she completely understood why neither he nor the Hightowers had been forthcoming about their activities on the island. No way would a now-married congressman want the public to know what he'd experimented with in his youth.

"Evan kept your secret all these years?"

She nodded. "And I kept his. I never told anyone what Evan had done because it was too late for Becca, and I didn't want him to go to jail for something I did. *I* didn't want to go to jail. We made a pact to keep quiet, and so far as I know, he never broke it."

"Did you ever speak to him after that?"

Tracy shook her head mournfully. "He was the one who convinced his school to donate a plot so Rebecca could be buried at Forest Hills. Every once in a while, he'd send a note, asking how I was. A card at Christmas. Flowers on my birthday. But the memories were so painful, I could never bring myself to respond. After a while, he stopped trying to contact me."

Marisela ran her hand through her hair, tugging at the roots to waylay the threatening headache. "He must have kept your pact, even if you did ignore his attempts to contact you. Craig Bennett didn't know what Evan had done, I'm sure of it. But then—how did the assassin find out?"

Tracy grabbed the dashboard in front of her. "I never told anyone, I swear. Except . . . "

"Your brother?"

Tracy squeezed her eyes shut. "Yes, but he was grateful to Evan for protecting me. That's why he stopped pushing the prosecutors for indictments, why I know Parker would never dig all this up again. He kept blaming the guys for Rebecca's death just to keep up appearances. He knew the truth."

Marisela decided to look at the situation from another angle. "Okay, so maybe Parker didn't tell your secret. Who else could have? You were on drugs for a long time. Maybe you told someone while strung out and you just don't remember."

Tracy's shoulders sagged as she pressed her lips tightly together. She nodded and her crying renewed. "Evan didn't have to die! None of them did. They didn't do anything! I killed her, accident or not. If anyone deserves to die, it's me!"

With gentle force, Marisela grabbed Tracy by the shoulders. "Stop it, okay? Stop it! You *don't* deserve to die. It was an accident and you know it. Trouble is, the assassin doesn't know it—and until I can find her, you might just be next."

After an emotional debriefing at the Titan office, Marisela rode along as Max deposited Tracy in a safe house tucked into a well-guarded Boston neighborhood and posted four guards—two inside the house and two outside—to watch out for her night and day. They'd taken a circuitous route, doubled back three times and worked in conjunction with at least four separate vehicles who'd acted as both decoys and lookouts. By the time they'd tucked Tracy away, Marisela was relatively sure that Tracy was safe. Ninety-nine percent. But it was that errant one percent that could get her killed.

She rendezvoused with Frankie, and after he recounted his findings from his interrogation with the barn patrol, they decided that interviewing Parker Manning was their next move. Frantic telephone calls from his sister had yet to yield any response—the guards were monitoring Tracy's cell phone—so they decided it was time to return to the guy's pigsty apartment.

The minute they exited the stairs onto Parker Manning's floor, the hair on Marisela's neck stood on end. Frankie must have experienced the same sensation because his arm immediately shot out, stopping her before she could take another step.

It was the music.

It was loud, too loud to be contained behind a closed door.

Which was why she wasn't surprised to see Parker's door gaping open.

They pulled their weapons, but kept them partially hidden beneath their jackets. Behind them, the elevator slid open and someone exited. Marisela dashed behind a tall potted plant and Frankie turned, gun returned to his holster, his smile friendly.

The guy, a twenty-something in jogging shorts with an iPod strung from his ears, started at Frankie's presence. He recovered quickly, pulling himself up to his full height, which wasn't that impressive.

"May I help you?" he asked, popping out his ear buds.

"Nah, man," Frankie said, jerking his thumb over his shoulder. "I'm a friend of Manning's. Thought it might be him riding up."

The guy eyed the elevator doors. "How'd you get up here?"

"Stairs."

The young guy sniffed haughtily. "Well, tell your pal to turn down that . . . music." He disappeared into his apartment without so much as a backward glance.

Marisela came out from her hiding place. "Not exactly the curious sort, is he?"

"No, but we'd better be. Clearly, Manning cut out without our guy's noticing. He runs with a dangerous crowd. He wouldn't leave his door open."

"Meaning?"

"Meaning maybe he didn't go by choice."

"How'd our guys miss a kidnapping?"

"Didn't say they did. But they were watching the exits, not the apartment. Someone experienced could have snuck him out."

"Experienced? Like the mob?"

Frankie shrugged.

They looked inside, but didn't enter. The apartment was a bigger mess than before—completely and totally ransacked. Drawers and file cabinets were upturned and broken. What was left of his laptop computer lay in a puddle of components on the floor. The stereo blasted on a hard rock station, making Marisela flinch as the guitars screeched and drums pounded with grueling, bass explosions.

"Stay here and watch the hall," Frankie said. He pulled surgical gloves out of his back pocket and snapped the booties plumbers use over his black athletic shoes before drawing his weapon and slipping inside.

Wow, look at him. Mr. Prepared.

Marisela volleyed her gaze between following Frankie as he slipped through the apartment and monitoring the hallway for any unusual activity. If someone called the cops to complain about the noise, then she and Frankie might be suspected of causing the chaos. Once Frankie turned off the blaring radio, Marisela knocked on the nearest neighbor's door.

"No answer," Marisela reported, holstering her gun. Frankie brought her gloves and booties, explaining that with the precautions, they wouldn't leave any evidence of their presence if the cops showed up. She entered Parker's apartment cautiously, noting that the lock bore no signs of a break-in. Frankie came out of the back bedroom. "No sign of Manning."

She pointed to the papers strewn around the room. "That his book?"

Frankie winced. "Now it's confetti."

"Think someone took him?"

"*Yo no sé*," Frankie replied. "But it doesn't look good."

Marisela strolled around, looking for anything a second set of eyes might pick out, trying to ignore the fact that if Tracy Manning had followed her advice earlier that afternoon, she might have stumbled into her brother's apartment just when the damage was being done. She also thought about the promises she'd made to Tracy to retrieve her errant brother—the last remaining member of her family. What kind of damage would his sister sustain if Parker Manning couldn't be found?

To distract herself from that line of thinking, Marisela pushed the play button on Manning's answering machine. The light hadn't been blinking, but she wanted to see if Manning had gotten his messages earlier that day. A mechanical recording announced the date and time and played the last message received. Today. Four hours ago.

Then, the message. The voice, female and distinctly Hispanic, rattled Marisela's soul.

"Señor Manning, it's time we meet face-to-face.

The mood has changed and there is more I want. Go to the Alhambra, tonight, at ten-thirty P.M. Don't be late."

Frankie pushed the stop button, then rewind, and played the message again. Marisela locked her gaze with his as the words replayed. The sound, the intonation, the accent. All familiar.

All Yizenia.

"¡Coño! He did hire her, that son of a bitch," she said.

Frankie held his hand up, palm out. "Don't jump to conclusions. This could be a setup."

Good point. "For us?"

He pocketed the tape. "Pretty clever way to manipulate us, *verdad*? Make us think we're close to catching the killer when she's the one catching us?"

"To kill us?"

Frankie shrugged and continued looking around.

Great. Marisela was the first to admit she preferred being the hunter rather than the hunted. And yet, she knew this was an opportunity they couldn't ignore.

"The new message light wasn't blinking," Marisela pointed out. "Parker has heard this message."

"Or someone else has."

Who'd heard the tape didn't matter. The chance that the message was left as bait didn't matter. Not to Marisela. At ten-thirty tonight, she would be at the Alhambra. At ten-thirty tonight, she'd finally stop Yizenia Santiago—one way or another.

❖

Prepping to intercept Yizenia at the restaurant took about two hours, giving Marisela and Frankie time to return to the hotel and change before heading to the Jamaica Plain restaurant called Alhambra. Frankie entered first, but was still waiting to be seated when Marisela strolled inside.

The space was both intimate and exclusive. The cuisine was Hispanic fusion, a varied mixture of dishes from Spain, influenced by the native cultures she had conquered. From the Moorish archways to the paintings of Spanish conquistadors on the walls, Marisela found the décor rich and exotic. As if she'd stepped into another world.

"*Bienvenidos a la Alhambra*," the hostess greeted, her accent shaky. "Do you have a reservation?"

Frankie shifted into the ruby light beaming over the hostess's podium, giving Marisela a chance to admire how *delicioso* he looked. His black shirt, black pants, and black tie, paired with his still sinfully long hair and trimmed moustache, made him look every ounce a Hollywood-style hood. He spoke in hushed tones to the hostess, and it was no surprise to Marisela that in about ten seconds flat, he had the woman flushed, giggling, and rushing to find a table for him despite his lack of a reservation. It was just after ten fifteen. As per their plan, Frankie would take a position near the back of the restaurant. Marisela would linger near the front.

The hostess returned, fanning herself with the wine list.

Marisela turned her back toward the hostess stand and pretended to comb her hand through her hair. When her watchband was level with her mouth, she whispered into the communications device. "Any sign of Parker Manning?"

"No," Frankie reported, his voice clear and crisp in her earpiece, hidden by her hair. "Yizenia?"

Marisela turned, careful not to make eye contact with anyone. She scanned the open dining area for any women sitting alone, catching sight of two. One was an older woman, in her seventies at least, who after a few minutes was joined by a younger girl who could have been a granddaughter. The second, with her back to Marisela, had long dark hair. She looked about the right height and build, but it was hard to tell since she was sitting.

Impatiently, she walked to the entrance where she looked out the window, as if she were waiting for her dining companion to arrive.

"Check out three o'clock," she suggested to Frankie. "Black hair, burgundy dress."

A pause. "Looks a little young, but you've seen her, not me. Wait for Parker, then we'll make a move."

Marisela acknowledged his plan, then continued to wander near the front entrance. A foursome came in. The hostess seated them. Marisela checked the time. Ten-twenty. She glanced outside. No sign of Parker.

The hostess finally approached. "May I seat you?"

Marisela turned on her friendliest smile. "No, thank you. I'm early. I told my date I'd meet him here. I guess

I should have let him pick me up so I wouldn't be so antsy right now."

The act clearly worked. The hostess, who had wise blue eyes set off by her short, blond bob, grinned back and waved her hand knowingly. "Oh, first date. How about if I get you something from the bar?"

"No, thanks," Marisela replied. "I need a clear head."

"You sure? A little white wine might take the edge off."

The woman's accent was distinctly Bostonian. She didn't sound like the Gordon's Fisherman, but there was a slight widening of vowel sounds that made Marisela smile. "Actually, this is a blind date. I've got to be sober in case I need to make a quick getaway."

Another couple walked in, forcing the hostess back to her job for a few more minutes and allowing Marisela a chance to glance out the door. From behind, she also watched the dark-haired woman still sitting alone at the table. The waiter had brought her a glass of red wine. When she lifted the goblet to her lips, Marisela could have sworn she saw a flash of red on her wrist, tucked beneath a gaudy, beaded bracelet.

It was her.

She moved to alert Frankie when the whoosh of the front door opening from the sidewalk forced her to spin out of the way. The man grumbled loudly as he fought to extract himself from his raincoat, and Marisela instantly looked for cover.

Parker Manning had arrived, cigarette dangling from his lips.

"Sir! Sir! I'm sorry, but we do not allow smoking in here," the hostess said, charging forward and shaking her finger like a nun catching her students chewing gum on the playground.

The distraction gave Marisela a chance to disappear. She spied the half-door of the coat-check room and without hesitation slipped inside.

She listened as the friendly hostess soothed the man's objections and escorted him to his seat.

"See Manning?" she said into the watchband.

"Yeah," Frankie answered.

"Does he see you?"

Marisela leaned out of the half-door and watched as the hostess attempted to hand Parker Manning a menu, which he waved away and immediately barked an order for a beer. He had his back to Frankie. Perfect. As soon as the hostess headed toward the bar, Parker leaned in close to his dinner companion—the brunette in burgundy. With his eyes narrowed and his lips strained into a line as he spoke, he was clearly trying to control both his volume and his temper. He might be meeting Yizenia Santiago, but he wasn't happy about it.

Behind them, Marisela saw Frankie lean back in his seat, perusing what she assumed was the wine list, as if he had endless knowledge of vintages, when in truth, if it didn't come with a twist top, Frankie wouldn't drink it. When the waiter came out of the bar with Manning's beer, Frankie waylaid him with a quick whistle. The waiter hurried over, and through her earpiece, she heard a riveting discussion of which wine went best with tonight's special filet mignon.

The waiter set down his tray, giving Frankie the chance to slip a miniscule listening device onto the bottle of beer. Not fifteen seconds later, it was delivered to the table where Parker Manning and Yizenia chatted. The waiter poured the beer into a frosted glass, then, thankfully, left the bottle on the table.

"I'm going to drink this and then get the hell out of here. So you'd better talk fast."

That from Manning.

"Having second thoughts?"

For an instant, Marisela thought the question came from Yizenia—until she spied the restaurant hostess looking at her in the coat-check room with about a dozen questions dancing in her eyes.

Marisela scooted out of the closet.

"You could say that," she replied.

"Life is funny, isn't it?" the hostess said, inviting Marisela closer to her station with a quick nod of her head. She shoved a silver bowl overflowing with rainbow-coated chocolate mints across the top of the podium. "You finally get the invitation to the big date, you go out once or twice and find the experience interesting. Exciting. But little by little, you want more. More thrills, more passion. More . . . purpose."

Marisela nodded and popped a few mints in her mouth. Splitting her attention between the hostess and the conversation at Parker Manning's table made her head spin.

"I don't know what you're talking about," Parker insisted.

"Of course you do," Yizenia replied, though the sound of her voice rankled. There was an accent, yes. But a fake one. More Frito Bandito than Frida Kahlo.

It wasn't her.

Marisela started into the restaurant, but the hostess stopped her. "Do you see your date? Don't tell me your destiny has been waiting for you the whole time while you've been talking to me?"

Frankie locked eyes with Marisela. He stood and started toward the table. Slowly, casually. The whispered conversation between the fake Yizenia and Parker Manning never faltered. He either didn't know he was talking to an imposter, or the whole deal was a setup as Frankie had believed.

Marisela grinned at the hostess. "No, but I see an old friend."

The hostess grabbed her by the arm, her grip tight. Marisela opened her mouth to demand release, but the woman stopped her objection mid-syllable.

"Just don't settle. There are so many choices in the world for women like us. Remember that."

Who was she? Dear Abby? Marisela nodded and turned away, making slow progress through the restaurant, trying not to draw any undue attention. If Parker Manning saw them, he might run.

Her guess was right. In the seconds between Manning making eye contact with her and his leaping to his feet, Frankie had positioned himself directly behind the reporter. Frankie pressed gently down on Parker's shoulders, and with a friendly slap on the back, confined the man to his seat.

The woman made no move to run. Marisela wanted to grab the imposter's wrist and yank her out of her chair, but instead she dragged a chair over, sat down with a laugh, and complimented the woman on her gaudy bracelet.

"I've been looking for one like this for so long! It's beautiful."

With a twist, Marisela turned the woman's wrist toward Frankie. Yeah, she had a tattoo, all right—one drawn on with Magic Marker. Perfect from a distance, but useless from close-up.

The woman looked downright terrified.

"Who are you?" Marisela asked.

The woman only stuttered.

"Who hired you?" This time, Marisela twisted her wrist for emphasis.

Parker Manning objected loudly. "Let her go! You're interrupting a business dinner."

"We're interrupting a sting," Frankie said.

"What are you talking about?" Parker asked.

"You think this is her, don't you? The hired killer taking out those guys who hurt your sister? But they didn't really hurt your sister, did they?"

Manning sat back, his body language cocky. "This woman offered me her story and I took her up on it."

"When?" Marisela asked.

"Right after she popped Cole. She called."

"And you failed to share this detail with the police? Or with us?"

The woman tried to stand, but Marisela had not released her wrist. She whimpered. Marisela silenced her with a deadly look.

Manning swigged his beer. "I wanted the story. And I wanted her to succeed. Those creeps might not have killed my sister, but they drove her and Tracy to ruin their own lives. Maybe not Bennett so much, but Hightower for leading her on. Using her to cover up what he was. And Cole. He dumped my sister in a marsh."

"He saved Tracy from being publicly blamed for Rebecca's murder," Marisela corrected.

"It was an accident!" Parker insisted. "She would never have been charged."

"Maybe not, but Evan Cole was trying to protect Tracy and you know it. He didn't deserve to die."

Manning's eyes sparked with hatred and recrimination. Toward whom, Marisela wasn't sure and she didn't care. Right now, she simply wanted Yizenia Santiago—the real Yizenia Santiago—in her clutches instead of this poor excuse for a look-alike.

"Who ransacked your apartment?" Marisela asked.

He glanced longingly at his beer. "I couldn't find my recorder."

"The loud music? The door left open?"

"I was in a hurry, okay?"

"Bullshit," Marisela snapped. "You wanted us here and you set us up to think you might be in trouble. Little nervous about meeting with a killer, maybe? Wanted us as backup?"

He didn't deny the accusation, but the point was, his motives didn't matter. He still didn't realize he'd been duped.

"If she was really selling you her story, why'd she send an imposter to meet with you?" Marisela asked, turning toward the woman she still held tightly in place.

"You're hurting me," the woman insisted.

"No kidding, really?" Marisela asked, her tone ice cold.

The woman's eyes widened. "Who are you?"

"Someone who can make the woman who hired you tonight look like Mother Theresa, that's who. Answer our questions and you'll get out of this with all your bones intact, ¿comprendo? We just need answers."

The woman's face paled. "She said the whole thing was a joke, to teach a reporter a lesson about asking too many questions. She paid me to give him the runaround, make him look idiotic if he printed anything in the paper! That's all! I swear! Look, if my boss finds out, I'm going to lose my job."

"Boss? What boss?"

"The owner of the restaurant."

"You work here?" Marisela asked, a tingle dancing its way up the back of her spine. "Oh, God." A realization hit her.

Marisela glanced over her shoulder. As she suspected, the friendly hostess was gone. The one with the blue eyes. Contacts. And the hair? Either a quick dye-and-cut job or a very convincing wig.

"I'm the hostess."

Marisela growled as she tore to her feet, causing a clatter of flatware and china and crystal. Patrons of the restaurant turned to gawk, but Marisela was through the crowded dining room before anyone could stop her. She reached the hostess's stand to find it deserted. Well, almost.

Propped up in the bowl of chocolate mints was a flower. Deep red, trumpet-shaped, with ruffled edges on a dark green stem.

Yizenia had escaped yet again.

Or had she?

Sixteen

MARISELA DASHED OUT of the restaurant, startled when a dark burgundy sports car screeched to a stop in front of her. The tinted window slid down and Ian, his pale green eyes intense, motioned to the passenger door.

"We have her," he said. "Get in."

Marisela hadn't even slammed the door when Ian pulled back into traffic. He maneuvered the vehicle with skill, practically leaping over the potholes and elevated manhole covers and weaving around slow-moving cars.

"You picked her up?"

He shook his head, his grip firm on the steering wheel and stick shift. "Not yet. We needed confirmation, which you just provided."

Marisela opened her palm. The silk flower was crushed in her hand.

"How'd you spot her?"

"Brynn was stationed on the roof across the street with night-vision binoculars. She recognized Yizenia when she fled the restaurant. We've tailed several women tonight, but the minute I heard you on the com system, I knew we'd found our killer."

Marisela couldn't miss the keen determination in Ian's voice. He clearly had a personal vendetta to settle. What she didn't know was why he'd waited to retrieve her before he made his move on Yizenia.

"She doesn't know, does she? About Tracy? About the fact that the guys were innocent?"

Ian shook his head. "Brynn is convinced Yizenia has no idea, that she bought whatever line her client fed her. If Yizenia knew the real story, she never would have pursued Craig Bennett or Raymond Hightower."

"She would have hit Tracy, for certain. Evan, too, maybe, for dumping the body."

"Exactly," Ian confirmed.

Figuring out the truth had only plunged them deeper into a web of lies and death. Before, they had an assassin on the loose who was following a relatively clear-cut pattern. Now she was a wild card, operating

on who knew what kind of faulty information. Tracy
was in a safe house, but Marisela wouldn't rest until
Yizenia was stopped from her misguided mission—
once and for all.

"Is Yizenia still under surveillance?"

Ian touched the screen on his GPS system. A red
dot flashed.

Marisela whistled, impressed. "You tagged her?"

Concentrated confidence ratcheted up Ian's smile.
"Max called it a classic twist on the bump and run."

Pickpocket slang. Just what had Max done before
he joined Titan?

"She's on foot, probably headed home," Ian informed her, after touching his earpiece. He had agents
up ahead of them. No way would they lose her.

Marisela's brain swam as her eyes focused on the
blinking red dot. They were so close. Close to catching the killer. Close to ending the case. "What was
her point of the meeting in the restaurant? She never
actually spoke to Parker Manning and I don't think
she intended to. The stand-in she hired thought the
whole thing was a joke. The only person she spoke to
was—"

"You," Ian said.

He cut around a corner a little sharp, throwing
Marisela sideways. Their shoulders touched. The look
he gave her, though brief, brimmed with speculation.

"What?" she asked defensively.

"Why did Yizenia speak with you and no one
else?"

"You heard the conversation," she reminded him, not liking the accusatory tone of his voice. "She didn't say anything that even made sense."

He glanced at the GPS and made another turn through a dark alley, slowing to avoid the trash cans piled along the walls. "I was listening. Were you?"

She frowned. "Only halfway. To me, she was just some chick making small talk. I was trying to focus on the conversation at the table, remember?"

Ian pulled out onto a narrow street, then slowly eased into a parking space, slipping into the tight spot with ease. The red dot had stopped moving. He put the car in park, then contacted Max and asked him to cue back the conversation Marisela had had with the fake hostess—with Yizenia.

She winced as her voice, Yizenia's voice, Parker Manning's and the duped, genuine hostess's overlapped.

"Max, isolate Marisela's conversation with the hostess," Ian ordered. "Play back Yizenia only. The real Yizenia."

"You finally get the invitation to the big date, you go out once or twice and find the experience interesting. Exciting. But little by little, you want more. More thrills, more passion. More . . . purpose."

Marisela listened carefully. "She wasn't talking about men, was she?"

Ian shook his head. "I believe she was talking about Titan. About your career choices. After you shared your theory with Max regarding Yizenia's coming to your rescue last night, I pinned my sister down for more information regarding her old friend."

"I would have liked to have seen that," she quipped.

He smirked. "Figure of speech, I assure you. Shortly after I hired you, Brynn requested a copy of your dossier. She also remembered that she'd been with Yizenia when she read it and that she mentioned you in conversation."

Marisela wasn't sure why, but the whole idea creeped her out. "Why would she do that?"

"My sister thought I was losing my mind."

Marisela didn't like that answer any better. "Nice. What did Brynn tell her about me?"

"Do you honestly care?"

She took a second to think about it. There was nothing a Titan dossier could tell her that she didn't already know about her own life. "Not particularly."

"The bottom line is that Yizenia seemed very interested in you, asking all sorts of questions, which according to Brynn struck her as idle conversation between friends. Her opinion has since changed. It seems clear that Yizenia set up this meeting tonight to draw you out. Talk to you."

"What does she want with me?"

Ian grinned, opened the glove compartment on the sports car and extracted a long, thin leather case. "That's what you're about to find out."

❖

Yizenia dialed the number one more time. When the recording came on yet again, she slammed the phone down on the cradle. Disconnected? How dare he! In all her years, a client had never treated her with such disregard. The remainder of her fee had shown up this morning in her Swiss account, yet how could he possibly believe the job was completed?

One man remained. The man who had been key to the whole sordid tale.

Bradley Hightower.

Yizenia dragged her fingers through her hair, disconnected the clips that held the blond hairpiece in place and threw it across the table. She massaged her scalp, trying to ward off the suspicions surging through her bloodstream. Why would her client back off now? That they hadn't found Bradley Hightower yet was simply a setback. A delay. He'd clearly hidden himself well, likely because he understood the true magnitude of what he'd done as a young man—first, lying to girls too naïve and too starstruck by his family's money and power to grasp the full breadth of his betrayal, and then killing one when she became inconvenient, thus dooming the other to a downward spiral of loss and despondency.

Her client had provided a detailed account of Tracy Manning's life. Locked in a cycle of self-destruction, the young woman had clearly never recovered from the tragedy of her sister's murder. Yizenia knew the girl's hopelessness. Her loneliness. Her rage. Didn't she deserve justice?

How could a man who claimed to have been Tracy's lover lose his stomach now for the violence of real retribution?

While Yizenia had hoped to have a message from her client awaiting her return, tonight hadn't been a total loss. She kicked off her shoes and reveled in the opportunity she'd had to watch Marisela work, up close. She could be crude, but effective. Under Yizenia's guidance, she could learn style. She could excel.

But how to lure her? What would a woman like Marisela Morales need in order to tempt her into the vocation of revenge for hire?

Yizenia was twisting her arms around her back to release her zipper when she heard the click. Instantly, the atmosphere in the room shifted. Someone had come into her apartment. Yizenia continued to undo her dress. No need to alert her intruder.

She moved casually toward her bedroom.

"You can stop right there."

When she heard the voice, Yizenia couldn't help but smile. She turned around, slowly, with her hands visible, since she assumed Marisela Morales had a gun.

She was right.

"You won't need that," Yizenia told Marisela, who held the weapon straight and steady.

"I'll be the judge of that, thanks." Marisela spared the apartment a quick glance. "You've moved up."

Yizenia grinned. Since abandoning her last apartment, she'd indulged in the nicest restored and furnished space she could find. This job in Boston had taken more time than she'd anticipated and she'd grown tired of living in squalor. The luxury of original polished hardwood floors, hand-carved masonry cornices, and luxurious hand-tooled leather furniture reminded her of home. The genuine Art Deco light fixture threw golden beams of light across the geometric patterns on the carpet and glinted like fire off the silver barrel of Marisela's LadySmith .357 five-shot revolver.

"I prefer to live in a certain style, *sí*. Nothing to be ashamed of."

"Okay, then let's try a little humility regarding your line of work."

Slowly, Yizenia lowered her hands. Marisela moved her gun only an inch, but her meaning was clear.

"I'm unarmed," Yizenia assured her. "I detest handguns. They lack elegance."

"They do the job."

Therein lay the difference between them. Yizenia admired the girl's raw courage, but she mourned her lack of sophistication. Still, standing in her presence electrified Yizenia with possibilities—and sapped her energy at the same time. Around Marisela, she felt both invigorated and old. The dichotomy fascinated her and repelled her, yet she couldn't curb her need to discover if Marisela was truly the one.

"Why did you follow me?" Yizenia asked. "The only way to stop me is to kill me. And if that were your aim, you would have done so by now."

"Not necessarily," Marisela said, her tone even. "First, I want to know why you sought me out."

"Are you so certain I did?"

Marisela rolled her eyes. "Why else did you lure Parker Manning to that restaurant when you had no intention of ever exchanging a word with him? You don't care about him. He's not your client."

Yizenia nodded. What did it matter if she shared this truth with Marisela? She had no intention of revealing her client's identity. She had a reputation to protect, standards to uphold. Protecting the identity of the client—even when the client had acted in ways that bordered on insulting—was as important to Yizenia as completing the job itself.

"How do you know you were my ultimate target tonight?" Yizenia asked. "Yes, I knew Titan was watching Parker Manning, and yes, I did initiate the meeting as a way to draw my opponents into the light. But perhaps I was simply looking for Ian again. I've been in this city longer than I planned. A woman cannot always fight her most intimate urges."

Marisela's mouth quirked. "Okay, yuck."

Yizenia laughed from deep in her belly. "You mean to say you do not desire this man? What's not to want? He's handsome, rich, powerful. No woman can resist that combination."

"You have no idea what I can and cannot resist. So if you're trying to make me jealous, you're wasting your time."

Yizenia laughed again. "*Mija,* I make it a rule never to waste anything."

"Then let's not waste any more words. Why did you

want to talk with me? What about me interests you?"

"Isn't it obvious?"

Yizenia raised her wrist, tugging back her sleeve so that her tattoo was bright and visible, even in the dim light.

"We are both so very much alike," Yizenia said.

Marisela's eyes narrowed. "So you have a tattoo. So do I. Big deal."

"It's not the marking itself, *mi hermana*. It's the symbolism. *El espíritu*. Your tattoo comes from your gang, *sí*? From the women who taught you the power of violence."

"And the consequences of it."

Yizenia sniffed. "You try to convince me now that you are peaceful?"

Marisela snickered. "Not likely. But I'm not reckless."

"And I am? Child, if that's what you think, you have not been paying proper attention."

"Oh, I'm paying very close attention. I want to know why you're in my business. What do I have to do with you?"

Yizenia glanced at her watch. She supposed the time had come to answer a few questions, to begin the dialogue she'd been toying with instigating for days now, perhaps months. She'd been intrigued by Marisela Morales since the first time she'd heard her name. The invitation to work in Boston had been a twist of fate— a dictate of destiny. Best to take advantage of the situation now rather than later. Because later, she will have slipped away.

"I will tell you what you need to know," Yizenia promised. "After you lower your weapon. You may hold it, of course, if it makes you feel . . . safer around me."

The dig sparked a snort. "Yeah, well, I think I will hang onto this, thanks. You being the big, bad, and all. See, not reckless."

American sarcasm. The lack of wit amazed her.

Yizenia gestured to a long couch in the parlor area. Marisela took the seat nearest the door, forcing Yizenia to sit with her back to the window. Yizenia admired the woman's keen strategic move and for a moment considered that her escape would be difficult. Yizenia had no doubt that Marisela had not come here alone. Her colleagues from Titan were likely monitoring their every move, listening to every word they exchanged. This annoyed Yizenia rather than worried her. She'd always planned this conversation to be private, but she'd reveal nothing of consequence—except to Marisela.

"Brynn is aware that I'm here?" Yizenia asked.

Marisela cradled the gun in her lap casually, but with the barrel still pointing directly at Yizenia and her hand still firm on the grip. "She helped us find you."

Yizenia smiled. "She's a smart woman. I had no illusions that she'd retain any loyalty to me once I betrayed her trust by seeking you out."

"Then there's that little matter of you trying to kill our client."

"Business is business. Next time we meet, I'll bring her a bottle of her favorite cognac. It's a very rare vintage and very expensive."

"Money doesn't impress me."

Yizenia leaned forward, looking deep into Marisela's onyx eyes. "What does impress you?"

"Why do you care?"

Single-minded. Another useful quality.

"You interest me."

"I'm not flattered."

"You should be. I'm a very discriminating woman."

"You're a killer. You take money and you gun people down in cold blood. How, exactly, does that make you believe you're so damned superior?"

"The people I kill have nothing but cold blood."

Marisela's mouth twisted derisively. "Right. You're this great avenger. Just out of curiosity, who died and made you judge, jury, and executioner?"

Yizenia bristled. "If you must know, my mother, my father and my two sisters. They were gunned down at the family dinner table by the agents of the Spanish government because my father dared to speak out against them."

Marisela's eyes didn't falter. "Why didn't they kill you, too?"

"Who says they didn't?"

Yizenia had answered too quickly. She hadn't guarded her words or her tone. She closed her eyes, took a deep breath, and regained her composure. Yizenia was no young upstart, overconfident and brash. She knew her limits, her weaknesses. Emotion was something she could not easily dismiss, but she had to hold her feelings close, keep them in control, or else she'd act in anger, haste, and ultimately, in error.

Marisela's expression was neither cold nor expressive, but somewhere in between. She too understood the advantage of restraint, though she wasn't as practiced in the art as Yizenia.

"It was luck, perhaps, that saved my life," Yizenia continued. "I prefer to think of it as fate. I was not mortally wounded. And when it was discovered that I had lived, the government decided to draft me into their service. My father was already dead—my death would have served nothing. So they spared my life. I learned my skills within the shadows of Franco's army, but once I was old enough and smart enough, I realized I should focus on pursuing my own interests. A change in regime made my defection possible."

"And you took up as a killer for hire?"

"I offered my services to others, yes, but only after I picked off, one by one, the *degradados* who killed my family."

Yizenia stopped trying to hide her disdain, her abject hatred, the emotion that had driven her here. Perhaps Marisela Morales was not the right woman to take her place. She hadn't tasted the bitter flavor of despair, of an anger so driving, her soul would surrender without a fight.

"You should be glad that I possess such talent or that man you sleep with, the one with the dark skin and intriguing hazel eyes, would be dead right now with a bullet in his back."

The look of triumph in Marisela's eyes was unmistakable. "So it was you."

Yizenia waved her hand dismissively. "Who else?"

Marisela arched a brow. "We were trying to track you down and you came to our rescue. Why?"

"You did not deserve death at the hands of *un criminal cualquiera*. He attacked first. You only defended yourselves."

"So it's true you never take on an assignment unless the targets deserve their fate," Marisela said.

"*Sí*," she confirmed with a nod.

"Then why kill Evan Cole? He wasn't on the island the night Rebecca Manning died."

"*Mentirosa*," Yizenia accused. "You know as well as I do that he was there."

Marisela arched a brow. "Actually, yes, I do. But here's the thing. *How* did you know? His presence was not common knowledge."

"I do not proceed without proof, Marisela. I'm not quick to believe the tales of angry men."

"But you're not imperfect."

Yizenia waved her hand dismissively. She supposed she was fallible, but she'd yet to be proven so.

"I'm human," she said.

"Some would argue with you on that," Marisela muttered. "Okay, then let's move on to Raymond Hightower, the younger brother? He was the first one you killed. What part did he play in Rebecca Manning's death?"

Yizenia considered the likelihood that she was

being recorded. Luckily, she knew enough about American laws to know that any recording would be inadmissible in the court system here. If the police needed proof of her involvement in the murders, they'd need to look no further than the bedroom, where she'd stashed her rifle.

"Raymond Hightower drove Rebecca Manning to her death. He coaxed her to the island on his brother's orders so they could kill her and dump her body in the swamp. Why are you asking me all this? You know the truth. You've interviewed Tracy Manning yourself."

Marisela turned her body and sat back against the armrest. "Yes, I have. But obviously, you haven't. The truth you think you know has been twisted, Yizenia. You're killing without cause."

Yizenia scoffed, but the sparkle in Marisela's eyes— so confident, so suddenly clear, as if the pieces of the puzzle had finally fallen into place—caused a shiver up her spine.

"I've no need to speak with Tracy. Someone contacted me on her behalf."

"That may be, but whoever contacted you is a liar."

Ian watched from a distance as Marisela led Yizenia out of the apartment building, the assassin's rifle, encased in leather, slung over her arm. Her own weapon, the muzzle obviously pressed against Yizenia's back, remained out of sight. Marisela had done exceptionally well. Yizenia, likely for reasons she'd never share, had spoken openly with his agent. The deaths of Raymond Hightower and Evan Cole, the critical injuries of Congressman Bennett, the chaos reintroduced into the lives of Parker and Tracy Manning had been sparked by nothing more than lies.

His passenger door opened and Frank slid inside.

"Where's Manning?" Ian asked.

"On ice. Wants to see his sister," Frank replied, his eyes trained on Marisela as she put Yizenia in the back of Max's sedan and the car pulled away from the curb. Ian didn't start the ignition, but instead turned to the agent beside him.

"What do you want, Frank?"

"Out."

"You had your chance," Ian said. He'd wanted nothing more than to rid himself of this macho asshole for years, but Brynn had forbidden his dismissal. After Frank's shooting in Puerto Rico, he'd given the agent another chance to walk away on his own, with a hefty bonus that would have kept him in gold chains and guayaberas for the rest of his life. Frank had turned him down. "You chose to stay."

Frank's expression, aimed out the windshield, was dark and inscrutable.

"I thought Marisela needed me," Frank replied.

"I could have told you otherwise."

"Your opinion don't mean shit."

"Honestly?" Ian asked, exaggerating his offense. "And all this time I thought I'd been your mentor."

"Fuck you," Frank shot back.

"And that's what this is all about, isn't it? Who fucks whom?"

Frank's rage was carefully checked, but the fire behind his eyes told Ian he'd better proceed with caution. They had Yizenia in their custody. For the time being, Craig Bennett and the elusive Bradley Hightower were safe from her bullets of retribution. He couldn't allow Frank to divide his focus.

"Life's all about who fucks *whom*," Frank replied.

"Right now, my life is simply about retaining Titan's stellar reputation for investigation and personal protection."

"You sent Marisela in, alone, to talk to a killer who may or may not have some freaky obsession with her."

Ian contained a grin. "You better than anyone know that Marisela is incredibly resourceful, that she can take care of herself. Don't pretend you were worried about her."

The sharp snap of Frank's eyes could have sliced right through him. "What does that bitch want with her?"

Ian wished he knew the answer to Frank's question. The tone in Yizenia's voice had raised his hackles, but Marisela seemed to handle the situation with aplomb. He'd underestimated his newest operative once—and Ian wasn't the type of man to make the same mistake twice.

"We'll find out soon enough, I suppose. Right now, the only question we should concern ourselves with is what do we want from Yizenia?"

"The name of her client," Frank responded.

Ian pursed his lips. "She'll never talk."

Frank chuckled. "She's never dealt with Marisela, *verdad?*"

Despite his best efforts, Ian grinned. "I can't argue that point, even with you."

Seventeen

"WE DON'T HAVE A CHOICE."

Marisela slammed her hand on Ian's desk. Frankie watched Ian and Brynn exchange glances that if he wasn't wrong bordered first on confused and then on understanding. He shut his eyes tightly. *Dios mio,* they were finally beginning to understand how Marisela ticked, how she thought, what pushed her and prodded her to need to win, no matter the price.

He'd understood her for years, but a damn lot of good it did him. As much as he wanted to deny the truth, he knew now they were on different paths. He was ready to jump off this train and she was panting after a longer, faster ride. He wanted to do what he wanted when he wanted—she'd already lived that life. He'd tried to care about this case, but the only thing he really cared about was protecting Marisela. And since she'd done a damned good job of that on her own—facing down a professional killer and coming out on top—he had to stop fooling himself. His excuse for staying was gone.

Except that he still wanted to work with her, be around her, make love to her whenever he had the chance. But what would that make him if he stuck around in a job he hated just for that?

"I agree with Marisela," Frankie said. "Tracy Manning is tougher than you think. Look at all she's been through."

"Her brother won't allow it," Brynn said.

"Her brother doesn't have a fucking choice," Marisela insisted. "Let me talk to her. I'm telling you, she wants to know the whole truth. She's folding under the pressure of knowing that Evan Cole was killed in her honor. She needs to confront Yizenia. And only after Yizenia sees how wrong she is about what really happened that night will she give up the name of her client."

Frankie watched Ian. He was listening, considering, working out the logistics of Marisela's plan. Frankie could practically see the cogs turning behind those cold blue eyes. Frankie knew Ian would still screw Marisela the first chance he got—or screw her over—

but he'd do it knowing that he'd lose a good agent in the aftermath. Maybe that would be enough to keep him from jumping her at the first opportunity.

"Listen to her, Brynn," Frankie said, making eye contact with the reluctant Blake twin. "Yizenia isn't going to give up her client's name until she's convinced she was tricked. That her honor has been betrayed. And the only person who can do that is Tracy Manning."

Brynn stood in the corner near the bookcase, her frown marring her china-doll face. "Yizenia will suspect that this is all a ruse. And even if we do convince her, she won't care. She'd go to prison before she ruined her reputation."

"Maybe ten years ago," Marisela said, her eyes narrowed. "Maybe thirty when she was first building that reputation she's protecting. Going to prison now for murder means dying there."

"And her client will only hire someone else to finish the job," Frankie added.

Ian rubbed the darkening shadows on his chin. They'd been in deep discussion since returning last night from Jamaica Plain. None of them, with the exception of Yizenia, who was being held in the penthouse apartment above the office, had gotten any sleep.

"We'll let Tracy state her case to Yizenia," Ian decided.

He glanced over his shoulder, but his sister had ceased her objections. She simply shook her head as if the exercise would be a waste of time. She knew Yizenia best. Frankie suspected she was right and that Yizenia would not trade the name of her client for her freedom, which would leave them with nothing.

"What about Brad Hightower?" Frankie asked. "Max said he had a lead."

Ian nodded. "He's following up right now. I think we should all get some rest and reconvene at the safe house at five o'clock. This show will be even more effective if we have the final player in the game."

Frankie stood and left, barely slowing when he heard Marisela behind him.

"So?" she said, knocking him in the shoulder. "I was right, wasn't I? About Yizenia shooting that guy in the alley? Saving your life?"

"Couldn't wait five seconds to remind me of that, could you?"

"No," she said, surprised. "Why should I? I was right."

He couldn't help the half-smile tugging at his lips. "Maybe you're right about a lot of things."

She stopped him by grabbing his sleeve. Her dark eyes narrowed and she crossed her arms tight, enhancing her chest until his mouth watered. "What else am I right about?"

Behind them, Ian and Brynn emerged from the office, their heads bent in serious discussion. Frankie grabbed Marisela's arm and led her around a corner, then swiped his key card, leading her into an unoccupied office. He didn't bother with the light. In the dark, he held both of Marisela's hands behind her back and nuzzled her neck, inhaling her scent, so rich and addictive. She surrendered to his assault for a moment, then twisted out of his hold.

"What else am I right about?" she repeated.

A sliver of light glowed from the motion detector in the corner, slashing across her face and illuminating her plump lips. Sweet lips. Lips he'd miss.

And her eyes. So brown and rich, like fresh-brewed *café*. And so full of suspicion. She knew him so well. Knew when he was kidding around. And when he was dead serious.

"About me."

"What about you?"

"You said I was like a caged animal."

She blinked. Did she not remember? "So?" She slid her hands around his neck. "Does that mean more fun at the hotel before we catch up on our z's?"

Instantly, his body hardened. He found himself gritting his teeth, biting back the words he knew he had to say. She was always ready for a quick roll, even when she pretended to resist. But that wasn't enough for Frankie anymore—one more reason why he had to leave.

"That's up to you." He splayed his hands around her waist, up her back, across her shoulder blades, pressing her close so that her breasts tortured him and her *concha* slid across his dick and awakened every nerve ending in his body. "I take it you've forgiven me for not listening to you about Yizenia saving my ass?"

"No," she said, her face so close to his, he could see her eyes glittering. "But I can let you make it up to me."

She kissed him and her mouth was so hot and her tongue so aggressive, he decided to drop his bombshell later. After he'd made love to her. For the last time.

From a shadowy corner of the room, Marisela watched Yizenia pace back and forth in front of Tracy Manning, who sat on the couch of the nondescript safe house, weeping into her brother's chest. Parker Manning, for all his previous nastiness, melted in the wake of his sister's grief. He whispered to her soothingly, patted her hair, and interrupted his sister's confession only long enough to promise that he'd personally kill anyone who implicated Tracy in Rebecca's murder.

The threat fell on deaf ears, since no one in the room (Marisela, Tracy, Parker, and Yizenia) and no one listening in (Ian, Brynn, and Frankie) had any reason to want Tracy arrested.

They simply wanted Yizenia to tell them who had hired her.

When Yizenia's pacing swung her close to Marisela, she reached out and grabbed Yizenia's arm.

"Convinced?"

Yizenia's nostrils flared. "*Yo no soy estúpida. Sé la verdad cuando yo la oigo.*"

Marisela gave a curt nod. No, Yizenia wasn't stupid. But she'd thought her client had been telling the truth, hadn't she? And she'd been dead wrong.

"Will you tell us who ordered you to kill?"

"No one orders me," Yizenia insisted.

"He paid you," Marisela insisted. "He gave you just enough information to lead you to the wrong conclusion."

Yizenia yanked her arm out of Marisela's grip. "And for that, he'll pay."

"Give us his name," Marisela insisted. "We'll do the rest."

Yizenia's laugh was a derisive snicker. "What will you, the high-and-mighty Titan International, do that I cannot do better? You are bound by laws and lawsuits. And without me, you have no proof against him. Your court system will bring you no justice. He's not poor and unconnected. His power likely reaches far, just as that of those boys' families did so long ago."

Marisela narrowed her gaze, not liking where this conversation was heading. "You let Ian and Brynn worry about the court system and the influence of money and power. They've got a shitload of that, too."

Yizenia's tsk was narrowly close to a scornful spit. "I know Brynn. I've known Ian," she said, her voice suddenly husky. "But they're powerless to stop the inevitable and you know it."

Yizenia made a move toward the door, but Marisela blocked her path. Incensed, she stalked to the other side of the room and tucked herself into a corner much like Marisela had, only Yizenia's corner wasn't anywhere near the door, a window, or any other means of escape.

Sadly, the assassin had a point. Without her testimony and evidence, which would have to include her admission of guilt on her part in the attempted murder of Craig Bennett and the murders of Evan Cole and Raymond Hightower, they'd have an uphill battle proving a client even existed. But Marisela had survived enough uphill battles to not be deterred, especially once the door opened and Max strode in.

Their ace in the hole walked in directly behind him.

Bradley Hightower.

He was just as tall and handsome as Marisela had guessed he'd be. The last fifteen years had been kind to him in many ways. He was buff, tanned, and perfectly dressed from his tailored cotton shirt cuffed at the elbow to his loose linen slacks and twelve-hundred dollar John Lobb shoes. He wore aviator sunglasses, which he instantly ripped off his face, then waited for his eyes to adjust to the muted light. When the process was complete, he instantly spotted Tracy on the couch. He stepped toward her, but Parker jumped to his feet and blocked his way.

"Get away from her. You started all this. You're to blame!"

Bradley took a step back and sighed. "You're right. Evan and my brother are dead because of me." He spoke with the kind of assuredness that only men comfortable in their own skin could manage. He glanced back at Max, who stood stoically near the doorway, and continued, "I hadn't spoken to Raymond in years.

He'd become quite the daredevil, so his death on that mountaintop didn't surprise me. No one knew it was murder until the body was recovered, least of all the brother he hated."

"So you come out of the woodwork now, after your friends start dropping like flies?" Parker spat.

Though his generous lips quivered, Bradley Hightower folded his sunglasses and slid them into his pocket. "Tracy, I had no idea what you've gone through. Had I known, I would have come home. After my father sent me off to Europe to ensure that none of his rich friends found out his son was a fag, I promised myself never to return, never to dredge up that awful time again. Craig and I never meant to hurt anyone. We were just stupid kids fooling around. He wasn't gay. He deserved to live his life honestly and to have a career in politics without risking it all because of teenage experimentation. And you. That night burst your illusions about a lot of things. Did you really want me hanging around, reminding you every day of how I'd used you? I swear, Tracy. I was a stupid, selfish kid. You didn't deserve my lies. I'm so sorry."

Marisela tore her gaze away from the scene long enough to catch Yizenia take a tentative step toward Bradley Hightower, her fists clenched. Yizenia knew she no longer had the right to kill him for his supposed crimes, but the instinct hadn't yet died in her entirely.

Tracy grabbed Parker's arm and pulled herself to her feet. "I do understand."

"What?" Parker's skin flashed bright red and the veins in his temple and neck bulged. Marisela took a step forward, glancing to her left to ensure Max was still there, keeping Yizenia from taking off, but he signaled for her to remain where she was.

"Parker, please," Tracy said calmly. "Bradley didn't want any of this to happen. He cared about his friends. He loved his brother. Rebecca ruined *him*, remember? She outed him to hurt him—in front of me and his brother. She wanted to tear him apart—not the other way around."

Tracy opened her arms and Bradley immediately fell into them. Marisela watched, part entranced, part unnerved, by their instantaneous weeping. She heard Brad apologize, though she wasn't sure for what, while Tracy tried to explain how her sister could have been so cruel as to use his sexuality against him. Parker, frozen with shock, dropped back onto the couch. Yizenia had her back to them all.

Marisela decided that Tracy's capacity for forgiveness trumped anyone else she'd ever seen. Bradley Hightower used her and Rebecca—leading them on so the whole world thought he was straight when he wasn't. His actions, coupled with Rebecca's vindictiveness, had put in motion the events that led to Rebecca's death. Maybe all the tragedy in Tracy's life had given her the gift of mercy. Blaming Brad for covering up his sexual preference when he was likely no more than a scared, confused kid wasn't going to help her heal—and for fifteen years that had been her only goal.

The young girl who'd accidentally caused the death of her sister, who'd lost her friends and her parents, who'd been shipped off alone to battle demons and drugs, had come out on the other side without losing her humanity. Was it too late for Yizenia?

Marisela strolled over to her nemesis. "You were wrong," she said, her words crisp but not accusatory. Simply a statement of fact.

Yizenia glanced over her shoulder. "Wrong? There are worse things to be than wrong, *mija*."

"How about tricked? Duped? Deceived? You killed two innocent men."

"They aren't blameless. They lied, covered up."

"Yes," Marisela agreed. "Whatever Brad and Craig did in that tent that night was *their* business. Fifteen years ago, their lives would have been ruined if the whole world found out they were gay—or at least, that Brad was gay and Craig was confused. What teenager isn't? And what about Raymond? He was just a kid who worshiped his big brother and had his whole family torn apart first by Rebecca's revelation and then by accusations of murder that weren't true."

"Evan Cole dumped her body in a cold, icy swamp," Yizenia argued.

"Yes, he did. But that shallow playboy's only crime was trying to protect the young girl he loved but for whatever reason felt he couldn't have."

Yizenia sneered. "You make it all sound so *romántico*."

"I'm just telling it like it is. The truth was twisted. Bent and broken until the bastard who hired you got what he wanted. Has this happened to you before? Have you ever been this betrayed?"

Yizenia remained with her back to Marisela. She shook her head, the movement quick. Sharp.

Marisela slid her hand onto Yizenia's shoulder, then down her arm. When she reached Yizenia's wrist, she latched on tightly, encircling the bracelet Yizenia wore over her tattoo. "Tell us who fucked you over, Yizenia. Turn over whatever information you can and help us bring this *hijo de puta* down."

Yizenia turned around slowly, her eyes sad and . . . tired? Suddenly, Yizenia looked her age—still stunningly beautiful, but her gaze possessed a weariness that Marisela prayed she'd never experience, not even if she managed to live beyond sixty. With a quick jerk, Yizenia extracted herself from Marisela's grip.

"I came to Boston to achieve two goals," Yizenia said, her voice laced with irony. "First, to avenge the death of Rebecca Manning. Second, to meet you and recruit you to be my protégée. Can you imagine? You, studying to be a killer under a woman as gullible as I?"

"Craig Bennett and Bradley Hightower are still alive," Marisela reminded her. "If you leave them alone, will he hire someone else to finish the job?"

Yizenia's shoulders sagged. "I don't know. He convinced me he had been in love with Rebecca Manning and wanted to avenge her death. He told me he'd been too poor as a young man to push the police, but now that he had money and power, no one cared about a fifteen-year-old murder. He gave me articles and files filled with evidence that proved those boys killed Rebecca and were simply never prosecuted because of their wealthy families."

"Fake evidence, clearly," Marisela surmised.

Yizenia nodded. "From what I've heard here today, assembling such evidence wouldn't have been hard. The police did pursue those *muchachos* as the killers. Even the authorities never suspected Tracy."

"Thanks to Evan, the man you murdered."

Yizenia's eyes flashed with anger, but she blinked in rapid succession until the emotion faded. "My client paid me in full," she admitted, "even though the job is incomplete. The telephone number I used previously to contact him is no longer in service. I have no idea of his true motives. I'm no longer of any use. To him or to you."

Marisela stepped closer. "You can give us evidence. Let us work out how to make it stick."

"And lose the last thing I have? My freedom? *No en esta vida.*"

Max cleared his throat, then gestured to Marisela to bring Yizenia to him. She complied and no other words were exchanged. A few minutes later, Parker stormed out of the room, unable to listen as Tracy and Brad mourned for their lost friends and loved ones. Parker had spent many years blaming Bradley Hightower for ultimately causing the destruction of his family. Marisela could understand why he couldn't let go of his anger so easily.

Marisela dug her hands into her pockets. Now what? Without Yizenia's help, they couldn't identify the source behind the contract killings. Craig Bennett would not be free until the man who wanted him dead was found and turned over to the police.

Her determination to see the case through forced her to intrude on Tracy and Bradley's hushed conversation.

"Tracy, we're not done," Marisela said.

Tracy looked up at her with eyes liquid with confusion. "You know the whole story."

"Did you have any other boyfriends in high school? Someone poor who's now made it big?"

Tracy shook her head. "No. Only Brad."

"No secret admirers?"

Tracy scoffed. "If any boy would have shown an inkling of interest I would have been all over him. You've caught the killer. What more do you want from me?"

Bradley started at the mention of the killer. "Who? That woman? She killed my brother?"

Marisela nodded, blocking Bradley's path when he started to stand. "We'll take care of her, believe me," she insisted, though she had no idea how they'd pull it off. That plan, thankfully, was for Brynn and Ian to fight over. At this point, Marisela had to concentrate on milking the last bit of information she could from Tracy. She introduced herself to Bradley Hightower and explained what they knew so far.

He sat back on the couch, winded.

"So someone went to all the trouble to hire a paid assassin to take us all out, but then fired the killer before they got to me?"

"Looks that way," Marisela confirmed. "The man who wanted you dead may have simply decided to change tactics. Just because one assassin is out of the picture doesn't mean you're safe."

Wide-eyed, Bradley listened, then gave a curt nod. "I don't have a death wish. I'll cooperate however I can."

Marisela gave Brad a half-smile. "It's not your help I need. Tracy, there is one bit of information we haven't fully explored. You were the only one who knew that Evan Cole had been on the island that night. You said you told your brother," Marisela pointed out, cutting Tracy off before she could protest Parker's innocence again. "I know you believe he never told anyone and I agree. He went to a lot of trouble to hire goons to protect you. He never would have blabbed about Evan and risked implicating you. But that still leaves us with the question of who else could have known."

Tracy glanced up at Brad, embarrassed.

"I know all about your past, Tracy," he said softly. "Just like you know about mine. I mean, yeah, I'm gay. Craig wasn't," he explained, his eyes darting between Marisela and Tracy. "We were young. Did some experimenting. I didn't know what it really meant to be gay back then, I just had these feelings I couldn't cover up."

"But you tried," Marisela said.

Regret glossed Bradley's eyes. "Yeah, first with Becca, then with Tracy, not to mention all the other girls I made sure were hanging off my arm so no one ever suspected what I was. I'm ashamed of how I handled my sexuality back then, seducing a friend, but we were stupid kids. We made mistakes."

Tracy sat forward, her head in her hands. Marisela gave her a few minutes of silence, noticing how Tracy didn't balk when Brad ran his hand supportively up and down her spine.

"I opened up a lot when I was in therapy," Tracy admitted, "especially this last time. I was approved for one-on-one therapy. The doctor and I dug down deep."

"Hypnosis?" Brad asked.

Marisela's hackles rose. She didn't know much about hypnosis except what she saw in the movies or on those television specials where the magician got members of the audience to act like chickens in front of the whole world. But she knew a skilled psychologist could coax deeply buried memories to the surface. She hadn't known that Tracy had undergone the procedure. The files she'd read from Windchaser Farms contained no reference to hypnosis.

Tracy lifted her head. "Yeah, I've tried everything. The doctor said if I could completely relive the event that had scarred me so deeply, then maybe I could move on."

Sounded like a bunch of shit to Marisela, but what the hell did she know?

"Tracy, this could be the break we need to find out who ordered the hit on your friends. What was the doctor's name?"

Tracy blinked wildly. "Um, I'm not sure. I was really strung out when I first got there. I saw three to five psychologists and psychiatrists and counselors every day."

Marisela dropped to her knees, putting herself eye to eye with the woman who might hold the key to the investigation. "But only one of them coaxed you into dreamland to pick through your brain. Give us a name, Tracy. Give us somewhere to start."

Tracy pressed her lips together. "Selig. Doctor Selig," she answered finally. "Andrew, I think."

"And this was at . . . ?"

"Windchaser. I always went to Windchaser."

Seconds later, two agents arrived. They instructed Tracy to pack her things as they were moving her and Bradley to a new safe house. Marisela trotted down the stairs, slipping on her sunglasses as her eyes were blasted by the late afternoon sun. She spotted the limousine and dashed inside, not surprised to find Max and Frankie typing away on twin laptops.

Frankie spoke as soon as Marisela slammed the door.

"Andrew Selig is no longer listed on the staff roster at Windchaser Farm."

Max continued typing.

"Where are Brynn and Ian?"

"Took Yizenia back to the penthouse," Frankie replied.

Marisela scooted over so she could better see Frankie's screen. He was paging through the main web site for Windchaser Farm, the in-patient and out-patient substance-abuse facility where Tracy Manning had been treated several times over the years. Suddenly,

Frankie's screen went blank, then re-emerged a bright blue. The text that scrolled across the screen looked more like code than words.

"I'm in," Frankie said.

Max grinned, his eyebrow arched. "Yes, I can see you. Through their system."

"Damn," Frankie cursed, then immediately backed out before any security protocols alerted the server to his illegal presence in their system.

Marisela switched seats. Max had already infiltrated the facility's main computer system. "Looks here like Dr. Andrew Selig was transferred to a facility in Germany six months ago."

"About the time Yizenia was first contacted?" Marisela asked.

"Looks that way," Max confirmed. "Let's see who authorized this transfer."

Max typed and Frankie and Marisela waited. Time ticked by slowly, despite Max's lightning-fast keyboarding.

"Damn," he cursed. "The records indicate that Andrew Selig's transfer was voluntary. Frank, check his bank accounts."

Marisela watched, her eyes wide, as Frankie complied. She had no idea Frankie had honed his computer skills so thoroughly. He had, of course, trained under a master. No wonder he was so ripe to leave Titan. He clearly knew all sorts of shit Marisela hadn't begun to study yet.

"Aren't you full of surprises?" she said.

Frankie's grin was pure sensual sin. "Even outside of the bedroom."

Max cleared his throat. Frankie returned to his computer. Max transferred the entrance codes to the facility's system, allowing Frankie into the payroll accounts. From there, Frankie worked his way into bank accounts.

"No overly large deposits," he announced. "Not six months ago."

"Trace back every month before that," Max ordered.

Frankie complied. "Nothing. Wait," he said, scrolling down a screen. "A year ago, he stopped directly depositing money into his savings account and canceled his 401(k)."

"What does that mean?" she asked.

Max looked up. "Means the man no longer had reason to take deductions out of his paycheck to ensure his future financial security. He must have an offshore or overseas account."

"Can that be traced?"

Max shook his head. "Not easily."

Marisela sat back, fighting off a dark and sour mood. They were so close. If they were correct, Selig had extracted the information about the night of Rebecca Manning's death through hypnotherapy, then gave the information to someone who used tht little known facts to build a case to present to Yizenia, including the secret participation of Evan Cole in the night's events. Yizenia's client had paid her off and clearly wanted her to abandon the hit, but they had no way of knowing why. Craig Bennett was struggling for life in a hospital, his political career effectively halted. Evan Cole and Raymond Hightower were dead. Bradley Hightower had been flushed out by Titan. Was that enough?

"Who is the target?" she asked aloud.

Frankie looked at her sidelong. "What do you mean?"

"Initially, we thought all four men were targets because of their involvement with Rebecca's death. We now know that no one who was there that night or who was affected by the aftermath had motive to want those men dead."

Frankie stopped fiddling with his computer, but Max continued.

"You think the 'Remember Rebecca Manning' deal was a smokescreen?"

Marisela bit hard on her lip before answering. She was putting herself out on a limb here, but so far, acting on her instincts had been fairly successful. "What else could it be? Yizenia's client could have used the old scandal to throw any investigations off. Hiring Yizenia, because of her reputation, implied that the murders were to settle an old score. But what if it's a new score that he's trying to settle?"

Frankie eyed Max, who was still typing away, even as he plugged in to his team back at the office, making requests and giving them instructions all while listening to Marisela's supposition.

"Raymond Hightower did nothing with his life but make and spend money," Frankie said, pulling up the reports transferred from the Stockholm office. "Our contacts said he was incredibly well liked and stayed away from pissing people off."

"Scratch him, then," Marisela said. "What about Evan Cole?"

Frankie didn't have to look at the computer this time. He'd done all the checking on Cole himself. "Lived mostly off his trust fund and investments. He has a couple of angry husbands in his wake, but I can't see any of them making such a show of killing him. He wasn't worth Yizenia's expensive fee."

"He's a possibility, I guess," Marisela commented, though she doubted that was the case.

"Then we're back to either Bennett or Bradley Hightower."

"Wait," Max said, finally joining their conversation. His colorless eyes flashed with what Marisela could best describe as fire.

"I think we've got something here."

He turned the screen toward them. Marisela squinted at the tiny type on the screen featuring a scanned copy of an old government document.

"What is that?"

"The board minutes to a foundation established five years ago by a consortium of political lobbyists looking to ramp up their moral stature," Max answered.

Marisela exchanged glances with Frankie. "In English, *por favor*?"

"A group of men who played politics by donating money to charitable causes," he clarified.

"Gotcha."

Max used a stylus to tap to a small name on the corner of the screen.

Her eyes widened. Wow. Maybe she was cut out for this shit after all. With a smile, she turned to Frankie. "See? Not so dumb."

"I never said you were dumb, *vidita*. Just gullible."

She sneered. Okay, maybe she could be easily snowed every once in a while. 'Cause when she'd met Leo Devlin, she'd thought him a cool guy, not a cold-blooded killer.

Eighteen

MARISELA AND FRANKIE marched into Ian's office together. Max had already informed him of the information they'd discovered, and he was staring at his computer screen and talking on the phone simultaneously.

"And so Mr. Devlin is very hands-on at the clinic?"

He listened to the response, waving Frankie and Marisela closer.

"Really? That's fascinating. Sounds as if he truly goes above and beyond for the patients there. Yes, yes. Sounds exactly like the kind of information we need for this Man of the Year award. Would you mind putting it all in writing? A glowing letter of recommendation? That would be fabulous. Yes. I'll send the email address to you immediately. Thank you. Your testimonial has been invaluable."

He hung up the phone, grinning slyly.

"The director of Windchaser Farm. Leo Devlin might have tried to hide his association with the clinic behind several foundations, but apparently, he's well-known by the staff. Likes to hang around, volunteer with the patients. All while remaining anonymous, of course."

"Of course," Marisela said, sliding into her usual chair. "Wouldn't want patients like Tracy Manning to know he was trolling for information he could use on his political enemy."

Frankie stood behind her, his hands on the backrest.

"Exactly," Ian confirmed. "We're dealing in speculation, but I'd say that while digging into Congressman Craig Bennett's past to find dirt he could use to get him to back off on his prescription drug plan, Leo Devlin found out about the scandal and that Tracy Manning had once been a patient at the clinic."

"How'd they get her back there?" Frankie asked.

Ian shook his head. "Dumb luck? Outreach? Any number of ways, I assume. Devlin's foundation owns a stake in hundreds of clinics across the U.S., apparently as a way to push addiction-fighting drugs. He could easily have gotten to Tracy at any number of facilities. And he has the power to coerce the doctor into doing the hypnotherapy to allow Tracy's full disclosure of the night's events. That's likely how he knew about Evan Cole."

Marisela shifted in her seat, the speculation making her uncomfortable. They had no proof, but the facts were piling up.

"Why not use the gay stuff?" Frankie asked. "I mean, couldn't he have ruined Craig Bennett's credibility by outing him?"

"Even the press needs proof," Ian replied. "Without Bradley Hightower to verify or deny the accusation, especially against a high-profile married man, the mud wouldn't stick. Massachusetts isn't a red state. Bennett's constituents likely wouldn't give a damn if he pitched for both teams so long as he got them cheaper prescription drugs. Besides, Devlin clearly wanted Bennett out of the way permanently. As Marisela hypothesized, Devlin may have used the entire sordid tale as a smokescreen, as a way to lure Yizenia Santiago to take on the case. The other men's deaths were nothing more than collateral damage, meant to send anyone off the trail of a political hit, plain and simple."

"How did he find out about Yizenia?"

Ian tapped more on his computer. "We'll likely never know unless she tells us. Brynn is upstairs, speaking with her. With any luck, she'll convince her to—"

Alarms blared. Marisela jumped, covering her ears. Ian and Frankie beat her out of her office, where Ian's assistant consulted a flashing grid of lights on her computer screen.

"Where?" Ian asked.

"The penthouse," she informed.

They dashed toward the stairs.

"What is that?" Marisela yelled.

Ian answered as he swung around to the landing on the top floor. "Panic alarm. Brynn's in—"

The door was wide open. Brynn sat on the floor, her hand pressed against the back of her head. Frankie slid onto the ground beside her.

Ian stopped up short. "What happened?"

"She clocked me," Brynn rasped, pointing weak fingers at a shattered crystal vase in the middle of the room. "Got my purse."

Which meant Yizenia had Brynn's gun.

Marisela vaulted across the room, to the window she saw was wide open. The fire escape below was rickety, but would have held the weight of a woman as lithe and quick as Yizenia. Marisela made sure her Ladysmith was still firmly in her waistband, then slid out the window.

"Marisela!"

She turned quickly. "Go around front," she yelled to Frankie. "We'll cut her off."

Back in her bounty hunter days, Marisela had shimmied up more than her fair share of fire escapes to catch bail jumpers, but she couldn't remember ever going down one.

She took a deep breath and traversed the shaky metal ladders and landings as quickly as she could. Once she jumped the last eight feet to the bottom, she looked around. The alley below was sandy and barely used. Yizenia's footprints were easy to spot.

Moving quickly, Yizenia hadn't spent time covering her tracks. Didn't take Marisela more than half a minute to figure out that the wily assassin had jimmied a window to break back inside the building. Titan agents were likely swarming the neighborhood by now and Yizenia was simply waiting for the perfect time to make a break for it.

The window, ground level into the basement, was still open, so Marisela slid to the dirt and then lowered herself inside, feet first.

The room she landed in was nothing more than a storage closet, filled with stained coveralls, stacks of motor oil and various filters, belts, and plugs. The door, which she guessed led into the underground garage, was slightly ajar. Marisela walked quietly to the opening and gazed into the parking area. She wasn't entirely surprised when she heard Brynn's Jaguar purr to life.

Yizenia had her purse, which meant she had the keys.

A garage door at the far end of the bay—the one that emptied into a narrow side alley—began its silent scroll upward. Guessing Yizenia's gaze would be trained outside, Marisela dashed out of the closet and headed for the driver's side door. With her right hand, she leveled her weapon at Yizenia. With her left, she pulled at the door handle.

Locked.

Yizenia grinned and punched the gas.

Marisela cursed and ran alongside the car as Yize-nia maneuvered out of the garage. Leaping onto the top of the car, Marisela spread her arms and legs wide for traction. She dug in her fingers and toes as best she could, yelping when Yizenia bounced up the drive, then closed her eyes and held on when the car spun onto the cobblestone street. Yizenia sped quickly to the end of the road, ran the stop sign, and continued on until she slammed on the brakes a few blocks later, sending Marisela rolling onto the slate sidewalk. She grunted as the air wooshed out of her lungs and her shoulder smacked hard against the rock.

The tires squealed as Yizenia jammed on the gas. Marisela rolled, pulling out her gun as she dropped onto the street. She fired continuously, hoping to hit the tires. As Yizenia turned the corner, a bullet pinged off the shiny alloy rims.

The car disappeared. Marisela cursed, pounded her fist on the pavement, and reached for her watch. The communication mechanism was as busted as the digital face. She'd have to walk back to the office, and that was going to hurt. She rolled off to the side seconds before a car, one she didn't recognize, came barreling toward her. The driver had the gall to roll down the window and yell at her after she barely made it out of his way.

He was kidding, right? Did he think she was lying in the street to be cute?

She pulled her bruised and aching body into a sitting position on the curb when she heard a gunshot and a crash from the next block over.

Cursing with pain, Marisela ran across the street, then cut through an alley to find the Jaguar smashed against a tall, iron lamppost on Boston's famous Freedom Trail, marked by a thick red line on the sidewalk. The driver's side window had been shot out and from what Marisela could see from a distance, there was blood spattered on the spiderweb of shattered glass.

People started to gather. Marisela figured they had moments until someone called 911. She dashed across the street, flashed her gun, and claimed, without a badge, of course, to be with the Boston police. She jumped the hood and slid to the passenger side door.

Still locked.

She banged on the glass with the butt of her gun. "Open it up, Yizenia. You can't run."

Yizenia was dazed, but very much alive. She pressed the door lock, then groaned in pain. Marisela reached across the passenger seat and turned Yizenia so she could examine her injury. Yizenia grunted, but bit back a full scream. Her arm was bloodied, the skin and muscle ripped, but it looked like a flesh wound. Marisela tore what was left of Yizenia's long sleeve and knotted it around the gash to cut off the bleeding. This time, Yizenia's eyes watered.

Marisela grabbed Yizenia under the arms and pulled her into the passenger seat, backing out to make room. "What happened?"

Yizenia stared at her with eyes that only focused for a few seconds at a time. "Ironic, isn't it?" she rasped.

"Shot in the car. Just like Evan Cole. Only he was innocent. I am not."

Her breath came in shallow pants, but Marisela knew that once the numbness set in, Yizenia would be lucid. Right now, the pain was driving her to focus on things that were not important.

Marisela slammed the door, ran around to the driver's side and got in. She assured the burgeoning crowd that she had everything under control and that she was taking the injured woman to the hospital herself. If she could get the car to run.

"Who shot you?" she asked, fumbling for the ignition. The crowd that had gathered around took a few tentative steps backward as the engine purred to life.

Yizenia managed to arch a brow. "I'd guess Titan agents."

Marisela glanced through the windshield. She couldn't imagine a Titan operative aiming for the driver of a car on a street full of pedestrians. It was a wonder Yizenia hadn't mown anyone down as it was.

"No way," Marisela assured her. "Titan wants you alive to testify. Guess again."

Yizenia's eyes widened. "Bradley Hightower?"

Marisela smirked. "He and Tracy and Parker are all still in our protective custody. You have one more guess or you lose the prize," she teased, hoping a little humor might offset Yizenia's agony.

Yizenia's sneer reflected her pain. "I never win anything," Yizenia said breathlessly, her accent so innately American that Marisela nearly laughed.

Nearly.

"Then why not guess your former client? That's where my money goes."

"*¿Qué dices?*"

Yizenia slid into a full sitting position. The bleeding had ebbed and the color was starting to return to her cheeks.

"You know his identity," Marisela said. "He doesn't know that, so far, you haven't shared that information. And even if you gave us his name, without your testimony, the police won't have shit to build a case against him. Doesn't seem much of a stretch to guess he'd order someone to kill you and shut you up. Hell, he hired you, didn't he?"

Yizenia's eyes narrowed.

Marisela put the car into reverse and backed up a few inches, convincing the crowd that she was serious about leaving. They dispersed and she was able to pull the car off the curb. She glanced at her watch and cursed, then twisted toward the back seat and yanked out Brynn's stolen purse.

"If you're looking for this," Yizenia said, pulling Brynn's gun from her jacket pocket. "I had dibs."

Marisela smirked and continued to drive. "I'm steering this smashed-up rust-bucket. You shoot me and you die, too. I'm looking for the cell phone."

Yizenia coughed, the sound a painful croak. "I tossed it back at Titan."

Marisela reached for the radio.

"Jammed that with a screwdriver before I left the

garage. And the GPS locator, in case you're wondering."

"Very efficient," Marisela griped. "Anything you didn't think of?"

"I didn't want Brynn talking me out of doing what needs to be done."

"And what needs to be done?"

"A man needs to be taught a lesson."

"And would that man be Leo Devlin?" Marisela asked.

Yizenia's color rose again. "Excellent detective work, Ms. Morales."

"*Gracias.* You see, that's what I do best. Took me a while to figure it out, but it's not the fighting or the killing that makes me useful in Titan. I'm a protector, not a killer."

Yizenia twisted again in her seat, taking a deep breath and releasing it slowly. "You've proved that."

"So let me protect you and return you to Titan."

Yizenia shook her head, turning so she could point the gun directly at Marisela. Though Marisela didn't believe Yizenia would shoot her, she simply couldn't be sure. With her hands on the wheel, she couldn't reach her own weapon, and a close-range firefight would only end up with both of them dead.

"No, you're going to drive me to see our friend Mr. Devlin. It's been a long time since I've taken on a personal vendetta. Feels good."

"It won't feel so good when you're arrested for first-degree murder. If you just give us what information you have, help the police build a case against Leo Devlin for murder and conspiracy to commit murder, I'm sure Brynn and Ian have lawyers that can work it so you get some kind of deal. Help us put him . . . "

Yizenia raised her brow over bored eyes, forcing Marisela to drop her attempts at rational argument.

"Oh, who am I kidding?" Marisela said, punching the gas. Maybe she could stop Yizenia once they reached their destination. Maybe she could stop Yizenia after gathering enough evidence to turn Devlin over to the cops for conspiracy. Or maybe she'd stay out of a battle that wasn't hers to fight.

Marisela killed the engine, allowing the Jaguar to roll to a silent stop beside a stone fence. She turned to Yizenia, who was effectively blocked inside the car. Marisela moved to reach for the LadySmith, but Yizenia jabbed the barrel of the semiautomatic pistol into her arm, putting a halt to her plan.

"We have matching tattoos, but if you want to add matching bullet wounds, I suppose you could continue with this childish ruse."

Marisela rolled her eyes. "You don't have to kill him."

"You seemed all for it before," Yizenia said.

"I was humoring you."

"Then continue. Get out."

Marisela complied. As she turned, Yizenia took the LadySmith out of Marisela's waistband. With a curse, she watched, impressed, as Yizenia pressed the lever that released the car's convertible top. It folded out of the way, allowing her the space she needed to exit the car, her good arm supporting the weight of her weapon. She'd left Marisela's on the seat.

"Go back to Brynn and tell her that while I appreciate the use of her car, I'm sorry I couldn't return it in pristine condition."

"Guess you owe her a whole case of brandy," Marisela said, spying the crunched hood and fender.

"It's cognac," Yizenia teased, "but you're close enough."

Marisela shifted, missing the weight of the Lady-Smith in her waistband. But retrieving her gun would not stop the assassin. Marisela had no reason to shoot Yizenia and no reason to stop her from shooting the man who had orchestrated the deaths of Evan Cole and Raymond Hightower simply to feed his political ambitions against Craig Bennett. Tracy Manning's life had been turned upside down. She'd been used, manipulated, and raped of her memories all for a greedy pharmaceutical capitalist who already had more money than God. They'd returned to the scene of the original crime—the same Brookline mansion where the hit against Craig Bennett had gone down. With no way to communicate with Frankie or Brynn or Ian or Max, Marisela had to make her decision on her own.

Let Yizenia kill the man or try to stop her?

"How are you going to get in?" Marisela asked.

Yizenia's smile belied the pain Marisela knew she was feeling from her injury.

"Mr. Devlin is under the misguided impression that he covered all his bases with me. He believes I don't know his schedule, his security codes, the precise timing of the guards that patrol his vast estate."

"Clearly, the guy's wrong," Marisela commented.

"Dead wrong. Now, run along," Yizenia ordered kindly, gesturing with her gun. "You claim to be a protector, not a killer. I can respect that, *mi hermana*. We do have much in common, but so much more that is different. I almost wish to apologize for seeking you out, testing if you were the right woman to take my place, but I cannot in good conscience say that with truth. I'm glad we met."

A tightening in Marisela's chest reached up and grabbed her in the back of her throat. "Weird, but I am, too."

Silence lingered for a few seconds, with Yizenia wavering on her feet. "Look at me closely, Marisela. I'm what you might become if you allow hatred and vengeance to poison your soul."

Marisela shook her head. "No, I think you're what I'd become if someone murdered my family."

Yizenia swallowed thickly, the action visible as she closed the distance between them. "In any case, you have no need to be here any longer." She held out her injured arm. "Take this," she instructed, indicating the thick, beaded leather band encircling her wrist, hiding her tattoo from the world.

"Your bracelet?"

"Those are black pearls sewn into the leather," she said, her voice inflected with pride. "Very valuable."

Marisela did as Yizenia asked, but wasn't sure why. "That's an expensive gift to give to someone who's held a gun on you multiple times in the last twenty-four hours."

"Consider it payment for releasing me."

Her eyes suddenly dry and burning, Marisela wrapped the band around her wrist and snapped it into place. Again, Yizenia waved the gun at the woods behind them and waited. Deciding she had no further reason to stay, Marisela walked away. She'd get to the nearest house, borrow a phone and make a call. If Brynn and Ian wanted to save Leo Devlin's life, then they could alert the police, though she doubted either of the Blake twins wanted to expose the woman who had avenged their mother, no matter what she did to the man who'd betrayed her.

Once Marisela had walked ten feet, she heard a grunt. She spun around. Yizenia was gone. Over the wall, no doubt. Marisela stopped. Listened. Except for the breeze rustling through the tree branches, she heard nothing.

You claim to be a protector, not a killer.

But Marisela couldn't do much protecting from the other side of the fence, though, could she? And besides, she thought, glancing at the expensive bracelet, she had been paid a retainer.

Cursing to herself, Marisela slid into the Jaguar's

driver's seat. Took her ten damned minutes, but she was able to reactivate the GPS locator on the car. Figuring she'd wasted enough time ensuring that sooner or later, she'd get backup, she pulled her LadySmith and jumped onto the hood of the car so she could make it over the wall.

If Yizenia could figure out how to break in to this fortress, so could she. And though she couldn't justify helping the assassin achieve her objective, the least she could do was watch her back.

Nineteen

JUDGING BY THE TRAIL Marisela had followed across the lawn and into the same stunning mansion where the charity masquerade had been held, Yizenia might know her way around this place, but she must not have realized how badly she'd been hurt. Marisela spotted a smear of blood on a wall near the side entrance, and after wiping it clean, discovered the secret panel nearby that led her into the hidden passageways that wound through the house.

Marisela moved slowly, carefully, through the interior corridors, ignoring the cobwebs and dust skittering across her face and clogging her nose. She stopped after winding through what felt like miles of passageway, listening for sounds that were less like rodents and more like a killer on the prowl. She didn't dare call out, even in a whisper. Yizenia had been single-minded in her decision to take Devlin out on her own terms—so much so that Marisela feared the woman was making a huge mistake.

If she'd wanted to send Leo Devlin to the great drugstore in the sky, she should have hunted him as she'd hunted the others. From a distance. Instead, she'd barreled into the man's home, determined to remove him face-to-face. While Marisela could appreciate the purity of Yizenia's intentions, her plan of attack was reckless.

After stumbling her way up a staircase, Marisela finally heard voices on the other side of the wall. She hesitated. She couldn't distract Yizenia without putting her life at risk.

"You received your payment," a male, presumably Leo Devlin, said curtly. "Your services are no longer needed."

"I've received payment, *sí*," Yizenia responded. "In my bank account and on my body. Did you really think you could simply kill me and remove the threat to your safe, secure existence?"

Devlin laughed, and under the cover of the deep, throaty sound, Marisela activated the mechanism that released the lock on the panel. She held on to the corner, allowing the secret entrance to only slip open a quarter inch. Through the sliver in the door, she saw the white-haired Leo Devlin sitting behind his desk, Yizenia directly across from him with her gun aimed at the center of his forehead.

"That was the plan," he replied.

"Your plans are incredibly elaborate, *verdad*? Had I not been the one manipulated by your lies, I might have admired the cleverness of it all."

Devlin's face reflected no fear. Abject confidence lit the man's pale eyes, despite the sweat trickling down the side of his neck. Marisela moved so she could see the door. She stretched down the passageway to listen into the hallway on the other side. She heard no one riding to his rescue, despite his smug expression.

"I wasn't always a rich man, Ms. Santiago. I had to play dirty to get where I am. Craig Bennett stood in the way of my continuing the lifestyle to which I've become accustomed," Devlin explained. "If his bill to allow foreign medications in the American market-place becomes law, I'll be ruined. I considered reviving the scandal alone to tarnish his reputation, but the press wasn't interested. Old news. I needed something more . . . permanent . . . to shut him up."

"So you hired me," Yizenia said. "My reputation alone would point investigators back to the old scandal and away from his political enemies. Away from you."

"Ah, yes. Brilliant, wasn't it? When I heard about this avenging angel of *España,* I concocted my story about being a devoted admirer of Rebecca Manning and that I'd simmered for years with the need for justice. With my connections at Windchaser Farm, I was able to get the information I needed to convince you to help me from Tracy Manning. The rest was no more than greasing the right palms. The decision to have you eliminated only came about when you'd been in the custody of those meddlers from Titan for more time than I thought wise. You do, after all, possess the means to have me arrested. If it is any consolation, I regretted ordering your elimination."

"You must, since whoever you hired missed."

"Clearly, not all assassins perform on the same level, though at least with Bennett, you left him vulnerable. I've already hired someone to finish the job you botched. But I am sorry for the turn our relationship has taken. I have a deep appreciation for those courageous enough to exact revenge."

"I doubt you'll feel the same way when my bullet is in your brain."

Devlin's eyes flashed, but before Marisela could warn Yizenia, a security guard burst through the door behind her. Yizenia turned and fired. The guard dropped. Knees, then torso, then face. Yizenia stood for a moment, stunned.

Marisela pushed out of the secret passage. For a split second, her gaze met Yizenia's. Marisela saw despair cross through Yizenia's dark irises before another shot fired.

Yizenia jerked. Blood stained her chest. Marisela stepped forward just as the assassin fell into her arms. She pulled her close and, over her shoulder, saw the gaping bullet hole in Yizenia's back.

"*Dios mio,*" Marisela said, her heart pounding as she watched the life slip out of Yizenia's eyes.

"*Sí, sí,*" she agreed. And then, she died.

Marisela looked up and saw Leo Devlin standing, pistol aimed, pale blue eyes alight with satisfaction. She scooted back, laying Yizenia gently on the floor. She retrieved Yizenia's weapon and held it tight in her left hand.

Devlin dropped his gun on the desk and smiled. "It was self-defense, Ms. Morales. You saw it for yourself. I'm sure as I'm a former client, you'd be delighted to testify on my behalf."

"You can fuck that shit, Devlin. I know what you did to Craig Bennett."

"Her word against mine, don't you see? I'm a wealthy man with access to the best lawyers in the world. The situation will be twisted to my advantage and the only person who could have effectively contradicted me is now dead. Except you, of course, but you'll have to tell the truth. That she came here to kill me. That I shot her only after she breached my security and murdered my guard."

There was a laugh in his voice that slithered up Marisela's spine like a slimy scaled reptile. "You're not using me for your defense," Marisela insisted.

She raised the gun, which only caused him to shrug casually. "I'll do as I like, just as I always have. You're a professional, Ms. Morales. Put down your weapon and admit defeat. I doubt if your bosses at Titan would approve of you shooting an unarmed man."

For Evan, for Raymond, for Tracy, hell, for Yizenia, Marisela raised Yizenia's gun and pulled the trigger. Devlin crumpled to the floor.

"Wrong again, you son of a bitch."

Shouts and alarms rocked the mansion.

Marisela dropped to her knees, wiped her prints from the grip and then genlty placed the gun between Yizenia's cold fingers. She fired again. "There, *mi hermana*," she whispered. "*El montruo* is dead at your hand. *Descansa en paz.*"

Marisela barely had time to slip into the secret passage before swarms of guards spilled into the room. Sirens wailed and walkie-talkies squealed with chatter. She closed her eyes tight, pressed herself into the darkest corner she could find, and willed herself not to make a sound.

You claim to be a protector, not a killer.

Once again, Marisela had lied. To Yizenia, but most of all, to herself.

From her nest on the couch, Marisela watched her best friend, Lia Santorini, pad across her apartment to answer the door. A movie droned in front of her, one of Lia's favorite old flicks with Cher and Nick Cage about the Italian moon or something. She hadn't been watching. Not really. Mostly, she'd been pigging out on Lia's homemade *jujulainne* cookies, dipping them in Chianti or *café con leche*, licking her proverbial wounds.

Yizenia hadn't been so fortunate.

But then, neither had Leo Devlin.

Immediately after returning to headquarters, Brynn had sent Marisela home. Not home to the hotel, but to Tampa. Max had whisked her off on Titan's private jet and she'd immediately holed up with her best friend. Brynn had promised she would personally clean up the mess in Boston, and frankly, Marisela had been too shell-shocked to argue. In her arrogance, she'd insisted to Yizenia that she wasn't a killer, but not twenty minutes later, she'd shot the lying, manipulative, unarmed bastard Devlin without hesitation. What did that make her now?

"Well, look who it is!" Lia exclaimed.

She wasn't entirely surprised to see Lia return from the foyer with Ian trailing behind her. Even wallowing in her own self-indulging pity party, as Lia called it, she recognized a predatory spark suddenly present in her best friend's dark eyes.

Great. Mr. Charming meet Ms. Perpetually Charmable.

"What are you doing here?" Marisela asked, barely sitting up from beneath the comforter.

"Marisela," Lia admonished. "Mr. Blake came to check on you. Don't be so rude."

She loved Lia, she really did. But damn, she was the most gullible woman on the planet when it came to suave men like Blake.

To appease her friend, Marisela stretched out her leg and gave the dessert plate a little push with her toe. "Want a cookie?"

"You haven't called in," he replied. "Nor have you returned the messages we left on your cell phone."

Lia might be gullible when it came to men, but in all other scenarios, she was damned smart. She excused herself from the room, even though chances were high she'd be eavesdropping from the hall.

"I planned to call in today," she lied.

"And tell us what?"

She shook her head. "Hadn't figured that out yet. Where's Frankie?"

Ian bristled. "He had some business to attend to. He said he'd join me shortly."

"And Brynn?"

Ian frowned. In the dim, flickering light of the television, he looked almost as miserable as she felt, if that were possible.

"She's on her way to Spain. She has taken it upon herself to ensure Yizenia receives a proper burial."

Marisela nodded, glanced down at her wrist. She was still wearing Yizenia's bracelet, though she wasn't sure why. How could she honor a woman who killed for a living? And yet, how could she not when the woman had provided justice for children like ten-year-old Ian and Brynn, when their mother had been brutally kidnapped and murdered?

Marisela realized that for at least a brief time, she'd considered herself better than Yizenia. Not in skill, but in moral fiber. Now she knew that her own moral fiber could be torn apart as easily as rice paper.

"How's Tracy?"

"Back in therapy," Ian replied, "though not with anyone associated with Windchaser Farm, which is being investigated for ethics violations. She wanted me to give you these," he said, reaching into his coat pocket and extracting a truly horrendous looking pair of gardening gloves with little strawberries on the fabric.

Marisela accepted them with a genuine laugh—the first she'd experienced in a week. "Okay, even off drugs, that chick is weird. I like her. Hey, it's the thought that counts, right?"

She tossed the gloves onto the couch. When she turned, she caught Ian eyeing her warily before he assessed Lia's apartment, which featured an inexpensive but incredibly cool décor. He strolled over to a set of classic movie posters she'd had framed, three in a row. Marisela preferred her movies in color, though she had to admit the old gangster flicks were a hoot.

"And Craig Bennett?"

"On the mend." Ian nodded at the posters approvingly. "The doctors expect a full recovery, and now that the story of Leo Devlin's manipulations is out, written, incidentally, by Parker Manning, he's never experienced such a high approval rating. I have a feeling he could ask Congress to change the minimum wage to a hundred dollars an hour and they'd pass a law."

"On behalf of former Wal-Mart clerks everywhere, I'll give him my vote," Marisela quipped. "What about the assassin Devlin said he hired?"

"Not as slippery as Yizenia, that's for sure. He was picked up casing the Bennetts' home and sang like a proverbial canary. He'd gotten his money up front, and with Devlin dead, we believe Bennett to be safe."

"And Bradley?"

"Mr. Hightower has slipped back into his anonymous life. All is right with the world of the Boston elite again. Now, we just have to work on you."

"I'm fine. Just needed a little R & R."

He clucked his tongue. "You've been out of contact."

"I needed time," she explained. "You didn't have to come all the way to check on me. You could have sent someone else."

"And you could have raked me over the coals for sleeping with Yizenia and believing she was you," he replied.

"Excuse me?"

He gave her the kind of withering look that only a man of unimpeachable masculinity could pull off. "You're not going to make me say it again, are you?"

"I don't know," she replied, her ears thrumming with the surprise. He'd hinted at this the other day, but she hadn't taken him seriously. While she'd always known Blake had had the hots for her, and she'd made no secret of the fact that at least in a physical sense, she thought he was *mucho caliente* herself, acting on their forbidden attraction was different. Especially when he'd apparently acted on it with someone else. "Torturing you has become one of my favorite pastimes."

"You're very good at it."

"Why tell me this?"

Ian slipped his hands into his pockets and casually strolled closer. Marisela glanced down at herself, wearing three-day-old sweats and a T-shirt with pizza-sauce stains. She wasn't even sure when she'd washed her face last, though she had brushed her teeth after Lia shoved a Crest-infested toothbrush in her mouth as a way of waking her up. Still, she suddenly felt incredibly grimy. She hugged the comforter tighter and nearly had a stroke when Ian crouched down so they were at eye level.

"Honesty isn't something we've ever had between us, except when it's been necessary to complete our jobs. With Yizenia dead and with you so deeply affected, I wanted you to know, in case you wondered, why I slept with her."

No, she hadn't wondered. Okay, she'd wondered a little. But for him to admit something so intimate—she shook her head, trying to clear the suddenly dense fog gathering there.

"So you slept with her because you wanted me."

Ian licked his lips and nodded. For the first time in a while, Marisela noticed how nicely shaped his mouth was. How perfect for his face.

"Do you regret sleeping with her?"

His mouth quirked into a half smile. "I know this woman. She's Latina, headstrong, foulmouthed. A real pain in the ass. You'd like her," he teased. "But the thing I admire about her most is that she lives her life without regrets. She does what she needs to do at any given time and then moves on."

His confession inspired her to scoot over on the couch and pull the comforter out of Ian's way. On his short journey to sit beside her, he snagged one of the sesame-seed-encrusted biscotti that Lia had made the day before.

Marisela suddenly felt very hot and uncomfortable. She didn't like Ian talking about her in such glowing terms. Made her skin crawl. Not because he was being insincere, but because admiration had never been something she and Ian had shared. Hell, she'd rarely shared that emotion with anyone.

"That's a pretty shallow way to live," Marisela quipped. "Never weighing consequences against purely emotional reactions?"

Ian took a bit of the crumbly cookie, chewed, swallowed, and hummed his appreciation. "If it works for you, who am I to judge?"

Marisela leaned back in the soft cushions of Lia's couch and forced a tiny smile. All around, her life had taken a strange turn. The boss she'd practically hated on sight months ago had just admitted he admired her—even though she'd likely jeopardized his company's stellar reputation by killing a respected Boston philanthropist, though the evidence she'd left gave Yizenia credit for the kill. Credit she would have wanted.

Marisela whipped off the blanket, stretched in her ratty sweatpants and T-shirt, attempted to hand-comb her unbrushed hair, and decided enough was enough.

"Okay then. So I'm not fired?" she asked, hands on hips.

Ian chuckled. "Did I miss a termination worthy offense?"

"Leo Devlin? Gun? Blood? Brain bits? Ring a bell?"

With a shake of his head, he snagged another cookie. "He ordered the deaths of innocent men and shot Yizenia in the back. The man was a coward. No one at Titan holds your reaction against you, if that's what you've been thinking."

A knock on the front door sent Lia scurrying by them to open it, but Frankie didn't wait for an invite to come inside. With a duffel bag slung over his shoulder, he stopped and eyed Marisela up and down.

"Ever heard of a shower?"

He softened his remark with a slow smile that spawned a flush of heat from deep within her. Yeah, she'd heard of showers. Had had a really interesting one with him what seemed like a lifetime ago.

Ian stood, straightened his unwrinkled slacks, and cleared his throat. "I'm off, then."

Marisela smirked. "You came all the way to Florida just to fill me in on the postmission details?"

"I have other business here," Ian replied, his eyes twinkling in Lia's direction. Twinkling? Marisela stood up straighter, trying to hook into the vibe shooting between her boss and her best friend. Okay, what's up with this shit? He just confesses to wanting her and now he's flirting with her friend?

Just like a man.

"Your cookies were delicious, Ms. Santorini," Ian complimented.

Lia smoothed her hand over her long, dark hair.
And was she blushing?

"Thank you. Anytime you want a batch . . . "

Marisela cleared her throat, trying not to blanch.
Lia responded by crossing her arms tightly over her
chest.

"Where are you off to, Mr. Blake?" Lia asked, ignoring Marisela's guttural warning.

"Ian, please."

Marisela and Frankie exchanged nauseated glances.

"My sister has suggested that for a while, perhaps
Marisela would benefit from running a few less taxing
operations. We're reopening our temporary Tampa office. We'll offer private investigative work. No guns,
explosives, car chases, assassins, or malevolent, power-
hungry political backstabbing."

Marisela frowned. "Sounds boring."

Ian grinned and walked toward the door. "With
you in charge, I doubt that will be the case."

He nodded and left.

"Me? In charge?" Marisela asked Frankie, who
shook his head in disbelief.

"*Brynn ha perdido su mente.*"

Lia strolled by Frankie on the way back to her bedroom, her scowl at Marisela's ex a deep contrast to her
flirtation with Ian. "She's not the only one who's lost
her mind."

"What was that about?" Marisela asked once Lia
left the room.

He adjusted his duffel. "Lia's pissed at me."

"Lia's always pissed at you. And she usually has a damned good reason. What did you do this time?"

Dropping his bag to the floor, Frankie wrapped his hands around Marisela's waist and tugged her close. She was sure she smelled of cookie crumbs and coffee, with a whiff or two of wine and rum and the pizza she and Lia had ordered last night. Frankie didn't seem to mind.

Sensations surged through her, reminding her that blocking herself off from the world never worked. She needed to get out, party a little, maybe take a day trip to the beach. She was home. And now, she had a chance to work here for a little while, likely until any heat on Titan died down. So far as she knew, no one even knew she'd been at the Devlin mansion that afternoon. The bullet in Devlin's skull and the one in Yizenia's gun stolen from Brynn, matched. Once Titan explained their ties to Yizenia and how they'd tried to detain her, the whole mess would blow over.

And she still had a job.

"Will you be working under me?" Marisela asked, tilting her head back so Frankie could nibble on every inch of her neck.

"If I'm lucky."

She stepped back and slapped him playfully on the shoulder. "I'm serious. Are you going to be in the Tampa office, too?"

All signs of desire dropped from Frankie's face. "No, Marisela. I quit Titan. For good. I'm on my own now."

"What?" She stepped back for a second, regained

her equilibrium, and then shot forward, grabbing him by the arm. "Why?"

"I got a better offer."

"From who?"

He shrugged. "From me."

Marisela swallowed hard, trying to contain the swirl of emotion twisting through her. Frankie leaving? Frankie not her partner anymore? Frankie heading off into an unknown situation without her there to watch his back?

Her mind somersaulted back to her final showdown with Yizenia and Devlin. Circumstances had forced Marisela to handle the situation on her own, and while she'd been wallowing in what she'd thought were bad decisions, neither Ian nor Brynn seemed to second-guess her choices. Marisela still didn't know how she'd permanently reconcile her killer instinct and her quest to stay on the side of the good guys, but at least she still had the opportunity to find out.

If she stayed with Titan.

She'd miss Frankie. She knew that. Standing on her own two feet was the next step—just like Frankie cutting loose from Titan was his. Frankie was her friend, her lover, and . . . her safety net. It was time to drop the webbing and face life and her career on her own.

But just because she didn't need Frankie on the job didn't mean she didn't need him at all.

She grabbed Frankie's sleeve and yanked him forward, smashing her mouth to his in a kiss that would brand his flesh for a good long while. Behind her, she heard Lia's footfalls skitter across the hardwood floors, then the distinct sound of her bedroom door clicking shut.

"Remember that shower you mentioned?" Marisela asked. "I think I might need a little help with it." She whipped the old T-shirt over her head. Her breasts warmed under Frankie's heated stare. "The showerhead in the guest room is a little . . . tight."

Frankie licked his lips, and when she imagined that tongue flicking over her nipples, she nearly cooed.

"No one fixes tight like I do, *vidita*."

No regrets, Ian had reminded her. She'd lived her life that way for a hell of a long time and, so far, things had worked out pretty damned good. And the minute Frankie slipped his hands around her waist, she knew the future was definitely looking up. She merged her mouth with Frankie's, reveling in the demanding push and pull of his tongue with hers. Frankie might be striking out on his own, but he wasn't gone yet. And who knew? Maybe she could convince him to stick around just a little while longer.

Or maybe not.

Her future was wide open—and Marisela couldn't wait to dive in and see what happened next.

POCKET BOOKS
PROUDLY PRESENTS

Dirty Little Secrets

JULIE LETO

Available now from Downtown Press

Turn the page for a preview of
Dirty Little Secrets. . . .

One

"I REMEMBER WHEN you used to stroke me like that."

Marisela Morales punctuated her pickup line by blowing on the back of Francisco Vega's neck. She watched the soft downy strands on his nape spike and knew her luck had finally turned around.

His fingers, visible as she glanced over his shoulder, drew streaks through the condensation on his beer bottle. Up and down. Slow and straight. Lazy, but precise. He toyed with his *cerveza* the same way he'd once made love to her, and for a split second, a trickle of moist heat curled intimately between Marisela's thighs. For the moment, the part of her Frankie used to oh-so-easily manipulate was safe, encased beneath silky panties and skin-tight, hip-hugging jeans.

Tonight, she'd have him—but on her terms. The hunter had found her prey. Now, she just had to bring him in.

"I don't remember taking time for slow strokes when you and me got busy, *niña*."

Marisela sighed, teasing his neck with her hot breath one more time before she slid onto the bar stool next to his. She'd been trying to track the man down for nearly a week. Who knew Frankie would turn up at an old haunt? Since they'd parted ways, Club Electric, a white box on the outside, hot joint on the inside, had changed names, hands, and clientele a good dozen times. But a few things remained constant—the music, the raw atmosphere—and the availability of men like Frankie, who defined the word *caliente*.

Like the song said, *Hot, hot, hot.*

"We were young then," Marisela admitted with a shrug, loosening the holster strap that cradled the cherished 9mm Taurus Millennium she wore beneath her slick leather jacket. "Now, I'm all grown up."

Marisela wiggled her crimson fingernails at Theresa, the owner of the club. The way the older woman's face lit up, Marisela figured she was going to get more than a drink. *Damn.* Marisela loved Theresa as if she were her aunt, but now wasn't the time for . . .

"Oh, Marisela! *Mija*, how can I thank you for what you did?"

The sentiment was as loud as it was sincere. So she'd done a nice thing for Theresa. The world didn't have to know. Good deeds could ruin her reputation.

And a simple thank-you wasn't enough for Theresa.

She stepped up onto the shelf on the other side of the bar and practically launched herself into Marisela's arms. Rolling her eyes at Frankie, Marisela gave the owner a genuine squeeze. She deserved as much. She was a good listener, kept great secrets and mixed the best *Cuba Libre* in town.

"*De nada,* Theresa," Marisela said, gently disentangling herself. She appreciated the woman's gratitude, but she had work to do.

"Anything for you. Anytime. For you, drinks are on the house from now on, okay? You and . . . your friend."

Even as she tried to be the courteous hostess, Theresa's voice faltered when her eyes met Frankie's. Marisela's ex hadn't been in the neighborhood for years. And in that time, he'd aged. His skin, naturally dark, now sported a rough texture, complete with a scar that traced just below his bottom lip. His jaw seemed sharper and his once perfect nose now shifted slightly to the right—likely the result of an untreated break. Even if he hadn't matured from a devilish boy to a clearly dangerous man, he likely wouldn't be recognized by anyone but Marisela and a few others who'd once known him well—the very "others" Marisela had made sure wouldn't come into Club Electric again, on Theresa's behalf.

"I never say no to free booze," Marisela answered. "*Gracias,* Theresa."

Theresa blew Marisela a kiss, patted her cheek, then moved aside to work on her drink. To most people, a *Cuba Libre* was just rum and Coke with lime. To Marisela, it was a taste of heaven.

"What did you do for her?" Frankie asked, his voice even, as if he wasn't really curious.

Marisela knew better. She slid her arms on the bar, arching her back, working out the kinks in her spine while giving Frankie an unhampered view of her breasts. She didn't want him to waste his curiosity on what she'd done for Theresa; she wanted to pique his interest another way.

"Last week, *las Reinas* chose this bar as their new hangout. Not quite the clientele Theresa has in mind. Gangs aren't exactly good for business. I politely asked them to pick someplace else."

"Politely?" Frankie asked, his dark eyebrows bowed over his hypnotic eyes. "Last I remember, *las Reinas* didn't respond well to polite."

Marisela shrugged. She'd earned a great deal of respect from her former gang by choosing to bleed out. She'd used every fighting skill she'd ever learned, every survival instinct she'd ever experienced, to escape a lifelong bond to the gang. But she'd survived. Barely.

"They've learned some manners while you've been gone. Lots of things have changed. Like," she said, snagging his beer around the neck and taking a sip, "I don't settle for fast and furious no more."

Frankie didn't move a muscle. "Is that so?"

She smoothed her tongue over her teeth, then licked the lip of his bottle, careful not to smudge her ruby red lipstick. He snagged his drink back and chugged, his gaze locked on her mouth. Frankie always had a thing for her lips. Marisela thought they resembled something between Angelina Jolie's and a grouper, but Frankie considered her thick, pouty flesh mighty fine. A detail she intended to use to her advantage, now that she'd found the man.

Theresa delivered her rum and Coke, tall and icy

with a wedge of lime. After another wary glance at Frankie, she left them alone.

"So you come here a lot?" he asked.

"Where else am I gonna go? This is West Tampa, not Miami. We've got one club and this is it."

"There's always Ybor City."

"If you don't mind drunks who can't dance and ridiculous cover charges. This is still the neighborhood hot spot. You'd know that if you came around more."

"I've been busy," he answered, draining the rest of his beer.

She sipped her spiked cola. "And how *was* prison?"

He chuckled, slid his beer bottle away. "Big party," he quipped. "I got out two years ago."

"Really? I hadn't heard."

He snorted. He likely knew as well as she did that the precise location and activities of all the neighborhood kids—young, old, and in between—were reported, catalogued, and reported again from the shiny vinyl chairs of Viola's Beauty Parlor, two blocks south of Columbus Drive. Their mothers both had standing appointments every weekend. And thanks to Aida Morales's devotion to the Saturday morning religion of gossip and speculation, Marisela knew precisely what Frankie had been up to over the last decade as if she'd been there herself. Gang. Prison. Dock work in Miami. Nothing too complicated.

Then a week ago, he'd shown up in Tampa uninvited and unexpected. After less than an hour in town, he'd been arrested for possession. Thanks to his parents, he'd made bail—and then he'd promptly disappeared.

Which was why she was here.

"So what have you been up to, Marisela?"

Her turn to snort. "Nothing too exciting. I did nails for a while. Worked at Wal-Mart. Graduated to Saks. Did some phone work and filing for Alberto Garcia, on the side. Now, I'm looking again."

She conveniently left out the parts his mother couldn't possibly have told him. Hardly anyone knew that her work for Alberto went beyond answering calls and shoveling papers. The owner of AAA-Able Bail Bonds had helped her out when her gang activity landed her in juvie. Instead of processing the teen and sending her on her way, he'd promised her a job. A real job. One where she'd put her fighting skills and gun experience to good use. She'd run little errands for him and trained her ass off until she turned twenty-one. Then, he'd put her in enforcement. For seven years, she'd tracked down bail-jumping bozos all across the state.

But Alberto had been careful not to send her into her own neighborhood to pick up strays. Called it a conflict of interest. So her secret life was safe. A good thing, too, since Frankie might not be so anxious to relive a little heat from their past if he knew she still carried a gun.

Illegally, but that was a fact she continued to ignore. She'd lost her license to carry and immediately thereafter, her position with AAA-Able. But she hadn't given up her piece. What the cops didn't know wouldn't hurt them, but ditching her weapon could get her killed.

"So, you're short on cash," Frankie said with a nod, his lips slightly pursed, hinting that maybe he knew more than she'd hoped.

"Who isn't?"

"Chasing deadbeats doesn't appeal anymore?"

Damn. Frankie might have been away for a while,

but he obviously still had contacts. Still, she wiggled her newly polished nails, the index fingers tipped with tiny fake diamonds, and hoped to play down his knowledge of her enforcement activities. "Too hard on the manicure."

He chuckled. "Were you good?"

She sipped her *Cuba Libre*, enjoying the burst of the sweet carbonation against the smooth tang of the rum. "I'm good at lots of things."

"I remember."

Man, Frankie had some incredible eyes. Technically, they were hazel, but the flecks of green glittered as deep and vivid as fine oriental jade. Offset by his swarthy skin, his irises simmered with hot intentions—every one of which Marisela could imagine in great detail.

"Wanna dance?" she asked, flicking a glance at the dance floor. At Club Electric, the music pulsed as hard and bright as the neon lights. The minute Marisela allowed herself to acknowledge the sounds, the rhythm seeped into her veins. Her shoulders and hips rocked and her feet itched to hit the dance floor and work off some of the fiery vibe slashing between her and Frankie.

"No," he answered.

She didn't hide her disappointment, pushing her lips into a thick pout. "Why not?"

"Not in the mood."

She leaned forward, her lips inches from his ear as the crowd around them whooped and sang a chorus of "Yo Viviré," a cover of Gloria Gaynor's "I Will Survive," by Celia Cruz. "I can always put you in the mood, Frankie." She shimmied her shoulders ever so slightly. "Like no other woman ever could."

"We were young, Marisela. Didn't take much to put either of us in the mood."

She laughed, punched him in the shoulder then downed a few more gulps of her drink. A flush of warm heat surrounded her skin and she didn't know if the reaction stemmed from their proximity to the writhing masses of dancers or from being so close, and yet so far, from her first love.

Back in high school, she and Frankie had melted more than one dance floor—not to mention the damage they'd done to various backseats. He'd loved her wild ways, her innate curiosity. She'd wanted to explore the world, find her place outside the tight community she loved, but still resented. To date, she hadn't gone anywhere too exotic, but her ambitions hadn't died, even if they were harder to pursue with bills hitting the mailbox like baseball-size hail.

Even after he'd chosen his gang over her, he'd kept her secrets. He'd never popped off to his *hombres* about her sexual appetites. The worst thing he'd ever done was break her teenage heart.

Now she was about to screw him in the worst possible way. Or maybe, the best way? Didn't matter. Bottom line—she was going to royally piss him off, although for a good cause.

A very noble cause. The noblest. Marisela may have skirted the law from time to time—well, she'd actually flashed and mooned the law on one or two occasions—but give her a benevolent purpose and she could be downright patriotic. And ruthless. Not that she needed a good reason to spend a little quality time with sexy, dangerous, Frankie Vega. But lucky for her, she had a good reason all the same. He was about to jump bail and she was going to stop him.

She finished her drink, slipped her fingers into her jacket pocket, threw a ten onto the bar, and nodded toward the door.

"If you don't want to dance, let's go."

She twisted off the bar stool, but Frankie moved only to tilt his head toward hers so she'd hear him over the music and the crowd.

"How do you know I'm not waiting for someone?"

Surrendering to her instincts, Marisela drew one of her long fingernails over Frankie's angular jawline. "I don't. But you just got a better offer."

Knowing she had to seal the deal, she dropped her touch slowly down his neck, until the ruby red enamel on her nail sparkled beside the gold chain he'd worn since his confirmation. Unlike the other Cuban-American males in this part of the world, Frankie didn't dangle a crucifix or saint's medallion from the necklace. No sense in contradicting his daily activities. He wore the gold serpentine necklace flush to his dark skin, even if the links probably pinched the hell out of his chest hair every once in a while.

Marisela grabbed his open collar and with surprise on her side, yanked him to his feet. Frankie wasn't the tallest man in the world—just shy of six feet—but to her tall-for-her-genes five foot seven, he towered over her just enough so she could glance through the veil of her eyelashes when she spoke.

"Do you understand what I'm offering?"

Before he could answer, she slipped her free hand between them and cupped her palm over the bulge in his jeans. She smiled, a thrill streaking through her like lightning.

He was hard. As a rock. Thinking he'd want her again was one thing. *Knowing* stole her breath.

Like the charmer he was, Frankie seized her winded moment and kissed her. Not hot and impatient like he used to. Oh no. The son of a bitch took his time, pressing his lips against hers like a warm iron on a silk blouse, careful not to scorch her by pressing too hard. His hands inched from her hips to her ribs, his fingers tantalizing the bared skin of her midriff with hungry, yet contained caresses.

Harvesting all her self-control, Marisela forced a step back, breaking the connection so quickly, Frankie's lips were still puckered.

He had the audacity to grin as if he'd been the one to push her away.

"Blast from the past too much for you, *vidita*?"

Marisela slipped her hands into the pocket of her jacket. Feeling the handcuffs she'd hidden there, she remembered the true purpose of this seduction.

She scooted away from her stool, away from him—knowing he had every motivation to follow. "Too much for me?" she asked, sassy and doubtful at the same time. "I'm just getting started."

TWO

DAMN IF MARISELA'S ASS didn't look even better aged ten years. He pushed through the crowd to keep up with her, knowing that if he'd had any sense, he'd realize that meeting up with her tonight was no accident. Maybe Blake moved in without Frankie's answer? Not plausible. Ian Blake was desperate, but he wouldn't act haphazardly.

Still, before Frankie left town tomorrow, he wanted to make sure Blake didn't pursue Marisela for his operation. Why Frankie cared, he didn't know. The *chica* could take care of herself. But Frankie had been the one to bring her name to the table and since he was ditching the deal, he'd decided to make sure she wasn't sucked in to a dangerous, treacherous world without him there to watch her back.

And yet, he couldn't ignore the fact that she'd come to the club armed. Maybe Blake had made contact. Maybe he'd sent Marisela to lure him back to the fold. Or was she simply being Marisela, ready to protect herself from the lowlifes he'd heard weren't too happy with her job hauling in criminals for cash? She'd tried hard to conceal her piece under that sexy black jacket, but Frankie'd become quite good at spotting guns. *¡Coño!* He didn't need this distraction!

His arrest last week had been the final straw. Yeah, he'd left Miami seriously entertaining Ian Blake's job offer, but being booked for possession five minutes after he cruised into town had changed his mind. He'd had enough of the life. Serving six years in prison for armed robbery, most of the time spent doubling as a DEA mole, had cut out the last of his cancerous obsession with high stakes thrills. Now, he just wanted to lay low until his hearing tomorrow morning, take care of business, and then get the hell out of town before he burned his cojones on the big trouble brewing so close to home.

Trouble that seemed to follow him wherever he went. Trouble Marisela didn't ask for. And probably didn't deserve.

Maybe he was just being paranoid. Maybe his running into his ex had been a simple stroke of good luck. And maybe Marisela's flirting was just because she was hot to trot, and for once in his hard-luck life, he was in the right place at the right time. He might as well take advantage while he had the chance. Once he left Tampa this time, he was gone for good.

Marisela waited for him at the exit, leaning suggestively against the door, one foot flat against the surface, her knee drawn up, sexy and bold. She always did have a way of broadcasting exactly what was on her mind at any given moment. Lying and manipulating took too much time and effort. With Marisela, what he saw was what he got.

And man, he liked what he saw tonight.

He slapped his hand on the door above her shoulder, then eased forward, inhaling her spicy scent as his nose neared her neck. "You want to start right here or take it outside?" he whispered, brushing his lips across her fragrant skin.

She chuckled softly, but enough so that her breasts bounced gently against his chest. "Either way, we'll have an audience."

He ran his tongue against the cool gold of her hoop earring. "Does that turn you on?"

"Who says I'm turned on?"

In a flash, she'd ducked away from him and pushed into the thick, outdoor air. The bouncer pretended to ignore the overheard exchange, but as Frankie strutted past the oversize cue ball of a man, he caught the glimmer of lust in the man's eyes. That same hungry shine reflected in the stares of the half-dozen or so punks hanging out with their backs to the wall, swinging their Colt 45 malt liquors. He smirked, confident that Marisela not only wanted him, but that for the first time in a long while, every guy in this joint wanted nothing more than to be in his *zapatos*.

As Marisela predicted, the parking lot outside Club Electric was jammed with nearly as many hot bodies as inside. Under-aged girls sat on the hoods of cars driven by boys they had no business messing with, boys with knives in their back pockets and oversize beer cans clutched in angry hands.

It wasn't so long ago that he'd been one of those jerks. In a lot of ways, he still was. But now he had the chance to jump back to a simpler time in his life— when the only thing that mattered was hot sex and cool living.

He caught up with Marisela as she approached the one-of-a-kind rust bucket his mother called her second car. Most of the time, she tooled around in the practical four-door Chevy Malibu she'd bought herself after hitting good numbers on the lottery. But to accommodate any one of her six children who often returned to the nest with one sob story or another, she kept the beat-up Impala. Frankie hadn't thought much about the car parked perennially in his mother's garage until he'd found himself in quick need of wheels to make a fast escape, his own ride impounded.

"Why does your *mami* keep this old thing?" Marisela asked, running a tentative finger over the oxidized paint of the dented outer shell.

He leaned one hip on the door, knowing he looked just as cool now as he used to back when Marisela thought he'd owned the world because he had wheels at his disposal. "*Yo no sé.* I think she's sentimental. I may have been conceived in this car," he said, half-joking. The Impala hadn't been around quite that long, though he wouldn't doubt if some of his brothers hadn't spawned a few of his nieces and nephews in that spacious backseat.

Marisela rolled her eyes, and then leaned in through the open window to inspect the interior more closely, giving him a view of her backside that made his cock tight.

No way was that move unintentional.

"What the hell are you doing, Marisela?"

She wriggled back out. He had to adjust the seam of his jeans. He didn't try to be sly about it, either. Why should he? She certainly wasn't.

"Just seeing if the old juices still flow between us," she explained.

"I could be an old man sitting in my wheelchair on the front porch and you'd get my juices flowing, *vidita*."

Marisela stalked toward him slowly, allowing him time to appreciate every soft bounce of her unbound breasts, every swing of her sexy hips.

"Why don't you let me taste some of those juices, Frankie? I'm thirsty. Aren't you?" When she stood toe-to-toe with him, her nipples brushed against his chest. His entire body tensed, hard and electric—as if he was on the job, ready to jump, react, strike, flee.

He swiped his tongue around his lips, then yanked Marisela close and pressed his mouth over hers. In an instant, she soothed the parched thirst crackling through his body. Just as fast, they were in his car, barreling out of the parking lot and over the half-bricked city streets of the old neighborhood. She climbed onto his lap, laughing her deep, throaty laugh, kissing his ears, sucking his neck, untucking his shirt, popping buttons so she could dip her fingers into his waistband.

Several skidding turns and rolling stops later, Frankie killed the engine, allowing the momentum of the car to propel them up the driveway beside his mother's house. When he'd first hit town, he'd planned to take up residence in the tiny apartment above the detached garage, but his arrest changed all that. Instead, he'd crashed in some flea-bit motels on the port side of town, avoiding Ian Blake and his far-reaching grip. Instinct alone steered him here, to the same apartment where he'd lost his virginity to Marisela—and she to him—all those years ago. He fished the key out of the flowerpot beside the door and by the time he turned to Marisela, she'd kicked off her boots and jeans, right there in the open air.

Lust surged and he grabbed her, not thinking about anything but feeling her naked against him. They fell into the apartment, landing half on the bed, half on the floor. Before Frankie could remove his own shoes and pants, Marisela lost her jacket and her T-shirt. For an instant, he spied the black holster she'd worn around her shoulder and waist, but the minute she crawled onto his bed, wearing nothing but pale pink panties, he willingly forgot about her gun. She hooked her hands under the lower rod of the cast-iron headboard, tested the strength of the metal with one wanton tug, then waited, her breasts round and tight-tipped, her areolas dark, her mouth slightly parted and still a blurry red from his kiss.

Frankie stopped, just for a fraction of a second, to drink in her illicit beauty. He tore off his own shirt, but swallowed a grin when her deep brown eyes sparkled with appreciation. Not much for a man to do in prison but work out, and his last job on the docks had enhanced his physique. He wasn't some scrawny school-boy anymore—if he'd ever been.

"Jesus, Frankie. You look good," she said, slicking

her tongue over her lips. He loved her mouth. He'd always loved her mouth. How it felt pressed against his skin. How she could use all that hot, wet flesh to drive him insane.

"*Vidita,* I could come right here, just looking at you."

She glanced down at her own prone and posed body, then shifted into the moonlight streaming in through the window.

"That would be a big waste, wouldn't it?"

The glow emphasized the gloss of sweat forming over her skin. The air inside the apartment was hot, stuffy. He hadn't noticed. He glanced at the dormant air conditioner unit shoved between the window and the cracked wooden frame.

In a rush, he marched to the window, pressed buttons, turned knobs, and cursed until the ancient unit kicked to life, blasting tepid air against his naked chest. He adjusted the thermostat, breathing easier when the temperature dropped just enough to let him know the junker still worked. But the last thing he wanted to be was cool. He spun around, just in time to catch Marisela fiddling with the pillows, propping them purposefully against the slender wrought-iron bars of the old headboard.

"Comfortable?"

She snuggled into the cushions, patting and fluffing as she spoke. "Not as comfortable as I could be." When she had the bed arranged as she wanted, she stretched her arms toward him. "Come here," she said, her voice husky.